Should You Ask Me

Also by Marianne Kavanagh

For Once in My Life
Don't Get Me Wrong

For Matt

First published in Great Britain in 2017 by Hodder & Stoughton
An Hachette UK company

A CIP catalogue record for this title is available from the British Library

Hardback ISBN 978 1 473 63933 1
Trade Paperback ISBN 978 1 473 63934 8
eBook ISBN 978 1 473 63935 5

Typeset in Plantin by Palimpsest Book Production Limited,
Falkirk, Stirlingshire

Printed and bound by CPI Group (UK) Ltd, Croydon, CR0 4YY

Hodder & Stoughton policy is to use papers that are natural, renewable
and recyclable products and made from wood grown in sustainable forests.
The logging and manufacturing processes are expected to conform to the
environmental regulations of the country of origin.

Marianne Kavanagh

Should You Ask Me

HODDER &
STOUGHTON

Should You Ask Me...

Should you ask me of D-Day, I would say
'Cataracts', for that night the sky roared, pulsing
Wave upon wave of heavy-bellied engines;
And afterwards, in blue morning, crimson roses,
I found, had fallen from their fence-board moorings,
Falling, cascading – not like blood, nor rubies,
Nor fire, nor any metaphor...
     just roses,
A waterfall of English roses...

   Then
Came the third cataract, a lone lark singing,
High, high above the empty plane-ways, hidden
Among the sunbeams...

Vera Rich, 1936–2009
Poet, journalist and translator

Author's Note

Should You Ask Me was inspired by a story in Rodney Legg's *Purbeck Island*, and by photographs in *Purbeck Camera* by Mike O'Hara and Ben Buxton. It also draws on historical references found in *Wareham's War* by Terence Davis, and *Wareham: A Pictorial History* by Lilian Ladle. But while some of the characters take their names from people who once lived on the Isle of Purbeck, *Should You Ask Me* is a work of fiction – an imaginary version of a past that could have happened but never did.

Monday

Two hours after the Sherman tank rolled through Wareham, the cellars of the King's Arms flooded. Water rose higher and higher, seeping through the iron gratings on to the pavement above. Outside the garage, in a dip in the road, the pool was soon ankle deep. Carts, cars and Jeeps splashed down North Street, spraying the passers-by.

Vic Smith's dog – a mongrel with traces of greyhound or whippet – barked a series of warnings before circling fast, chasing its own tail.

As a brilliant sheen settled over the town centre, and the Cross turned into a shallow lake that glittered in the May sunshine, Wareham police station filled with protesters. Sergeant Mills, leaning over the high Victorian counter, struggled to make himself heard. No, he said, it was probably a coincidence. A burst pipe. Nothing to do with thirty-two tons of steel flattening the high street. The army had been informed. Yes, they were working on it now. Yes, the barrels of beer had been hoisted to safety. Yes, they might need to shut off the mains.

In the end, tired of the hubbub – because there was nothing more he could do – he straightened up and banged the ledger shut. Most of them took this as a signal to leave. But a small knot stayed outside, muted but rebellious, their voices floating back through the open window.

'It had to be a Monday morning, didn't it,' said the sergeant, 'when the whole town's doing its washing.'

Now that the crowd had gone, William could see that an elderly woman in a black hat was sitting in one of the chairs

3

against the far wall. A large leather handbag was balanced on her knees.

'They're on edge, that's the problem.' Sergeant Mills picked up a pile of brown envelopes. 'Can't blame them.'

She looked at William. He looked back.

'A military camp full of Americans, that's what we are. The whole of Dorset packed in tight, just waiting for something to happen.' The sergeant – who had been speaking increasingly loudly – glanced up. 'Miss Holmes. I'm sorry. I didn't see you there.' He cleared his throat. 'What can I do for you?'

She said, 'I've come about the bodies.'

'The bodies?'

'I read about them in the newspaper.'

The sergeant frowned.

'Up by Acton. In the fields by the quarries. One of the stone-cutters found them.'

'Ah, yes.' The sergeant straightened up. 'Some kind of burial site. We don't have any more information, I'm afraid, at the moment.'

'I do.'

'And what sort of information would that be?'

'I know who they are.'

'You know who they are.'

'Yes.'

Sergeant Mills leaned forward. 'They're very old, Miss Holmes. Very old. They've been buried a long time.'

The door banged open. A boy of about ten, breathing hard, stood on the threshold. 'Sergeant, you're wanted in North Street.'

The sergeant sighed, came out from behind his counter and bent down over William's desk. 'Constable, take Miss Holmes into the office and ask her to make a statement, would you?'

At the door, he turned back and glanced in William's direction, opening his eyes wide in mock panic. Something secret was being communicated. It was complex, urgent and alarming.

It also made Sergeant Mills laugh.

———

The room smelled of old bacon. Light filtered through from a narrow window looking out on to a brick wall. There was a telephone booth, a grey enamel gas stove, a square white sink and a scrubbed deal table with two benches either side. In the corner, a bare staircase led up to the floor above where William and two other constables slept, each with their own iron bedstead and coat hook on the wall.

William pulled forward an upright chair for Miss Holmes and set it at the end of the table. He sat down with a thump on one of the wooden benches, his leg sticking out to one side, and opened his notebook.

She said, 'You're very thin.'

His mouth trembled.

'I expect it's the war.' She nodded at his stiff leg. 'Dunkirk?'

'You want to make a statement.'

Underneath the black hat, which had a small silky bow to one side, her hair was a silvery grey. The skin of her face was so criss-crossed with tiny lines that it looked like soft paper that had been crumpled and re-crumpled many times. She was wearing a black coat, with a pink scarf tucked in at the neck, and cream woollen gloves, buttoned at the wrist. 'You hear so many stories. My neighbour next door, her cousin's fiancé lost all his clothes swimming out to the boat. Came back in nothing but a Union Jack and a pair of women's boots. They couldn't pull them off so he sat all afternoon with his feet in a basin of hot water. And the water turned red. After all that time.'

Her accent was old Dorset, a hum of long vowels.

William took the cap off his pen.

5

She said, 'Maybe it wasn't Dunkirk. Maybe it's more recent than that. You might have been in Africa. In the desert with Monty. Or Sicily. You know, a lot of the Americans fought in Sicily. Most of them didn't expect to get out alive. They must have been so pleased to get to Dorset. They must have looked round and thought they were in heaven.'

They both sat in silence for a moment.

Then she said, 'I have a lot of time for your Sergeant Mills. Old soldier. That's how he lost those two fingers. Did he tell you that? Blown off in France in the Great War. He should be retired by now. But they couldn't let him go. Because there's no one left, you see. Not with his kind of experience. And we need it so badly at the moment, don't we? They were drinking in the Pure Drop, the Americans, and some of them had had too much and wouldn't leave. And your sergeant said, Come along now, let's be having you, and one of them stood up, ready to start a fight, and your sergeant said, If you're going to do anything with that pint glass, I'd drink up first if I were you, because beer's in short supply, and they all laughed, and drank up, and went back home as quiet as lambs.'

William said nothing.

'Of course they say the beer's too warm. But they like the pubs. Playing darts. Cribbage. Listening to all the old tales of Wareham. Cromwell. Judge Jeffreys. Five men hung, drawn and quartered on Bloody Bank. And they're so generous, aren't they? Threw a party for Marjorie Brewer on her twenty-first. Her family couldn't have done it. Not with rationing. But they invited her down to the chapel in Church Street and there were pies and ice cream and fritters and meat sandwiches, all piled up on the table. A feast. She'll never forget it as long as she lives.'

William said, 'Miss Holmes—'

'Although the barbed wire up on the walls is covered in French letters. And that's got to be the Americans, hasn't it? They get them free. In shoe boxes.'

'Miss Holmes, do you want to make a statement?'

'Overpaid, oversexed and over here. And what they say back, of course, is underpaid, undersexed and under Eisenhower.'

William closed his notebook. 'Perhaps it would be better to come back when you know what you want to say.'

She considered this. 'You could ask me questions.'

'Is that what you want?'

'It might make it easier.'

He leaned forward. 'The names, Miss Holmes, that's all we need.'

'Did you see it in the newspaper?'

He shook his head.

'I expect you've heard all the news before it gets into the *Chronicle*. And there's no point reading what you already know.' She opened the silver clasp on her bag and brought out a green tortoiseshell spectacles case. 'I've got the cutting here if you want to see it.'

'Miss Holmes—'

'Although it doesn't give much away. You end up with more questions than you started with.' She put on her glasses and reached back inside her bag for the small rectangle of newsprint. 'HUMAN REMAINS FOUND NEAR ACTON. That's the headline. Then it says, Human remains have been uncovered in Acton's open-cast stone quarries during excavation for a new mine shaft. Mr Jack "Hog" Bower and Mr Eddie Harding, both stonecutters from Langton Matravers, reported their discovery to the police on Friday. The burial is not believed to be recent.' She glanced up. 'Which could mean anything, couldn't it? Stone Age, Civil War, sixty years ago.' She paused. 'I knew Eddie's father, you know. Robert Harding. Drove a lovely Singer Ten. Six-cylinder. But he had a bit of a squint. Some of the girls didn't like that. They couldn't tell where he was looking.'

William opened his mouth to speak.

'You can see why they stayed hidden for so long. Just fields

7

and farms for miles. And the cliffs and the sea. They could have stayed in peace for ever.' She took off her glasses and put them back in the case. 'A honeycomb of mines round there. You hear it whenever you pass by, the sound of chisel on stone. Like music almost. And the piles of white rock, and the dust in the air. And then there's the cliff quarries, of course. Winspit and Seacombe and Dancing Ledge. The smugglers used to land their boats there. Bring in kegs of brandy from the sea. Store them in the roof of the church. So you'd be sitting there on Sundays, worrying the whole lot was going to fall in your lap.'

'Miss Holmes—'

'You're not from round here, are you?'

He took a deep breath and let it out slowly. 'Dorset, yes. But not Wareham.'

'Where in Dorset?'

'I've been working in Dorchester. Police headquarters.'

'But where were you born?'

'Miss Holmes—'

'You know, the walls in Wareham are very old. Built by Alfred the Great. To fight off the Danes. We would have fought off the Germans, too, if they'd invaded. Although Mrs Elmes said she'd kill herself and both her daughters if the Germans even crossed the bridge. That would be the way they'd come, wouldn't it? Across the Channel, land at Kimmeridge Bay, up through Steeple and Creech. They'd be over the river before you even knew they'd arrived. Of course, most of the bombers that come this way are heading for Bristol. We used to have sirens going off every night. Wareham was hit once. December 1942. Injured three people and blew the back legs off a goat.'

'Miss Holmes—'

'Wouldn't they have you back? Your old station? Because I think what happened, after your injury, is that you left the army, and they looked after you in police headquarters for a while, and then they found you a job where you wouldn't need to use that leg. A desk job. Because you sit there all day doing reports, don't you? Which suits Sergeant Mills, because he doesn't like paperwork. I don't expect you go out on the beat much any more. Well, you can't, can you? You can't walk, and you can't ride a bike. Which must be hard on the others, if they're out in all weathers. They probably feel you're not pulling your weight.'

He put both hands flat on the table in front of him, ready to push himself to his feet.

She said, 'You could say that I killed them.'

He paused, looking at her.

'I can't just tell you, Constable. I can't just reel it off. Because it's a long story. And I've kept silent for more than sixty years.'

'Are you saying that you committed murder?'

She looked at him directly. Her eyes were a milky brown, like chocolate. 'Yes.'

'And you want to confess.'

'It's more a case of having to. Now they've dug them up. They're going to want to find out who they are, aren't they?'

'How many bodies?'

'Two.'

'And you know their names?'

'Yes.'

With great care, William opened his notebook again. 'Is there anything that links you to the bodies?'

'Apart from being the person who killed them?'

'What I mean is, you could have kept quiet. They've been buried all these years. You could have stayed silent.'

She smiled. 'I'm eighty-six years old. I'm tired of being quiet.'

'In which case—'

'And the guilt eats away at you. A lifetime of telling lies.'

He paused, studying her face. 'Let's start at the beginning.'

'That's not always the best place.'

'Miss Holmes—'

'How old are you?'

9

He shook his head. 'That's not really relevant.'

'To me it is.'

'Twenty-four.'

'So young to be so badly injured. What does your mother think?'

'Miss Holmes, you have just confessed to murder. You need to answer my questions. Or I may have to place you under arrest until such time as you feel more able to cooperate.'

'Call me Mary.'

William shifted position and winced.

'You're still in pain, aren't you? Can't they do anything?'

'I don't think you understand the seriousness of the situation.'

'You have a problem with hearing too, don't you? I noticed your sergeant leaned right over your desk when he spoke to you. I think you're all right if you're quite close and you can read people's lips. But I don't think you'd manage in a noisy room.'

William didn't speak for a moment. Then he said, 'Miss Holmes, if you don't want to start at the beginning, where do you want to start?'

'I could tell you about the shipwreck.'

'All right.'

She smiled.

'But first I have to take a few details.'

'Mary Holmes. Langton Cottage, North Street. Born March 1858. No surviving relatives. I ran the garage until 1934. Did you know that? And before that a smithy. And before that a pub. Although not here. In a village. Langton Matravers. I'm telling you this because you asked me, but you don't need to write it down. It's all common knowledge. Ask anyone round here. I've lived in Wareham for sixty-two years. I used to serve Lawrence of Arabia at the garage. Clouds Hill, that's where he lived. Came off his Brough Superior SS100 trying to avoid two boys on bicycles. He called it George V, his motorcycle. I have no idea why. And of course his effigy is in St Martin's.'

'Miss Holmes—'

'Mary.'

'This will be a lot easier if you could keep your answers relatively short.'

'It all comes of living alone. I don't often have a nice young man to talk to.'

'At this stage, I just need the facts.'

'I end up talking to myself sometimes. I don't even realise I'm doing it. It's all going through your head anyway, all the memories, and every so often you just say it out loud. Especially the things that make you laugh. Those memories are the best.'

'Miss Holmes, human remains have been discovered in the fields by the quarries in Acton. You say you know who was buried there. I would like you to start by giving me their names.'

'May I have a cup of tea?'

He stared.

'Given we're in the kitchen.'

'This is the charge office.'

'It has a stove and a kettle.'

'You want a cup of tea.'

'It makes your mouth dry, doesn't it, all this talking.'

For a while, William just sat there. Then he got to his feet, holding on to the table for balance.

'How did you get injured?'

His progress across the room was slow. He had to bend to the left from his waist in order to swing out his stiff right leg. Then he would stop, re-balancing his weight, before stepping forward with his left foot again. Once he caught his breath in a kind of gasp, quickly suppressed.

'Looks like you got shot. Or perhaps it was a shell.'

William's hands were shaking as he filled the kettle.

'It's worse seeing it all when you're my age. Because it makes no sense. What's the point of hanging on to my life when so many young men are losing theirs? I'd gladly give away the years I have left. Imagine, a young man like you being cut down for no reason.'

He lit the gas.

'A waste, that's what it is. Although there are always some who profit from it. The shopkeepers, of course. And the publicans. They did well out of it the first time round. We had thousands of soldiers here in the Great War, in tents on the Worgret Road. It rained for weeks when they first set up camp. I remember thinking, Those poor boys. They always marched down West Street, you know. On their way to war.'

William reached out for the wall to steady himself.

As the kettle boiled, the whistle blew.

———

Running flat out through the half-open gate, William reached the train just as the conductor was raising his hand. He flung open the door and jumped inside.

She must have been late, too, the woman standing in the middle of the carriage, a leather suitcase at her feet, because she was breathing hard. On her lapel was a square enamel brooch painted with white daisies.

The whistle blew.

'Here,' he said. 'Let me.' He bent down, picked up the suitcase and swung it on to the luggage rack above.

'My mum says, give yourself enough time and you won't arrive all hot and bothered,' she said, collapsing into the seat by the window. 'But I never seem to remember somehow. Always leave everything right to the last minute.'

On the platform, two sailors in blue-and-white uniforms hoisted kitbags on to their shoulders. Behind them, next to a poster for Beecham's Lung Syrup, was a sign on the wall saying 'Jesus Christ: neither is there salvation in any other'.

With a jolt, the train started to move.

She glanced up as she took off her gloves. Her hair was dark and shiny, swept back from her face. 'So where are you off to in such a hurry?'

'On leave.'

'You and the whole army by the looks of it. The station was full of khaki.'

He leaned his head against the seat, smiling back at her. 'It's almost like there's a war on.'

She laughed. 'I'm going to see my sister. Just had her third. You keep seeing those signs, don't you, Is your journey really necessary? Well, they should try it. Three under five. And she's all alone. Her husband's a prisoner of war, captured at Dunkirk. She's worried sick. Hasn't heard a thing for months.' She laid her gloves on her lap, smoothing out the fingers one by one. 'I keep telling her, no news is good news. But that's just what you say, isn't it? Grab what comfort you can. Don't give up hope. Whatever you do, don't give up hope.'

The train chuffed, building up speed.

'So where are you off to, then?'

He didn't reply for a moment. 'London.'

'They've had it hard, haven't they? I can't bear to read about it. Bombing night after night, piles of rubble, broken glass, whole streets gone. They say you can't breathe for the smoke. Gets right in your lungs. I don't know how they manage.'

Outside, the edge of the town gave way to flat, icy fields. The November sky was powdery white, like a haze of dust.

'Visiting someone?'

He was silent.

'Ah,' she said, her eyes bright with flirtation. 'Like that, is it? I should have guessed. The best ones are always taken.' She gave an exaggerated sigh. 'So go on, then. Tell me all about her.'

He stared down at his black army boots.

'What's her name?'

'Stella,' he said, when he finally found his voice. 'Her name's Stella Allen.'

———•———

Mary said, 'The kettle's boiling.'

William jumped and grabbed the Bakelite handle at the top. The kettle crashed to the stove with a clatter.

'Be careful. You'll burn yourself.'

He reached up to the shelf for the big brown teapot and concentrated on small defined movements – opening the tea caddy, spooning in the black leaves, pouring the water. Limping back to the table, he placed the pot in front of Miss Holmes. He found cups and saucers, the sugar bowl, a jug of milk.

She said, 'I like it strong.'

He lowered himself on to the bench.

She said, 'Of course he had to tell it that way to get me to agree. He knew I would have said, it's not yours to keep. It's no different from brandy or kid gloves.'

William frowned. 'Who are we talking about?'

'So he made it sound like fate. As if he had no choice. He'd dived down deep, way down into the black water. And there was the cabin, door open, inviting him in. The dead woman, pinned behind the table, eyes wide, staring at nothing.'

'Is this the shipwreck?'

'A shiny mirror, a corner cupboard, the work of a moment to turn the key. Finding the soft bag, ramming it inside his shirt, lungs bursting for air, legs pushing him up, taking a breath when he thought time had run out.'

'When was this?'

'Back in the wreckage, the wind, the roar of the waves. Grabbing hold of a crate, any crate, swimming back to shore, using every ounce of his strength, finding the rocks beneath his feet, scrambling back to land. Heaving boxes and chests from the waves, wading out to sea again, thinking all the while of the soft bag against his skin under his shirt.'

'Who was this man, Miss Holmes?'

'A long line of villagers, the scavenging passed from hand to hand, trudging back home over the fields, once – just once – clasping his hand to his chest to feel it safe against his heart. Back at the inn, finding blankets, pouring brandy, stoking the fire, then outside to the garden, pushing the bag right to the bottom of the muck pile, among the peelings and the stalks – still with no idea of what was inside, but hoping, hoping. The memory of his daring keeping him wide awake all through the long night. Stealing back from the smithy the next day, with the whole village mending, building, setting to rights. Windows smashed, fences flattened, roofs blown away in the storm. Creeping into the earth closet, the soft bag covered in leaf mould and the smell of warm rot, shaking the contents into his lap.'

William said nothing.

Mary's eyes were dark. 'Because you share it out. Always. Take nothing for yourself. Or else who would save the survivors? If you worked for yourself, you'd forget the living. You'd let them die in the black boiling sea. Waves roaring like sea monsters. A fog of white spray. Broadside on, there was the ship, its sails in tatters. People still on board, screaming. Others clinging to the rocks. Ropes were let down from the cliffs, and we were hauling the poor souls to safety – sailors and officers and young women half dead from exhaustion, their hair streaming in the wind. The rescuers themselves were slipping and falling, in danger of being washed out to sea. I shouted at them to take care, but the wind just whipped my voice away.'

'So you were there, too, that night?'

'There was terrible loss of life. Forty laid out on the shore in rows. Some of them drowned. But most had died on the rocks, smashed to pieces like the wreck. I pulled at a shoe, tangled up in the cordage, and it came away as light as a feather, all by itself, with the foot still inside. And there, in the frothy scum, among the fragments of mast and spar, was something I couldn't make out at all. And someone said, What part of a man is this? And all I could do was stare. Because it looked just like the heart of a pig.'

'Miss Holmes—'

She stopped, frowning. 'Forgive me. I'm sorry. You don't want me going on like this. You'll have seen worse yourself, fighting on the front line. Bodies blown to bits. Terrible destruction. Were you in a tank? I don't think you were in a tank. I think you were infantry. Good with a gun.'

'So there was a shipwreck. And a man stole something.'

'I imagine you took to it well, all the discipline. Shouting orders. Marching about. Polishing your brasses.'

'What was his name?'

'The tea must be brewed by now.'

Their eyes met. Eventually he said, 'Shall I pour?'

It was only when she had stirred sugar into her tea and put the teaspoon back in the saucer that Mary said, 'Of course, he wouldn't agree it was stealing. It was payment in kind. He worked all night to keep them alive. And dug the graves for the ones who lost the fight, who faded away by the light of the fire. They were buried at St George's the next day, with the Reverend Mr Lester, rector of Langton, praying for their souls. And then we waited for the rest. Nine days it takes. Nine days for a corpse to float to the surface. The sailors were marked. Blue tattoos. Prayers, hearts, anchors, forget-me-nots. So the rector was able to describe them to the ship's agent when he came. They had come from all over the world, those men. But their final resting place was a country churchyard by the sea.'

'What about the woman?'

'The woman?'

'The dead woman in the cabin.'

Mary smiled. 'I didn't think you were listening.'

He waited.

'She went down with the ship. Buried at sea.'

From outside the window, in the passageway, came the sound of a baby crying.

———

William noticed the red coat first. Then the bright gold hair, caught by the sun. As he slowed down, got off his bicycle and positioned it against the brick wall, he glanced up. He could see her more clearly now. A young woman pushing a pram.

'Who's that, then?' he said, inside the shop.

Mrs Bradstock looked out over the village green. 'An evacuee. From London.'

'I thought we were just taking children.'

'Some of them,' said Mrs Bradstock, handing him his newspaper, 'came with their mothers.'

'Meaning?'

'Nothing at all, Constable. Nothing at all.'

'Where's she staying?'

'Number two. With Mrs Poyton.'

'Nice clean house.'

Mrs Bradstock gave him a knowing look over the top of her spectacles.

'It'll be company for her, won't it?' said William. 'With Mr Poyton away.'

'Not the kind of company Mrs Poyton wants.'

'What do you mean?'

'See for yourself.'

William glanced out of the window again. The young woman was bent over, as if pushing the pram was hard work. The wind caught the hem of her coat, making it dance like a ballgown.

She was a splash of colour in a grey landscape, a poppy against bare earth.

'Fur coat, no knickers.'

'What?' said William.

'I said, don't forget your paper.'

The next day, he was cycling back over the hill, the blue of the sea spread out beneath him, when he caught sight of her again. She was sitting on the fence by the side of the road. Same red coat, blond hair blown by the wind. By her side was the pram. As he came closer, he could hear the baby crying.

He got off the bike while it was still moving, as he always did, and stopped in front of her.

'Enjoying the view?'

Up close, he could see she was slightly older than he'd first thought. She was wearing red lipstick. 'Not against the law, is it?'

'Where are you from?'

'Can't you guess?'

'I'd say it was London.'

'East End.'

He said, 'Bit different out here, then.'

'You could say that.'

The baby was still crying.

'Yours?'

She kicked her heel against the fence. Her brown leather shoes were caked in mud. 'He'll go to sleep in a minute.'

'Maybe he doesn't like Dorset.'

'Maybe he doesn't.'

He said, 'What about you? Do you like Dorset?'

She just looked at him.

'Wouldn't you rather be indoors?'

'She doesn't like me there during the day.'

'Who doesn't?'

'Mrs Poyton.'

'Why?'

'I don't know. Maybe she thinks I've got fleas.'

He adjusted his chin strap. 'There's the Mothers' Union.'

'The what?'

'If you want somewhere to go. They meet Tuesdays and Thursdays. In the church hall.'

She laughed. 'The Mothers' Union?'

'Try it. They're always saying they want new members.'

'I don't think they'd want me.'

'Why not?'

'I'm the wrong sort.'

He smiled. 'You can be what sort you like.'

'How about the married sort?'

He didn't blink. 'No one knows you. Say what you like.'

She raised her eyebrows. 'Now there's a thing. A copper suggesting I lie.'

They assessed each other in the September sunshine.

She said, 'So where are you going now?'

'Back to the police house.'

She jumped off the fence. She didn't ask if she could walk next to him, pushing the pram. She just did.

After a while, the baby stopped crying. She bent over and pulled up the soft white blanket so that it tucked under the baby's chin. 'It's colder here than in London.'

'Not so many buildings.'

'Not so many people neither. How do you stand it?'

'I like it. Lived here all my life.'

'They said it's near Weymouth. A village near Chesil Beach. And I thought, That sounds all right, the seaside. But I can't get down there with the pram.'

'It's closed off anyway. And there's only pebbles. And fossils.'

She glanced up at him. 'Fossils?'

'Ammonites.'

She laughed.

'What's funny?'

She said, 'You're young to be a copper, aren't you?'

He smiled. 'You don't hold back.'

'What do you mean?'

'Just say what's on your mind.'

'Why wouldn't I?'

They walked on, keeping pace with each other, his bicycle making an elegant ticking sound. The baby, soothed by the motion of the pram, slept. Now they could see the outskirts of the village, and the steeple of the church.

She said, 'So what do you do on your evenings off?'

'I don't have any.'

She opened her eyes wide. 'You must do.'

'No. My sergeant was in the reserves. So there's only me until they find a replacement.'

'You can go to the pub, can't you?'

'Especially not the pub. Can't drink on my own patch.'

She gave him a pitying look. 'Maybe my life's not so bad, compared to yours. Even if she does kick me out every day.'

'You can't even sit in the kitchen and have a cup of tea?'

She shook her head. 'Says she's got to clean. Says she can't clean if there are people cluttering up the place.'

'Maybe you should offer to help.'

'I did. I dusted the front room. When I turned round, she was doing it again.'

As they reached the village green, he widened the distance between them, straightened his shoulders and set his helmet straight. He was about to say goodbye, but she was looking out over the grass and the little low grey cottages, her expression desolate. 'I'll go mad if I stay here.'

'It's safer than London.'

She turned to face him. 'But there aren't any bombs.'

'Not yet. It could happen any day. Or a gas attack.'

Her eyes were dark with misery.

'Look at it this way,' he said. 'Better safe than sorry.'

She bent down and released the brake on the pram. 'If you say so,' she said, and walked away without looking back.

———•———

Mary said, 'It wasn't his blood, of course. But what did they know? You tell people what they're looking at, and that's what they'll see. It was cold that year. Ice in the farm tracks. That blue light when the world has frozen over. He got to us late. Because he was a thatcher during the day. And the yard was lit with lanterns so people were black shadows against the walls. A great fire burning. And he got hold of her and stretched her on the cratch and tied her down with rope and slit her throat, and I remember the blood gushed out, spurt after spurt, and I couldn't stop watching because I thought, Look how much there is now, filling a whole pail, that will be plenty for what we need. And I picked up the bucket and took it to the scullery, and set it down on the cold stone floor. And then back to singe the bristles off her skin with burning straw, and slit the belly, and hoist her up on the beam. It smelled to high heaven, of course. But we breathed it in like a meadow full of cowslips.'

William stared at her, dazed.

'The pig-sticker. Killing a pig for Christmas. So I knew that part would work.'

He screwed his eyes tight shut, then opened them again.

'You can't get rid of them, can you? The pictures in your head.'

They sat in silence, listening to the clock ticking. They could hear nothing from the outer office. The police station seemed deserted.

Mary said, 'Are you married?'

'What?'

'Married?'

He didn't answer.

'I always think it's so hard for the women when their sweethearts come back injured. Happened a lot in the first war, of course. There was a young man in Langton who had a bomb blow up in his face. Skin pulled tight like a bat's wing. She still married him. Edie Best's daughter. Had six children. Two of them are fighting now.'

When he didn't respond, she said, 'I'll come back another time if you like.'

'No,' he said. 'No, let's get on.'

'You haven't drunk your tea.'

After a while, he said, 'What were you talking about just now?'

'Soldiers getting injured.'

'Before that.'

'Killing the pig.'

'Why?'

'It's part of the story.'

William narrowed his eyes. 'I don't think you're making this easy, Miss Holmes.'

'It wasn't easy when it happened. And it isn't easy to talk about now.'

'What was the importance of killing a pig one Christmas in – when was this?'

'I was twenty.'

'When you were twenty.'

'I did explain. But I don't think you were listening.'

William repositioned his notebook. 'Let's forget the pig for a moment. You were on the beach after a shipwreck. And a man found something, and took it back home. You haven't told me his name.'

'I can tell from your eyes when you're seeing the pictures.'

'When was this?'

'I know what it's like. I spent years trying to forget. But it's like trying to get rid of a bloodstain. You scrub and scrub, but it's still there. So you hide it away so that no one can see. And then you can't talk about it, even if you want to, because it's such a habit, keeping it secret.'

'Miss Holmes—'

'Of course, I nearly told the rector. Several times. All those long afternoons when we sat there in the Ship talking about resurrection and eternal life. And telling me tales, of course. He knew all the old stories, Mr Lester. Shipwrecks and sirens and Calypso and poor Penelope with all those men wanting to marry her even though her husband was still alive. And Aesop's fables. I loved those. The hare and the tortoise. The fox and the grapes. The boy who cried wolf.'

'Miss Holmes—'

'Right at the end, when he came to say goodbye, I wanted to tell him. I wanted to fall at his feet, bury my face in the dust and plead for forgiveness. But I didn't. I wish I had. All those years keeping it secret. Ashamed, I suppose. Frightened of what would happen to me. But I know you won't judge. You'll make up your own mind. And like I told you before, the sin was not in the taking. The Church frowned on it, but they knew they couldn't stop it. The sin was not sharing with the rest of the village.'

'Miss Holmes, what was taken from the ship?'

'If you went down to Swanage in those days, and looked out to sea, behind the stone bankers, ten foot tall, there they'd be, all the ships and steamers heading for the New World. People travelled with everything they owned. Some of them were quite wealthy, too. The younger sons of great families. The choices were very straightforward: the army, the law, the Church, or seek your fortune in America.'

William studied her face. 'Are you doing this deliberately?'

'I'm not sure I follow you.'

'You won't answer my questions.'

'I'm trying to tell you what happened.'

He shifted position, straightening his back. 'I understand that memories can become muddled as you get older. But I don't think you have that problem, Miss Holmes. We've been sitting here for half an hour, and so far you've told me nothing important. I'm beginning to think that there's nothing to tell.'

'That's not very kind, Constable.'

'Perhaps that's why Sergeant Mills asked me to interview you. Because he didn't want to do it himself. Perhaps he has experience of your confessions. I wonder, Miss Holmes, is this something you do to pass the time? Come down to the police station and make up stories?'

'What an unpleasant accusation.'

'You see my point.'

'Perhaps it's the pain. It must make you very irritable.'

'It's not my job to listen to old memories.'

'You have something more important to do?'

'Than sitting here drinking tea?'

'You're never that busy. I often look in when I pass. And it seems to me that the others don't talk to you. Give you a wide berth. Except for the nice sergeant. No one's come to ask for you while we've been sitting here. No one needs you. Because it's a bit of a made-up job you've got, isn't it? Just something to pass the time. I expect someone pulled strings somewhere, because of your war record. And the others resent it, given they're out in all weathers walking the beat.'

After a while, he said, 'I need to know the names of the people buried at Acton.'

Somewhere in the building, a door slammed shut. William flinched.

She said, 'It was always the three of us. All the time we were growing up.'

'Miss Holmes—'

'Arthur followed us everywhere. Here comes your shadow, my father used to say. Trailed after us whatever we did – fishing, finding birds' nests, climbing the rocks near the Pig and Whistle. All the girls in the village mothered him. He was so small. His clothes never fitted him. Moleskin trousers from a man twice his size, flapping round like a scarecrow. Boots tied up with string. His uncle had him working in the quarry when he was seven years old. All by himself in the cold and the dark with nothing but a candle for company. Eighty foot down. They kept the roof up with stone pillars. Sometimes there would be a sound like great guns, and they would split from top to bottom because of the weight they were carrying.'

William looked down at his notebook.

'A mutilated skeleton, they said. Up by Chapman's Pool, in one of the ancient barrows. Bronze Age. Well, that was enough for John. He had to see it. It was a long climb. And when we got there, we saw they'd put a wooden fence round to keep people out. But John just jumped over it. And so, after a while, did we. We were only children. I would have been ten, John and Arthur two years older. So we stood there, looking down at the white bones in the dark earth, and John said, She talked too much. So they killed her and ripped her jaw off. I don't know if it was true. John liked telling stories. But you could see it was only half a skull. Poor little maid with no mouth. And only half buried now. I knelt down, and bowed my head, because you must always show respect for the dead. And that made John mad. He wanted me to laugh at it, this butchered skeleton, and there was I behaving like I was in church. So he got down beside me and started working at the soil, picking at it, scratching away like a fox in the dirt. And he got the skull free. That was bad enough. I thought, God will punish us. God will punish us for this. But then, before I could stop him, he made it worse. He threw it up in the air and kicked it like a football. I cried out in shock.

25

'Arthur got to his feet. Looked at me, and then at John. And I watched as he stumbled away in his big black boots, tripping over the tufts and hillocks like a sheep scrambling on shale. He found the skull some way off, hidden in the long grass. Held it high like a prize. And then he slipped and skidded all the way back, coming to a halt by the grave, and he knelt down and buried the skull again, taking great care, patting the earth smooth when he'd finished. And all the while, John just stood there, watching him, just watching him. And then, when the job was done, Arthur looked up at me. He had such blue eyes. Bright blue, like the sky.

'It floored him, the first blow. Hit him on the side of his head. And then John was upon him, sitting on his back, beating him clout after clout where he lay. I pulled at him, yanking his hair and his collar. But I was nothing. A flea on a carthorse. So I grabbed hold of one of the posts, and it must have been hammered in by a lazy man, because it came free straightaway. And I raised it up and held it high above my head, and I shouted, You leave him alone! Or as God is my witness I will smash your skull! And he stopped, and looked up, and we stared at each other for a long time, and my arms were aching with the weight of the wood.

'And then, very slowly, he stood up, and I held my breath, because I couldn't have stopped him. But all he did was spit on the ground. Then he turned away, and climbed the hill, starting the long walk home.

'But I didn't trust him. I didn't move until he'd gone, until he'd disappeared from sight. And only then did I put down the post and crouch on the ground. Arthur was white, blood on his face, his eyes filled with tears. But he didn't say a word. He didn't say a word all the way home.

'And later I walked back through the village, and passed the smithy as quiet as a mouse, because I didn't want to see John. But he was there all the same. And he looked up, and one of his eyes was fat red and swollen, almost shut fast. So he laid about Arthur that day. But he came back to a worse beating himself.'

William waited. But she was staring down at the wooden table, apparently lost in thought.

He looked at his notebook. He had written down two names: Arthur and John.

———•———

'I climb out the window round the back. She doesn't know any different. I can hear her snoring from here.'

He could hardly make her out. Just the whiteness of her skin in the thick velvet black. 'What about the baby?'

'He's a good sleeper. He never wakes up.'

The tip of her cigarette glowed.

'What's his name?'

'Who?'

'The baby.'

'You don't know my name yet.'

'Stella Allen.'

'You found out.'

'It's my job. In case of an air raid. Names and addresses of our evacuees.'

'But they didn't tell you his name?'

'They hadn't taken a note of it.'

'Not surprising, since nobody asked me.'

The lit stub flew in the air and was ground out, her shoe scraping against the stone.

He said, 'You shouldn't be out at night.'

'What's going to happen? Pecked to death by an owl?'

'You're safer indoors.'

'Oh, have a heart, copper. It's like being buried alive. You know, the other day she asked me to stop singing. Said it gave her a headache. I ask you. My baby's as good as gold. But if he even whimpers there's a frost in the house.'

'Did you try the Mothers' Union?'

'What do you think?'

'You'll settle in. Give it time.'

'How long? They don't want me here. None of them. They hate evacuees. If I go in the shop, they stop talking. Look at me, then look down at the floor.'

'Maybe because you went to the pub.'

She must have turned away, because even the pale blur of her face disappeared. 'So you heard about that.'

'People talk.'

'What's wrong with going to the pub?'

'With the baby?'

'I can't leave him with her. She hates him. I peg out his nappies and she gives me the evil eye. What am I supposed to do? Wrap his bum in newspaper?'

After a while, he said, 'What about the others?'

'What others?'

'From London. The ones you came with.'

'They're miles away. I don't even know how to get to where they're staying.'

'You could borrow a bike.'

'How am I going to get the baby on a bike?'

He heard her sighing deeply. He said, 'It won't seem so bad in the morning.'

'I miss home. I miss everything about it. There's always something happening in London. People having a laugh. Music. Kids playing. Here it's dead. I walked round the green twenty times yesterday, and all I saw was the postman, a herd of cows, and you on your bike.'

They heard the dull clang of the church clock chiming the half hour.

'You didn't tell me what he's called.'

'Peter.'

He said, 'That's a good strong name.'

'Just had his first birthday. One whole year in the world.' There was a rustling of ivy leaves as if she'd leaned back against the wall. 'And before you ask, I've got no idea. He came in on a ship, and went out on a ship. Promised he'd come back and find me and never did. All the nice girls love a sailor. That's what they say.'

He heard the tune in his head.

She said, 'What about you?'

'What about me?'

'Got your eye on a nice girl?'

'There's not many would take it on. Policeman's wife. Life's not your own.'

She said, 'I don't know. Nice little house. Steady income. Doesn't sound so bad.'

'You'd do it, would you?'

'Are you asking?'

For a moment, he couldn't breathe.

She laughed. 'My dad's inside. Did I tell you? House-breaking. Seven years in Pentonville. Mum told him he'd cop it if he kept on. But did he listen? Always flashing his money around. Win on the dogs and he'd buy everyone in the pub a pint. Every bloody sod in Cundy's. We'd be sitting at home starving hungry and he'd be rolling back as drunk as a lord.'

'That must have been hard.'

She said, after a long pause, 'You're not like the others, are you?'

'What others?'

After a while, her voice came out of the darkness again. 'I did what you said. In the shop. Made up a story they might like. I said, My husband's in the merchant navy. I don't know when he's coming back. It's the war, isn't it? You're always the last to know. I'll see him when I see him. And in the meantime, it's my job to keep cheerful. That's what he'd expect. But when I turned round, it was just the same. They didn't believe a word of it. None of them said anything. But I knew what they thought. They speak with their eyes round here. At least back home they say it to your face.'

'They just don't know you.'

'I thought, Poor little bugger, he didn't ask to be born. And Mum stood by me. She said, What's done is done. We'll make the best of it. And we did. Held our heads high. And now they love him. Who wouldn't? He's never hurt anyone.'

He said, 'They don't mean to be unkind.'

'They don't like me. I'm not their sort.'

'Give it time.'

'You know what, copper? I don't know if I want to.'

There was a fluttering above them, a dark shape, a displacement of air. He said, 'They might bomb London. Any time.'

'They might not.'

'It's safer here.'

Something flew so close it almost touched him.

She said, 'You're the only one who ever talks to me. I've been here a month, and if it weren't for you, I'd never even open my mouth. They make me feel like something you wouldn't even wipe your feet on.'

The silence stretched out around them. 'Sounds like you've made up your mind.'

'Would you miss me?'

He said, 'There'd be a lot less to worry about.'

'You worry about me?'

'I worry about Mrs Poyton. She likes everything neat and tidy. And then you came along and turned her life upside down.'

The sudden movement startled him. She had reached up and was pulling his head down, her fingers cold on his cheek, her lips soft against his mouth. The kiss was urgent. She tasted of tobacco and something sharp, metallic. He felt a rush of surprise, of shame, of outrage, and a flood of heat and pleasure that he recognised, belatedly, as lust.

She pulled away. His hand went out to grab her back.

But it was dark, so she couldn't see.

She said, 'Goodnight, copper. Look after yourself.'

And then she was gone.

He stood there, feeling the ground beneath his boots. He waited until his breathing was regular again. Then he turned out of the alleyway – the one that ran all the way down the side of Mrs Poyton's house – and resumed the beat.

It was the last watch before bed.

———

William heard her voice first. It was as if someone was turning up the volume on the wireless bit by bit. And then he saw her again, Mary Holmes, sitting opposite him at the scrubbed deal table in the charge room of the police station in Wareham, her handbag on her lap, her eyes on his face. If she suspected he hadn't been listening – if she thought he'd missed whole sentences, whole paragraphs, whole pages of memories – she gave no sign.

She said, 'But you see, I never really knew him. I look back now, and it seems like a dream. Why didn't I wake up? I saw only what I wanted to see. I can't forgive myself. It's the kind of guilt that wears you down, like water on a stone. I thought I knew him. Well, you do, don't you, if you've grown up together. You think you know them inside out. It was like the time I was sitting with John on the stile, when we were children, and the wind was pulling at my skirt and flapping my bonnet, and I said, One day I'm going to see Africa and India and Australia, and I'll ride elephants and shoot tigers, and eat off gold plates and wear rubies and diamonds, and I thought he'd laugh at me. Because if anyone was going to see the world, it was him. John had no fear. Climbing the bell tower, braving the bull, diving off the cliffs like a plumb weight, hanging like a monkey from the old iron chain that held the bucket in the well. The rest of us were fat and lazy and would die in our beds. But when I said I was going to travel the world, he didn't laugh. He just said, I expect you will. I expect you will do that. And I was so shocked I nearly fell off the fence. You have a picture, don't you, of the way someone is. But then they surprise you, and do something different. And sometimes you don't know if it's your own imagining, or you've just seen the person they really are, beneath the skin, behind the eyes.

'I remember when Arthur's uncle died. We were sitting on Dancing Ledge, looking out to sea, with the waves crashing on the rocks, and Arthur said, I killed him.

'I couldn't believe my ears. I said, What do you mean?

'And he said, I wanted him to die. I killed him.

'And then I thought, Oh, he's taken more notice of Sunday sermons than I ever have. He's punishing himself for what he thinks in secret. Matthew five, verse twenty-eight: *Ye have heard that it was said by them of old time, Thou shalt not commit adultery. But I say unto you, That whosoever looketh on a woman to lust after her hath committed adultery with her already in his heart.* So I said to him, Why wouldn't you hate him, the man who starved you and beat you and never had one kind word to say to you? Of course you wanted him dead. Anyone would. But he wouldn't be comforted. He just sat there, staring into space. And I thought perhaps the shock had been too great, seeing his uncle crushed to death when the chain of the quarr cart broke and it hurtled back down the slide, breaking every bone in his body.'

The graveyard sloped down towards fields on the edge of the village. Far beyond, just visible, was a slice of blue sea.

Stella had her back to the path, head down, shoulders hunched, distancing herself from passers-by.

William walked towards her, pulled by invisible strings.

He said, 'You shouldn't be sitting on cold stone.'

She looked up. Her eyes were blank. 'Why?'

'I don't know. Something my mother used to say.'

The baby, tucked up in the high black pram, slept.

After a moment's hesitation, William sat down on a gravestone next to her. There were splashes of yellow lichen on the grey. 'So what are you doing out here?'

'Is she still alive, your mother?'

'No. They've both gone. You can see their headstones if you like. Over by the lych gate.'

But she just sat there, hugging her knees.

He said, 'I've got a brother. Older than me.'

'I saw him, didn't I? All dressed up in uniform.'

'He was home on leave.'

I'd give it up if I were you, Will. I can see the way you look at her. And I'm telling you now, she's not going to make a policeman's wife.

'He was staring at me in the shop.'

'Probably wondering who you were.'

You told me yourself. If you want to get married, you ask permission. And if the chief constable doesn't like her, that's it. Wedding's off.

She said, 'Maybe he fancied me.'

'Maybe he did.'

She's a good-looking girl. I'll give you that.

'So what did he say?'

'About what?'

'About me?'

She's not happy here. She wants to go back to London. And if you ask me, it's better she does. You don't want to take on another man's child.

'Nothing. Asked why you'd come. I said you'd come here to be safe.'

She put her head on one side. 'And am I?'

'What?'

'Safe?'

'Of course you are. They're not going to bomb sheep, are they?'

She laughed, her expression brighter. 'You never get it, do you?'

'Get what?'

'What I'm on about. I could be talking French. Oh la la and san fairy ann. Like the sailors at the docks. Jabbering away and you don't understand a word.' She studied his face. 'You wouldn't know you were brothers.'

'Why?'

'You don't look like him.'

'Can't all look like film stars.'

'Touched a nerve.'

'I'm used to it.'

'You're just young, that's all. Give it a few years and they'll be queuing up.'

It's your life – I know that. But I might not be back for a while. And I don't want to be worrying about you. Don't get yourself in trouble, Will. Think about what you're doing.

She said, 'Why did you join the police?'

'It's a long story.'

'You don't give a lot away, do you?'

They sat side by side, shoulders almost touching, looking out over the ancient jumble of stones jostled by centuries of wild Dorset winds, with letters so faded you could hardly read the names.

Stella let out her breath in a long sigh. 'I can't see you ever leaving Dorset.'

'Why would I want to?'

'Because you could die of boredom out here,' she said. 'That's why.'

———•———

Mary said, 'My father was everything. He was the rock I leaned on.'

Stella – so strongly remembered that William could still see the sunlight on the surface of her skin – began to fade away, becoming translucent, then nothing but air. He stared at the space she had occupied.

'My mother died when I was six years old. Scarlet fever. Just seven days, my father said, was all it took to snuff her life out. After she went, he protected me like the great hand of God. He had me by his side when the quarrymen came to drink the stone dust from their throats. At night, when I lay listening to the voices beneath me, he checked, with each strike of the quarter hour, that the candle burned until I slept. He taught me to sew and to cook, to skin a rabbit and to sing psalms. He taught me to swim from the rocks and dive down deep in the dark green water looking for lost gold coins. He knew the names of the birds and the trees and wild flowers and lichen. He told tales about pirates and ghosts and mad dogs and lost children.

'On the nights he led the smugglers, bringing down the brandy kegs from Spyways Farm, he couldn't leave me by myself, so he wrapped me up in a woollen shawl and carried me down to the churchyard where I huddled behind the gravestones, half sleeping, as the great shapes of men grew out of the darkness, rolling the barrels, every sound stopped, every footfall silenced. And the next day in church, I would lean against his shoulder, smelling the beeswax and the lilac, and the brown wood of the pew would rise up, darker and darker, and my eyes would close, and my head fall sideways, and my father would catch me,

35

nudging me upright, because no one must know, no one must know our secret.'

William looked up. Mary was staring at him intently. He opened his mouth to speak, to attempt to shape the monologue, but she began talking again before he could frame a question.

'And there were people who said a motherless child should be sent away, because what man can bring up a daughter alone? We muddle along, he said. We muddle along. And we did. We sang while we worked. We were Roman soldiers, Arthurian knights, Roundheads and Cavaliers. The windows were dull with dust, and mud and clay hung in the air. But no one cared. They came to drink in the Ship whether the floors were swept or not.'

William shifted position.

'We grew all the vegetables we could eat. We had a hive of bees and a run of chickens, and sold honey and eggs and spring greens at the market in Swanage. Standing on the shore side by side, we looked out to sea. We saw horses pulling carts of stone into the water, to the barges and the waiting ships. We saw steamboats with grand ladies in wide-brimmed hats, bobbing and dipping as they talked, and lifeboat men in jackets of cork. We saw fishing smacks heading for France, and schooners heading for Scotland, and cargo ships bound for the New World. And I'd look up into my father's face, and he'd look down into mine, and I felt we were standing on the edge of the world, just the two of us, looking out at new kingdoms, hand in hand.'

'Miss Holmes—'

Mary paused.

William rubbed his forehead. 'How is this relevant?'

'I thought you wanted to know about the bodies.'

'I do.'

She frowned, as if confused.

William took a deep breath. 'I don't need to know about your childhood.'

'Yes you do. Or it makes no sense. Half a story is worse than no story at all.'

William stared at her, exasperated.

After a while, taking his silence as acquiescence, she began talking again.

'So John grew up in the smithy, and Arthur grew up in the quarry, and I grew up in the Ship. John's mother died when he was fourteen. His father said she fell down the stairs. No one believed a word of it. Covered in bruises all the time, and only a stick of a thing. Not that anyone said so to his face. He was six foot four and built like an ox. Beat his wife, beat his son, beat anyone who disagreed with him. When the old man finally drank himself to death, John took over the smithy. Ironware for the carts and the horses, punches and chisels for the quarrymen. He wasn't wild any more. Worked hard, went to church every Sunday, kept himself to himself. But no one trusted him, because he always looked as if he'd rather thump you than pass the time of day. Never smiled. Stares you in the eye, my father used to say, like an angry bull.

'Arthur became a stonemason – a Purbeck marbler. Served his apprenticeship and became a member of the guild. It was seven hard years. But he was determined. Fixed in his purpose. I remember the time I passed by the quarry in Acton, and there was Arthur, ten years old, pulling at a donkey that wouldn't move. Leaning back on the rope, heaving with all his might. It just stood there like a tree, rooted in the earth. Tired out, prob-ably. Tired of walking round and round in circles, winding the chain round the capstan, dragging the carts of stone up the slide. But Arthur wouldn't give up. Face white, eyes full of tears, but he was going to have his way. That's how he was. Once he decided something, there was no stopping him. He became a skilled craftsman in the end. When Lord Eldon built the new church at Kingston, carving beauty from stone, Arthur made good money. He cared about his work. *Let your deeds be done as well in the dark as they are in the light.* Steady as a rock, said my father. You know where you are with Arthur Corben.

'Most of the girls left Langton to go into service. All the great houses had armies of kitchen maids and nursery maids and housemaids. Unseen hands doing unseen work. But my father wouldn't hear of it. He said he needed me at home. I propped him up, kept him steady, like a bean cane. I didn't want to leave him. Of course I didn't. But it was a small life. The village took care of its own. Neighbour helped neighbour. You knew who had gout, who had palsy, whose bones ached in the east wind. You knew each sagging roof, each cracked teapot, each silver spoon. You saw the same dress refashioned again and again, passed from mother to daughter, from daughter to baby, then ripped to libbets for the rag rug by the fire.

'Sometimes in the summer the bigger farms took on workers for the harvest. If I was doing errands in the village and heard there were strangers at the Ship, I'd come haring back, gasping for breath, and there they'd be, with their pipes and pints, full of tales from Wiltshire and Hampshire and Somerset and Devonshire. And once or twice when I was growing up, a fair would come to Swanage. It wasn't much – a few stalls selling ribbons and trinkets, an organ-grinder, a tent for marvels like snake-charming and fire-eating. But I couldn't keep still for excitement, clapping my hands, dancing from foot to foot. And my father would stand there, laughing, enjoying my delight.

'The summer I was seventeen, when Mr Lester had been rector of the parish for eight months, my father went off to market without me. I don't remember why I wasn't with him. We always went to Swanage together. But that day I stayed at home. He might have fallen asleep, or struck his head on a branch. No one knows for certain. But they think he fell to the ground and the horse reared up in fright and trampled him where he lay. He was dead by the time they found him.

'They brought him back on a cart and laid him out on the

kitchen table. I remember how white his skin was. It didn't look like him at all. He was always dark from the sun.

'And after that, I was only half alive, like a small animal, its guts spilling out in coils, dragging along in the dirt. I couldn't sleep. I couldn't eat. You could have hung me upside down from a hook, like a dead bird, for all I cared.

'Arthur was one of the coffin-bearers. John was too tall. He had to walk in the procession behind. They all came out, the whole village, every man, woman and child. Because they had loved my father.

'After the funeral, they wouldn't let me stay at the Ship by myself. Mrs Selby took me in. She was the local midwife. Delivered all the babies in the parish. Mr Lester came to see me often. We sat in her parlour as the light faded and he prayed with me. Arthur visited sometimes. He never said much. But he sat with me while I wept.

'It was a long time before I looked up and I heard what they must have been saying for months. Jem Bennett was doing a good job running the Ship, and he was a single man, although a little old at forty-odd and a face like a bag of spanners. What about Samuel Thompson's cousin? He plays the trumpet in Mrs Serrell's orchestra, and he's got a nice little farm up by Acton. There's James Bridle, Harry Thorne, George Burt. There's John Ball the blacksmith, too, but would you want to risk his temper? Like father, like son. And then there's Arthur Corben, of course. A Purbeck marbler, earning a good wage. What a fine young man he turned out to be. There were names from Stoborough, names from Creech, boys from Corfe, men from Worth. All from Purbeck. No one married a foreigner in those days.

'I said to Mr Lester, What should I do?

'And he said, Choose a good man, Mary. Choose a good man.

'Wherever I went, there were questions in people's eyes. It

felt like the whole village was holding its breath, waiting for me to decide.

'There was a tea party for the children that summer. At Mrs Frances Serrell's house. Mrs Serrell wasn't grand at all, in spite of her great connections. One Christmas, the carol-singers were so clogged with drink they could barely stand, and one of them wet his trousers, right there in front of her in the porch of Durnford House, and she just smiled and wished them all the compliments of the season. That afternoon Mrs Hobbs said she needed an extra pair of hands, so I helped look after the children, playing party games – blind buck o'Davy, pig-in-the-middle, the farmer wants a wife – while Mrs Serrell sat watching in the shade of the willow tree on the green velvet lawn. The children had tea – bread and butter, and lemon cake and almond biscuits – and afterwards we wiped their faces, and re-tied their ribbons, and found their lost handkerchiefs, and they lined up to shake hands with Mrs Serrell. And then, when the last of the stragglers had left, I helped carry the empty plates back to the cool dark kitchens inside.

'The minute I walked in, it went quiet. No one would look at me. And I knew they'd all been talking about me the whole afternoon, Mrs Hobbs and Mrs Abbott and Fanny and Maggie and Ada, about what I would do and who I would marry. And I wanted to cry, because the entire village had done nothing but gossip about me for weeks. So I turned on my heel and ran out of the house into the lane. And my eyes were blind with tears, and I kept stumbling on the stones, so I didn't see Arthur until it was far too late, until I'd run straight into his arms, so that we stood there under the great green linden trees, for all the world like lovers in a warm embrace.

'Arthur smiled, and said he'd walk me home. So I took a deep breath and straightened my dress, and after a while I felt calm and quiet again, as I always did with Arthur. And I said to him, They keep teasing me.

'He said, Why?

'I said, They want to know who I'll marry. And I'm tired of it. I have no peace any more.

'Arthur said, And what do you say, when they ask who you'll marry?

'And I said, I say nothing. What business is it of theirs?

'By this time, we had reached the end of the lane. Arthur stopped. The sunlight came through the leaves in little glints and shafts, turning strands of his hair gold. He said, You could always marry me. He made it sound so simple. He said, I'll look after you. You'll never want for anything. Not for as long as you live. We stood in the dancing light, staring at each other. He said, There's no hurry. Take your time. I'll wait for you. His eyes were so blue, blue like the sky.

'Back at Mrs Selby's cottage, I couldn't sit still. I swept up, and righted the rooms. I lit a fire, even though it was summer. And all the while I was thinking about Arthur. Was this what Mr Lester meant? A good man? I kept shivering. I got my shawl, and went to sit by the fire, but I couldn't get warm.'

———•———

It was icy. Total blackout. But the road ahead glistened in the moonlight, as smooth as a frozen lake.

He could see, down the alleyway, the red tip of her cigarette.

Twigs crunched underfoot. Cold leaves brushed his face. She was right at the end, tucked behind a creeper.

She said, 'Evening, copper.'

'Bit late, isn't it?'

'Late for what?' Her white skin gleamed in the cold light. 'I was going to come round and see you in the morning. To say goodbye.'

'You're going, then.'

'I can't stick it here.'

'Home for Christmas.'

She put the cigarette to her lips, a ghostly hand against a pale face. 'Will you miss me?'

'You asked me that before.'

'Maybe I want a different answer.'

'So ask a different question.'

She laughed.

He said, 'What will you do?'

'Go back to work. Keep busy. Be a good girl.' He heard her draw on her cigarette. The tip glowed. She was leaning forward, grinding the stub into the ice, when he pushed her back against the fence.

She said, 'Well, you took your time.'

He bent down to kiss her.

'Take your bloody helmet off.'

When he straightened up, she was standing there, waiting.

It was almost a collision, the force of it. He crushed her, mouth on mouth. They staggered backwards into the ivy. He kept nudging his face into hers, like a dog headbutting for attention, because the kiss wasn't big enough, wasn't swallowing her up. Once, when the slippery sliding of his mouth let her breathe, just for a second, she said, 'Hold on, copper. What's your rush?' But he didn't answer, just tried to push his hands inside her coat.

There was a moment when he thought they were fighting on opposite sides. Then he realised she was undoing the buttons for him.

When it was his turn, she undid his jacket and loosened the buckle of his belt, and her fingers reached down inside. He lifted her up, hands beneath her buttocks, as his trousers slithered to his ankles. Now she had her hands round his neck and her legs round his waist, and he fumbled and tugged and ripped at the clothes beneath her dress, slipping on the ice, steadying her against the wall.

She gave a little cry each time, one, two, three.

Then it was over.

He clung to her, sweat cooling on his skin, blood pounding in his ears, humbled and amazed.

She said, 'Move, can't you? I've got something sticking in me bum.'

So they uncoupled themselves and she pulled free of the ivy suckers and they re-fastened their clothes. William straightened his tunic, tugging at the hem, and adjusted the chin strap on his helmet. He was anxious suddenly, and put out his hand and said, 'Stella . . .' but she shrank back out of reach and said, 'Hurry up. I've got to get back.'

They slunk along the alleyway, heads down, close to the wall, like cats coming home from the hunt.

Just outside Mrs Poyton's back door, Stella close behind him, William looked up. The curtains of the bedroom – the one overlooking all the moonlit gardens, and all the alleyways in between – twitched shut.

———

Someone shouted, 'I can see what you're doing!' and the metal lid of a pig bin clattered shut. A dog started howling, a lone, wolf-like cry. William, startled, raised his head. The voice outside the police station shouted, 'I'll have you! You see if I don't!' and there was another percussive rattle followed by a frightened whimper.

William swallowed. He pushed his finger between his neck and the collar of his shirt, finding more space to breathe. The air in the charge room was hot and still.

Mary said, 'I didn't know what to make of it, Arthur wanting to marry me. Of course I shouldn't have been surprised. My father had liked him. The whole village thought he'd make a good husband. But in my head he was still that little white-faced boy falling over his feet, struggling to keep up. I thought it was my job to look after him, not the other way round. I couldn't think. I felt restless and confused. So I took to walking off over the fields and along the cliff path. Past all the quarries – Chillmark, Smokey Hole, Scratch-Arse. Climbing right to the highest point. You're on top of the world up there. Great green hills with the sea way down below, like God has taken a giant chisel to the land and split it from top to bottom. You stand on the edge, with the kestrels and the falcons up above, and you spread your arms, the wind on your face, and you feel like you could fly yourself. I remember Mr Lester saying that to me, one afternoon. Here's the village, low and grey, like a handful of stones on the surface of the earth. But look up, and there is the glory of God's heaven, the blue skies spread out around as far as you can see.

'One afternoon I climbed down the rocks to the cave behind Dancing Ledge. I should have worried when I saw the bones inside. Skeletons of sheep and deer, their ribs like the frames of old sculls. But I sat there, hidden away, watching the white spray flung in the air from the crash of the sea beneath me, and I felt safe and warm and happy. I thought, There's no point wearing myself ragged, worrying about the future. Who knows what will happen? It will turn out right in the end. It always does. And at that exact moment, I swear, a wave rose high in a thick glass wall and threw itself inside, like God was hurling out a pail of water. I stood up, my heart pounding. The sky had turned dark grey. The sea was dirty, whipped by the wind. Dancing Ledge had disappeared.

'I thought about swimming back. But I was frightened of being dashed on the rocks. By now the cave was pitch black. I remembered that galleries ran higher and higher in a spiral all the way to the roof, so I reached up and found the first with my fingers, and then, bit by bit, I pulled myself to the topmost ledge. The water kept rising. I was screaming, but the sound went no further than the walls of the cave, drowned by the wind and the waves, muffled by stone.

'And then he was there, shouting my name, in the water beneath me. He kept disappearing, coming up again, hauling himself higher and higher, until he was right up to the ledge where I lay, and he shouted at the top of his voice, Mary, we've got to go, take the biggest breath you can. And then we were under the surface, deaf and blind, and I felt him pulling me through the blackness. He never let go. He had the strength of ten men. He got me ashore, pushed me up the rocks, and when I fell, half dead from exhaustion, he wrapped me in his coat and carried me on his shoulders back up the cliff path, all the way over the fields to Acton.

'John saved my life that day. And I knew then that he'd been watching over me. All the time, when I didn't even know. That's how he knew where to find me. That's why he came looking for me when I'd been gone too long. He would always protect me. He would always keep me safe.

'I waited a few days to tell Arthur. I asked him to meet me in the churchyard. We sat down on a low wall and I told him I was going to marry John Ball. He looked so shocked. He said, When?

'And I said, As soon as the banns are read.'

There was a long silence. Mary sat, straight-backed, staring into space.

It was some time before the past disappeared.

William looked down at the notebook lying flat on the table. With great care he shifted its position, just a touch, to the right. 'You don't use your married name.'

'No.'

'Why?'

'No reason.'

He lifted his chin. 'Miss Holmes, I think you're telling me that Arthur Corben and John Ball are buried in the fields near Acton.'

45

She nodded.

'How did they die?'

There was a loud knock on the door. William looked at her. She looked back.

Sergeant Mills put his head round. 'Are you finished in here, Constable? We'd like to make our tea.' He didn't wait for an answer, but strode past the table to the square white sink. He filled the kettle and struck a match to light the gas. 'You wouldn't believe the excitement out there. If I've been told once, I've been told a hundred times. Private Joe Louis just paid a visit to the cookhouse. On his way to a boxing exhibition in Weymouth, and called in to see the soldiers of the twenty-sixth.' He sighed. 'The world heavyweight champion in Wareham, and I didn't even know. There could be Carmen Miranda on North Street and I'd be none the wiser.' He looked up. 'You know the one. Hat made of fruit. South American Way.'

William looked blank.

'One of those tunes that gets in your head. Especially the way she does it. Hi-yi, hi-yi.' The sergeant, reaching up for the tea caddy on the shelf, wiggled his hips. 'Dancing in the tropics. Kissing in the moonlight.'

Mary's eyes were bright with delight.

'From what I've heard,' said Sergeant Mills, peering into a sink full of dirty crockery, 'there's more than boxing going on with the Americans. Unofficially, of course. Bare-knuckle fighting. Fisticuffs. That's how they settle an argument in the ranks. No Marquess of Queensberry rules. Anything goes. A battle to the finish, with bets on the outcome.'

William said nothing.

Turning round, the sergeant caught sight of his strained expression. 'Perhaps Miss Holmes should come back tomorrow.'

William said, 'It might be better to continue now.'

'Ah, yes,' said Sergeant Mills. 'But I might need you, Constable. To write reports.'

Words unsaid hung in the air.

'In that case,' said Mary, rising to her feet, 'I'll leave you.'

'Would you like someone to take you home?' Sergeant Mills seemed to bow, like a footman in a stately home.

'No need. Although it's kind of you to offer.' She turned to William. 'Shall I come back in the morning?'

'About eleven o'clock would be good,' said the sergeant. 'After the morning rush.'

With difficulty, William pushed himself to his feet.

'Please don't get up,' said Mary. 'I can see myself out.'

William turned his head to watch her leave. She looked small and neat in the black coat, her back straight. She was still wearing her hat. She had kept it on the whole time, a Victorian lady going out for tea.

When he sat down, the bench shook, shuddering under the collapse of his weight.

'You can thank me later,' said the sergeant, looking round for the brown teapot and finding it on the table with the empty cups and saucers. 'Talks for England. Doesn't even pause to draw breath. More than an hour with Miss Holmes and you lose the will to live.'

'Her story seemed to hang together.'

The sergeant laughed. 'That's the beauty of it. Quite plausible.'

'She's done this before?'

'Famous for it. She told me once that she'd gone to London and met the King. When he was Prince of Wales, of course.' Sergeant Mills sighed. 'I don't mean to be rude. She was a fine businesswoman in her day. Ran the forge. Once cars came along, she turned it into the biggest garage in Wareham. There was nothing she didn't know about engines. She was proved right so many times, the men stopped arguing with her in the end. Accepted all her advice, as meek as lambs. And I think she misses it very badly, all that respect. Because people forget, you see. Once upon a time, she was a force to be reckoned with.

Especially after the last war. Kept her head through the Depression. Everyone admired her. And now she feels left out. Overlooked. Sidelined. She knows she's not as sharp as she used to be. So she's not above a bit of mischief-making.'

William watched the sergeant give the teapot a cursory rinse. 'When will we hear from the coroner?'

'When he's had time to examine the remains.' The sergeant frowned. 'But he'll be in no rush with this one. Not with a war on. You haven't met him, have you? Medical man. Very practical. Two ancient skeletons buried six feet down near one of the open-cast mines – it'll be an old quarrying accident. They've been mining round Acton since Roman times. There must have been hundreds killed there over the years. The marblers who found them weren't that surprised. It's a dangerous business pulling stone from the earth.'

'But you still want me to talk to Miss Holmes?'

The sergeant tried to look solemn. But, as usual, there was the hint of a smile round his mouth. 'Leave no stone unturned, that's what I say. You never know what you might find.' He lowered his voice. 'But keep your wits about you. She's an old lady with time on her hands. Clever enough to keep you guessing, and wicked enough to waste your time. I doubt she knows anything useful. I'd get rid of her as soon as you can if I were you.'

Tuesday

High in the air, black against the blue, swifts were flying above South Street. They screamed and called, hurtling onwards, racing north towards the flood plain beyond the town walls. For a moment the sky was full of aerial acrobats wheeling and diving like tiny fighter pilots. Then in a flash, fast and free, they were gone.

It wasn't yet nine o'clock, but already there were long queues outside Worlds Stores, the general grocer's, and Whittles, one of the butchers that always opened early. The frivolity of the morning sunshine was making everyone smile. Mrs Walbridge and Mrs Legg, distracted by gossip, stood deep in conversation, their baskets at their feet. A gaggle of boys ran past, shouting and waving catapults, late for school in Worgret Road. Outside Sansom's the ironmonger's, the rector of Lady St Mary's stopped to admire young Mrs Farwell's new baby, bending down low to peer under the hood of the great black perambulator.

At the police station, Vic Smith's dog stuck a thin nose round the edge of the door.

'Watch out,' said the soldier in a loud voice. 'We've got company.'

William looked up. The American was tall, blond and well turned-out – clean-shaven, tie properly knotted, khaki jacket buttoned. But despite the formality, he seemed relaxed and loose limbed, like someone used to working outdoors. He leaned back against the high Victorian counter, and the room around him shrank, becoming small and shabby and mean.

The dog sniffed the air. Mrs Bascombe, standing with her

back to William's desk, retreated one step further, hugging her wicker basket more tightly. Her dark green coat rose up like a hedge. William stared at the cloth, seeing the loops and flecks in the weave.

'He can smell something good,' said the soldier.

William, glancing up, saw that Mrs Bascombe's hair was bundled up in fine netting, and the weight of it bounced on her shoulders as she talked. He leaned forward, straining to hear her voice.

The soldier said, 'Sounds like scrapple. Something we make back home. Throw it all in. Pig heart, pig liver, pig kidneys – everything but the snout. Then slice it up and fry it for breakfast.'

The netting bounced again.

The soldier said, 'Indeed she is, ma'am. The best cook in Wilmington.'

William put paper and carbons in position and rolled the platen. The sudden grinding made Mrs Bascombe jump. She glanced behind and seemed surprised to see William sitting there. He began typing one-fingered, as if distracted by the handwritten notes to his side.

The dog had disappeared.

Outside, a jeep rumbled by, making the windows rattle.

'Just gone to fetch something for me, ma'am. Said he'd be five minutes.'

William picked out, '*is hereby authorised to drive a motor car, lorry, motor cycle or other mechanically propelled vehicle*'.

'So where are you from?' Mrs Bascombe was now sideways on, facing the American. William could see she was smiling.

'Wilmington, Delaware. Same as the colonel. The first state.'

'The first?'

'First to sign the Constitution.'

'And how do you like Dorset?'

'It's beautiful, ma'am. What I've seen of it, anyway. Dorchester.

Weymouth. And I was down in Swanage at the weekend.' He pronounced it Swan-Age, two equal syllables.

'Did you try the fish and chips?'

'We did. Wrapped in newspaper.'

'I always think,' said Mrs Bascombe, in her soft light voice, 'that it tastes so much better in the *Chronicle*.'

The soldier was still laughing when the door to the charge office opened, and Sergeant Mills bowled back into the room, holding out a brown envelope. 'This is what you need. Any more problems, get back to me.'

'Thank you, sir.' The soldier turned to Mrs Bascombe. 'It's been nice talking to you, ma'am. I hope I see you again.'

On the way out, he ducked, too tall for the doorframe.

'I don't think I've seen him before,' said Mrs Bascombe, gazing after him through the window.

Sergeant Mills banged a bundle of papers together. 'He's the colonel's driver. From Binnegar Hall.'

She shook her head. 'Such a sad story. It must have broken their hearts. But they never complained.'

Sergeant Mills cleared his throat. 'So what can I do for you, Mrs Bascombe?'

'Lilian says, can Annie come over for tea. Between you and me, she's got to a tricky bit in her pattern, and needs a bit of help.'

'I'll ask her. She'll be back at three.'

'And she says they're going to be showing a film in the Congregational Chapel on Sunday. One of the Americans told her. They're asking all the local girls.'

'I bet they are,' said Sergeant Mills under his breath as Mrs Bascombe left.

Before William had even framed the question, the sergeant said, 'Binnegar Hall at East Stoke. Lovely old place. Large grounds, a lake, woods. Owned by an elderly couple, Mr and Mrs Farrar. It was requisitioned last November – just before you got here. They turned it into the local HQ for the twenty-sixth. So the Farrars had to leave.' Sergeant Mills sighed. 'Their family home for years. But they're not the only ones. Not by any means. It was the same at Tyneham. Little village near Worbarrow Bay. All of them had to be out by Christmas – everyone from Mr and Mrs Bond to the postmistress. They needed a training area for the troops.'

Under the desk, William clenched his fists to stop the shaking.

'And when it comes to officers' quarters, communications, clerical staff – well, what can you say? The Americans have to go somewhere. There aren't many places big enough. The trouble was, the Farrars had been taking in evacuees since the war started. Four families at one point. Goodness knows how many children. Their chauffeur used to drive them off for picnics in the Purbecks. Waving handkerchiefs and cheering. But the army moved in, and they all had to go. Every last one of them. Some of them just packed up and went back to London.'

William said nothing.

'That seems the way of it these days,' said Sergeant Mills. His usual expression of geniality had disappeared. 'As soon as you get settled, it's all change. Hard to keep up. Nothing to hold on to any more.' There was a small pause. 'Maybe you should go, too.'

William was startled.

'To the chapel,' said Sergeant Mills, 'on Sunday. The Yanks get all the films before they're in the cinema. It'll be something new. You might enjoy it.'

Just before eleven, when Constable Fripp had come back to the station and gone out again, and Sergeant Mills was in the charge room on the phone to Dorchester, William put the cover on the typewriter and pushed his chair back from the desk. He found his notebook and flicked back over the past few pages, rereading his notes.

When he next looked up, Vic Smith's dog was in the doorway again.

For a long moment, they stared at each other.

Then William put out his hand. The dog sped forward, stopping just in front of William's one good knee. It rested its smooth brown head on William's lap, and William, absent-mindedly, stroked its ears.

'We felt like Noah in the flood that summer. The fields were lakes and the crops were drowning. Water as far as the eye could see. Poor farmers. Everything turned to mush. And then the sacks of cheap grain arriving from America. They couldn't make a living. It had always been hand-to-mouth. But now they were staring hunger in the face.'

Mary and William were once again seated at the scrubbed deal table in the charge room. The door was shut. Sergeant Mills had left them in peace.

'Mr Lester had his work cut out. Week after week he had to explain why God had abandoned us.' She shook her head. 'It was never easy for him in Purbeck. I remember the winter he arrived. I was sixteen. The church was packed. There he stood, gaunt and thin, eyes wide with terror. Kept falling over his feet, like a man in someone else's skin.'

William, his eyes on her face, nodded.

'Imagine what it must have been like for him that first Sunday, looking out from the pulpit. He had the Garlands in the front pew, of course, and Charles Garland was a cousin on his mother's side, so he would have felt at home with them. And next to them was Mrs Serrell from Durnford House with her hooked nose and black cape, and she was kind to everyone, from lords to laundry maids. But after that, a sea of faces. A mob. Laughing, coughing, shuffling feet. Loud whispers behind hymn books.

More like a music hall than a church. He kept dropping his prayer book, and losing his place. Leaned forward, trying to work out where we'd got to in the service. But he didn't understand a word we were saying. I remember my father laughing afterwards. He'll learn, he said. He'll learn. And he did, in the end. But he was never one of us. We took the clay from the heath, the stone from the cliffs, the guts from the earth that fed us. We were part of the land. It was our flesh and blood. He grew to love it. But he was always an outsider.'

Again William nodded.

'They were different days, you see, Constable. No railway from Swanage to Wareham then. No strangers in Purbeck. We didn't try to change laws. Not like Mr Lester. We just didn't take much notice of them. Ignored them completely when it suited us.' She stopped, her head to one side. She was wearing the same black hat, but the scarf round her neck was white with tiny blue flowers. 'No notebook today?'

'No.'

'Why?'

'Perhaps I was rushing you yesterday. You need to tell the story in your own way.'

'What a kind young man you are.'

'Thank you.'

She smiled. 'All lies, of course. You're not bothering to take notes because your Sergeant Mills has told you I've got nothing worth saying.'

William's expression was neutral.

'If only he'd listened a bit more carefully. He could have learned so much over the years. So many times I've told him about Mr Lester. And how brave he was. Only a country parson. I like to think I helped that first morning in church. When he looked up, lost, he would have seen me smiling at him. Only young himself. Like a fish out of water. I think that's why he tried so hard to help me later on. All that letter writing. Lobbying.

You'd think a policeman would be interested in what he did. Trying to change the law of the land.' Mary paused. 'I think you ought to write that down. About changing the law. Otherwise you'll forget when it comes to it, and you might miss a vital clue.'

William took a deep breath. 'Perhaps we ought to talk a bit more about lies, Miss Holmes.'

'Lies?'

'Yes.'

She said, 'Mine or yours?'

A kind of tremor shivered through him.

'You're in pain again, aren't you? Have you got pills you can take?'

'Miss Holmes—'

'Did you tell me where you got injured? If you did, I've forgotten. Was it France? Italy? North Africa?'

They sat in silence. Then William said, 'You didn't tell me the truth yesterday.'

Mary had her brown leather bag on her lap. She undid the clasp, took out a white lace handkerchief and pressed it against her lips. Then, carefully, she put it back. 'Proverbs twelve, verse twenty-two. *Lying lips are abomination to the Lord, but they that deal truly are his delight.*'

'Miss Holmes—'

'It was all true.'

'Are you sure?'

'I would have drowned if he hadn't come. He swam out from Dancing Ledge and risked his life to save me.' She gave a little shrug. 'I cut a few years, that's all. It happened when we were children. No one knew at the time. You wonder how children survive, don't you? So many accidents that nearly kill them. And of course you don't tell when you get home, because you know they'll shout at you for frightening them. Hug you to death and then give you a clout.' She paused. 'How did you know?'

'That you were lying?'

'I wasn't lying. I was summarising.'

He shook his head.

'You keep asking me to keep it short. So I chose the best example. I can give you a list of all his good deeds, if you like. All the times he protected me, kept me safe, put my happiness before his own. But we'd be sitting here for weeks.'

'There's something missing.'

'Is there?'

'You're a storyteller, Miss Holmes. And you didn't do this part justice. There was a moment when you made your decision to marry John Ball. And you left it out.'

For a while, she held his gaze, her expression defiant. Then she looked away.

'Miss Holmes?'

Her voice, when she spoke, was quiet. 'Mrs Selby went white when I told her. She said, Are you sure? As if I were going to marry the devil himself. And what could I say? They didn't know him as I did. It's true, he spoke with his fists as a child. But why wouldn't he? It was all he'd ever known. When he grew up, he was wary. Not sure who he could trust. Kept himself to himself. And they didn't like that.' She stared into space. 'When he saw he had a chance with me, the darkness fell away. Like a great black coat thrown to the ground. I hadn't seen him so alive since we were children. Hadn't heard him laugh for years. It was like watching a flower open up to the sun. Although of course no one knew at the start. And we kept it secret for weeks. Meeting at night. Hiding in alleyways. So it was a shock to them. Came out of nowhere. They said they'd never seen a man change so fast. One minute frowning, the next all smiles. Mrs Selby said, You loved him into being, Mary. Loved him into being.'

William stayed still, watching her.

She looked up. 'I didn't tell you about the fair in Swanage.'

'Yes, you did. When you were a child.'

'When I was sixteen. August 1874.'

William shifted. 'Is it important?'

'I'll tell you the story,' said Mary, 'and you can decide for yourself.'

———•———

'There were men wearing flat caps, wide-awakes, billy-cocks. Some in shirtsleeves and waistcoats, some with bright yellow neckerchiefs, velveteen jackets, the odd smock frock. Most of them dusty with earth, all of them drunk on cider. The midday sun burning hot. A rumble of talking and laughing, the smell of tobacco and woodsmoke and sweat. A tiny brown monkey begging for pennies. Right in the middle, a great white tent. On either side of it, stalls selling tin whistles, glass beads, coloured ribbons. Striped flags hanging from the trees, fluttering each time the wind blew in from the sea. Beyond it all, the sloping green of Ballard Down and the vivid blue of Swanage Bay.

'There weren't many women. Just a few, right on the edge of the crowd. One was still wearing her long cotton apron because she had come straight from gutting sprats on the quay, drawn by the shouting and the noise and the music of the fiddle.

'For once, I was alone. My father was at the market, selling honey and eggs and strawberries. Not far away – he was never that far away. But at that moment, sitting high on a wooden handcart, there was only myself to please. I knew the men were watching me. I caught all the glances. But I pretended not to see. They'd watched me earlier, too, when I stood at one of the stalls holding a locket to the light, turning it this way and that, seeing the sun spark on the silvery chain.

'There was a sudden drum roll. And on to the platform in front of the booth came the fighter, stripped to the waist, black moustache, black eyes, black hair greased back. And the barker raised the fighter's arm high in the air and shook it, because he was the unbeaten champion of Dorset, this scrawny man with muscles like rope, and a broken nose, and pitted blue scars on his face. Would anyone challenge him? There is a prize, gentlemen, a cash prize for anyone who can last three rounds.

'Laughter and cheers. Men pushed each other forward. But there were no takers. The barker said, Come along now. Come along. Which of you gentlemen will try his luck?

'Arthur, standing by one of the tent poles, flashed me a quick look. I opened my eyes wide, as if to say, don't you be so stupid, Arthur Corben, don't you dare. His face broke into a smile, and I laughed, too.

'Then someone shouted, I'll do it.

'The crowd strained to see who was speaking.

'John had been leaning, propped up sideways, against a high-wheeled cart right at the back of the crowd. So no one had noticed him until now when he stood up, head and shoulders above the rest. There was low murmuring, both approving and disapproving. They didn't like him, the surly blacksmith. At the same time, they wanted to see a fight. And he was the only volunteer.

'He walked to the front and climbed on to the platform. He was easily taller and heavier than the champion with the blue scars. Ten years younger, too. But fighting is about skill, tactics, experience. That's what they were saying in the crowd. And John Ball wouldn't be so quick on his feet, being such a big man.

'We have a match, said the barker, his voice ringing with triumph. And the crowd surged forward to the entrance of the tent, and people handed over their pennies, and they all crammed inside, standing round the makeshift ring. Money was changing hands, from pocket to pocket, from palm to palm, betting on who would win. Then the champion appeared. John was just behind him. He had taken his shirt off, too, and you could see his blacksmith's muscles, the cords in his neck, the thickness of his arms. The air was charged inside the tent, smelling of earth and warm grass and unwashed bodies. And the barker said, A fair fight, gentlemen, a fair fight, that's what we want, and the crowd cheered. He held them apart, John and the champion. He wanted you to think they'd be at each other's throats if he wasn't standing between them. And then, with a flourish, he stood back, and they faced each other in the ring.

'John's expression was set, almost angry. The champion showed no emotion at all.

'John threw the first punch, which hit nothing, just air, because the champion ducked. Someone laughed. John was ashamed, his face flushed red. He tried again. When his third punch failed, the crowd groaned.

'Then John staggered back from a blow to the chin. I caught my breath. But he rallied. And now they were circling each other, watchful. John lunged, but the champion stopped him with a punch below the ribs and John doubled up, folding like paper.

'The crowd was shouting now. John found his balance and threw himself forward. But it seemed the champion was waiting for this, for he dealt a blow to the side of John's head that made him spin round and fall to the grass floor, lying on his back with his arms outstretched.

'The barker stepped in. Round one, gentlemen, he said. That's it. On to round two. John sat up, dazed. There was a cut above his eye, and a ribbon of red blood trickled all the way down his neck.

'I put my fist to my mouth and bit hard on my knuckles.

'Arthur shouted, Come on, John.

'The crowd took Arthur's lead, and now everyone was shouting John's name, first singly and then in a chorus. John shook his head and got to his feet. The crowd roared its approval.

'John hit the champion on the cheekbone, and the blow threw him halfway across the ring. The crowd went wild. Now watch, they said to each other. His blood is up. The blacksmith is angry. Now we'll see a proper fight. John dodged the next punch and managed a short jab to the champion's stomach. The two fighters seemed evenly matched, trying feints and parries, testing each other's guard.

'Then the champion punched upwards, right underneath John's chin, and followed it with a sideways swipe to the head. John fell with a crash. He lay still. The crowd was hushed, waiting. John rolled to one side, tipped himself on to all fours, pushed himself to his feet. As people started shouting encouragement, the barker strode back into the ring. Round three, he said, looking from one to the other. When you're ready, gentlemen. When you're ready.

'John stood as still as stone. Then he shook his head, like a dog ridding its coat of seawater, and sweat and blood flew out in a fine spray.

'Arthur yelled, Only one more round!

'And now I found my voice. I shouted, John, stop. No more. But the noise of the crowd drowned me out. He didn't hear me at all.

'John lumbered forward. The champion waited, just for a second. And then he was punching John's head again and again, so that his skull seemed to bounce from side to side, from one fist to the other. He was blinded by blood. But though he swayed and stumbled, he didn't fall. The champion swung again. Now John's forearms were up against his face. He took blows to his ribs, his stomach, his back. He wasn't fighting any more – just standing there, stunned, taking a beating. One of the women in the crowd shouted out, For shame! That's enough! But the match couldn't end because John was still on his feet. The mood began to turn. The lad's only young. He's being battered half to death. It's not right. Someone shouted, Give it up, son! And John turned, and the champion's knuckles met the bone of his face, the socket of his eye and the bridge of his nose, and his neck snapped backwards.

'The barker strode into the ring, catching John as he stumbled, staggering under his weight. He held John's arm high in the air. Still standing after three rounds, he said. A noble winner of the challenge. Your very own champion in Swanage.

'There was clapping and cheering.

'John's face was a mess of blood, puffed out like a mound of dough. His eyes couldn't focus. He was unable to breathe. Someone took his arm. Bent over, he shuffled forward, and the crowd hid him from sight.

'Who's next? shouted the barker. Who else will take the challenge?

'I was desperate. I stood on tiptoe, dodging this way and that. But the crowd was too thick. There was a moment when the coat backs moved apart, but all I could see was Arthur, looking somewhere over my head, his face blank.

'Outside the tent, I searched everywhere. I ran from stall to stall, past shiny trinkets and flagons of cider and trays selling ribbons and lace. I kept asking, Have you seen John Ball? Have you seen the blacksmith? But people just shook their heads and turned away.

'I'd almost given up hope when I found him. He was sitting on the stone steps leading down to the quay, fully dressed, facing out to sea. But he saw nothing of the view, because one eye was tight shut, like a black slit, and the other was buried beneath a cushion of swollen flesh. Seeing him like that, broken and bruised, I was filled with rage. I shouted at him, Why? Why did you do it?

'He opened his mouth to speak, but there was only blood.

'I said, Wait here. I'll get my father.

'He put out his hand and touched my sleeve. With great difficulty, like an old man with arthritic hands, he reached into the pocket of his waistcoat.

'He drew out the silvery locket.

'In the hot afternoon sun, the light danced on the chain.'

———

'Silvertown,' said Mrs Poyton. 'That's where she lives, isn't it?'

William looked down at the polished black doorstep.

'No notice. Nothing. Just disappeared. I went upstairs, and the room was empty. Bed stripped, blankets folded, and the cot just a bare mattress. It was a shock. After all I'd done for her. Taken her in, given her a home. But what can you expect? No manners, the lot of them.'

'Did she take the train?'

'No idea.' Mrs Poyton, arms folded, fixed him with a cold stare. 'As I say, she told me nothing. Is there a problem, Constable?'

'Just regulations, Mrs Poyton. It's my job to keep track of the evacuees.'

She raised an eyebrow. 'So I noticed.'

William flushed dark red.

'How's that brother of yours? You must be so proud of him. I expect you feel a bit ashamed, safe and sound in the country while he's off fighting the war.'

'I can't join up until they've found a replacement for Sergeant Drew, Mrs Poyton.'

But she wasn't listening. 'I hope you're not expecting me to take on anyone else. Because I can't do it. Not now. Not with Harold away. I asked for a girl. That's what I wanted. A nice quiet little girl. Someone to keep me company and help round the house. I never said I'd take a baby. It cried all the time, you know. Morning, noon and night. I haven't slept a wink for weeks. My nerves are shattered.' She paused, remembering. 'She left something behind. I wasn't sure what to do with it.'

'I've got the address somewhere.' William kept his voice casual. 'I'll forward it on, if you like.'

Mrs Poyton turned and vanished into the shining depths of number two.

William concentrated on regulating his breathing.

'Here.' Mrs Poyton reappeared. 'And you needn't worry. It's quite clean. Boiled it and bleached it.' She pursed her mouth. 'Most of them were grey, you know. I don't think she even cared.'

William looked down. Mrs Poyton had handed him a towelling nappy.

———·———

'I never thought I'd marry him,' said Mary. 'Not at the beginning. There was always something between us. But I didn't like it. He made me angry. He assumed too much. So I wouldn't let myself think of him. And that's why I couldn't make up my mind. I look at it now and I can see what I was doing all those months. I was waiting. All the talk. All the knowing looks. I was tired of it. Tired of the whole thing. But I couldn't make a decision. Not until I knew what John would do.'

William focused with difficulty on Mary's face.

'Are you all right, Constable? You look very pale.'

'Why did you tell me about the fair?'

She frowned. 'So that you'd understand.'

William looked down at the scrubbed, bleached wood of the table.

Mary said, 'No one knew the whole story. Of course they didn't. All they heard was that John had lasted three rounds against the champion of Dorset. They were even more afraid of him after that. Didn't want to get too close in case he lost his temper and hit them.'

'What happened to the locket?'

Mary looked surprised. 'I didn't think you were listening.'

'John took a beating to buy it for you. With the prize money.'

'Yes.'

'Do you still have it?'

'Why?'

William said nothing.

'You want the evidence. Because you still don't believe me.' Mary sounded reproachful. 'You think I'm making it all up. A foolish old woman telling tall tales.'

'Tell me what happened to the locket, Miss Holmes.'

For a moment, her mouth was set, as if she didn't intend to answer. Then she shrugged. 'I threw it away.'

William stared.

'It broke. It was only tin. And I could never have worn it. A locket is a gift from your sweetheart. And he wasn't. Not then.'

There was a taut silence.

'You shouldn't judge. John knew from the beginning. Right from when we were children. But it took me a long time. Eighteen years. He didn't blame me for that. And neither should you. One Corinthians thirteen. *Though I speak with the tongues of men and of angels, and have not charity, I am become as sounding brass, or a tinkling cymbal. And though I have the gift of prophecy, and understand all mysteries, and all knowledge; and though I have all faith, so that I could remove mountains, and have not charity, I am nothing.*' She looked away. 'He called one afternoon. Soon after Mrs Serrell's tea party. Came in and stood in the front parlour, holding his hat, forced to stoop because of the low ceiling. Eyes on the floor. Black hair falling over his face. Shoulders so huge his neck had almost disappeared. He sat down in the ladderback chair, a giant in a doll's house. Mrs Selby said, He brought a rabbit that he caught this morning. Neither John nor I said a word. She said, He thought we might like it. And still we sat in silence. I stared at my lap. He stared at his boots. When he stood to go, the movement was so sudden that the chair fell backwards. And afterwards Mrs Selby said, What did he want, Mary?

'He called again a few days later. When Mrs Selby left the room, he looked up, his eyes fierce, and said, Is it true?

'And I said, Is what true?

'And he said, You and Arthur. That's what they're saying. Married before the year's out.

'I was angry – all the gossiping tongues. I said, They can say what they like. I've made no promise.

'John stared at me. He said, But you might?

'After that we could say no more. Just sat there like beaten dogs. The clock ticked. Outside, a wagon, piled high with stone, ground its way down the street to the bankers at Swanage. It got so late that the day began to fade away, but neither of us moved to light a candle. And suddenly I began to weep, because I felt so lost and so alone, and I wanted to speak, but I didn't know where to begin or what I wanted to say. It seemed so hopeless, all those years of fighting and fury just to end up here, in the half-dark, unable to say a word. I couldn't reach for a handkerchief in case the movement made him look up. So I just sat there, tears running down my face and into my lap. And when he did glance up, finally, his eyes opened wide with shock. He didn't know what to do. He moved towards me, and then stopped, and suddenly he was on his knees at my feet, pulling me to him, kissing me on the mouth. And he took my face and held it, and looked at me for a long moment before he kissed me again. And all I knew is that I wanted him to go on. We heard a sound outside in the passageway, and he got to his feet, and I put out my hand to stop him leaving, but he misunderstood and shook it instead, his great hand holding mine. And after he left, I stood there in the dark, my heart racing, wanting to run after him but unable to move. And Mrs Selby came in and said, But why didn't you light the lamps, Mary?

'At church on Sunday, I knew he was there, just behind me. I felt him breathing. I felt his presence like a touch on my skin. I turned round when we sang the hymn, and we stared at each other. Neither of us could look away. And for the first time since my father died, I didn't feel afraid. I knew my own mind. I felt free. Like breaking out from a dark room into sunlight. The joy of it made me want to laugh out loud. We were blessed, you see, by needing each other so badly. Once the fire was lit, it raged like a furnace. The past was burned, and the world around us was clean and new.'

William made a slight movement as if he were about to speak, but said nothing.

'When I told Arthur I was going to marry John, he looked as if I'd hit him. I saw the boy again, hurt and humiliated, blood smeared on a white face. It didn't stop me. Nothing did. People talked. Of course they did. But I didn't listen. I gave Jem Bennett notice, and Mrs Selby and I set to, cleaning the Ship from top to bottom. Mrs Adams made me a wedding dress of pink sprigged cotton trimmed with lace, and the banns were read three Sundays in a row. By the time Mr Lester married us, the third week in September, in a church filled with campion, cornflowers and harebells, I was so impatient to be John's wife that I almost grabbed the ring and put it on my own finger.

'That night, we had a party in the Ship. Toast after toast to Mr and Mrs John Ball.

'The only person missing was Arthur. One minute he was there, the next he had gone.'

The room was silent except for the ticking of the clock.

After a while, William said, 'So you were happy.'

'As happy as sandboys. Couldn't be apart. Not for a second. Twined round each other like ivy. The women didn't approve, of course. Wives were supposed to endure their husbands, not lust after them.'

William nodded. Then he said, 'How did he die, Miss Holmes?'

'It's quite warm today, Constable. Could you open a window?'

William got to his feet and walked stiff-legged to the sash window. He steadied himself against the wall. When he pulled down the top frame, he could feel the warm May air on his face.

From behind him, Mary said in a loud voice, 'I can hear the firing now the window's open. From Lulworth. From the gunnery school.'

His whole body started to tremble.

'Of course, they have to learn, don't they, these young men. You can't send them into battle without training.'

He held so tightly to the window frame that his knuckles went white.

'Can you hear it, Constable?'

When the shaking stopped, he turned and made his way back to the table. It took a long time. His stiff leg was dragging, as if it didn't quite have the strength of the day before.

She said, 'Young and fit. Bright new marriage. We should have been happy. But it all went wrong. That was the tragedy. Of course, times were hard. No one drinking at the Ship. Even the smithy was quiet. But that was the same for everyone. And we weren't starving.'

William sat down. 'So what happened?'

There was a knock on the door. Sergeant Mills appeared on the threshold. 'Constable, a quick word. I've got an appointment at the rectory, and then another at Baggs Mill. Your fellow officers are all out and about, so the desk is temporarily unmanned. I'll leave this door open, and you'll be able to hear if anyone needs attention.' He nodded at Mary. 'Morning, Miss Holmes.'

'Good morning, Sergeant.'

'Very busy, as you can see. Inspector Pearce unexpectedly called away this week, so just me and my four constables. Very long hours. Normal police duties, plus wartime extras. Petrol changing hands where it shouldn't. Movement of aliens. Crashed aircraft. Unexploded bombs. Security. Had to tell Mrs Jackson this morning that her mother couldn't visit a restricted area. What with the coast out of bounds. And no one allowed in the army training areas, of course. And then there's our American friends. The odd bit of translation needed here and there. So we might need to hurry you up a little. I'm sure you understand. It's very important to find out why those bodies were buried in Acton all those years ago. But there's a war on. And police time is limited.'

Mary, small and neat in her black coat and hat, just looked at him, saying nothing.

'So, Constable' – Sergeant Mills pushed the door open wider – 'you're in charge now until I get back at lunchtime. If you could finish with Miss Holmes here and type up the report, I'll see what needs to be passed on to the coroner's office.' He paused. 'Constable Meech's bicycle was missing again this morning. Any ideas?'

William shook his head.

'I have my suspicions. I'll be making enquiries.'

After Sergeant Mills had left, they sat in silence for a moment. Then Mary said, 'His daughter Annie works up at Holton Heath, you know. In the cordite factory. Making bombs. Lovely girl. Dark hair and blue eyes, just like her mother.'

William nodded. 'Before we were interrupted—'

'I think I'd be quite worried if I were Sergeant Mills. They have accidents all the time up there. Hands blown off. Terrible burns. One girl hanging out the window with half her insides gone. Hushed up, of course. Like the army training exercises on the beach at Studland. We've had the King and Mr Churchill watching from the cliffs, but we're not supposed to know, are we? So much you have to keep secret when there's a war on.' She stopped, looking anxious. 'I hope this doesn't count as careless talk. It's all right to talk about secrets with a policeman, isn't it? I don't want to be arrested.'

'Miss Holmes—'

'They like working there at the factory. The pay is good. And they're doing their bit for the war while the men are away fighting.'

William trembled, as if he felt a cold draught on his neck.

'It's not so private with the door open, is it? And so much noisier. You can hear all the people on South Street.' She hesitated. 'Although I'm never quite sure in your case. I remember reading once, years ago, that it's not so much the hearing. It's

70

that you have to concentrate so hard, if you're a bit deaf. And sometimes it gets too much, and you just want a rest, so you stop listening altogether.'

'Miss Holmes, you were talking about the time just after your marriage to John Ball. And I asked you what happened next.'

The ringing of the telephone in the booth startled them both. William got to his feet and struggled across the room. He picked up the receiver and leaned against the wall while he listened, his face tense with effort. Several times, he said, 'Could you repeat that, please?' At the end, he said, 'Fine. I'll tell him.'

He had made his way back, and was about to sit down, when Mary said, 'You must worry every time the phone goes, in case it's news of a raid and you have to sound the siren. I hear Plymouth is still being bombed. Poor souls.' She shook her head. 'Perhaps I should go. Sergeant Mills is quite right. You have so much to do. And the bodies are going to stay dead, aren't they? I'm not sure you would even be spending all this time on it if I hadn't come in here on Monday and told you I knew who they were.'

'You seem in quite a hurry to leave.'

'Not at all.'

William lowered himself on to the bench. 'This always seems to happen when I ask you a direct question.'

'As your sergeant said, you're very busy. I can come back another time.'

'I need to write the report. All I have at the moment is the names.'

'I could come back tomorrow.'

'Shall we run through what you've told me so far? You married John Ball.'

Mary looked down at the brown leather handbag on her lap. 'Yes, I did. September 1876.'

'But then he died.'

'Twice.'

William frowned. 'I'm sorry, what did you say?'

'No, you heard me. He died twice.'

'Miss Holmes, is this another example of wasting police time?'

She looked up. Her eyes were full of tears.

For a moment, neither spoke.

'Miss Holmes—'

'I have to tell you the whole story. I can't just pull out bits and pieces in a rush. Or none of it makes sense.'

William nodded.

'No,' she said, 'you don't understand. I have never told anyone before. It can't be done quickly. And the more you try to hurry me, the more confused I become. If you want to know what happened, you have to be patient.'

He said nothing.

She opened the bag on her lap, took out a white handkerchief, and carefully patted the skin beneath both eyes. Then she said, 'Of course in those days, you had to pretend that nothing was happening. You took out the seams of your dress and covered yourself in a shawl and no one referred to it at all. John was so proud. So happy. But he didn't like me being in the Ship of an evening. Not once I got bigger. So I spent many hours upstairs alone, sewing tiny stitches with a sharp needle, listening to the singing below.' She stopped, staring into space. 'I was washing the bedsheets in the tub when the pains started. So sharp I gasped and dropped the dolly peg. When I could breathe again, I went for Mrs Selby, and she brought me back and got me into bed. I lay there, torn limb from limb, wanting it all to stop because I knew it was early, much too early, a full two months to go. And then suddenly he came, in a rush, still in the caul. And Mrs Selby took him up and wiped his face and blew in his mouth. But there was no breath, no movement, no quickening of the spirit. She tried everything she knew. She massaged his tiny body. She splashed him with ice-cold water. But he was stillborn. And in the end, when there was nothing more she could do, she wrapped him in a clean cloth and put him in my arms, and I looked down at his little face and wept, because I had failed him, my body had failed him, and he hadn't been allowed one breath of life, not one breath of life at all.

'And John came and stood at the end of the bed, shoulders bowed, tired and bent like an old man, and I couldn't look at him because it was my fault, all my fault, and I couldn't bear to see his sadness. When he left the room, Mrs Selby said, They don't know what to do. And I said, Then they should stay away. But I didn't mean it. I needed him. I needed him so badly. But he did as I asked and kept his distance. So I hated him. And in no time at all, there was a chasm between us. We were like two people washed apart on opposite sides of a great wide river. If my father had been alive, he would have told me that grief makes you cruel. You turn on the person you love. But there was no one to help. We were frozen by sorrow. At night we lay side by side like stone statues in a church. And the more it went on, the worse it became. We started to fight. We picked holes in each other. All in public. They loved it in the Ship. You see, they said, that's what happens. Marry an angel, and end up with a shrew.

'Most of the time I was too numb to care. But sometimes the gossip made me angry. I thought, If you think I'm behaving badly, I'll behave even worse. So I'd put on a pretty dress, and flirt with any man stupid enough to play the game. And one night, one of the farm workers pulled me on his lap and gave me a kiss, smack on the mouth, and John picked him up by the scruff of the neck, like a cat, and threw him out the door so hard he screamed in pain. He must have broken his shoulder. And then John turned to me, fury in his eyes, and I took fright, and ran all the way up the street to Mrs Selby's house. And she gathered me in and dried my eyes, and I told her what had happened.

'And she said, Be careful, Mary. You're playing with fire.

'I said, He has no right to treat me like that.

'She said, He's your husband. Of course he's going to be jealous. What do you expect?

'I wouldn't listen. I wanted to hurt John. By that time I blamed him for everything, for all that had happened, even though I was the one who had sent him away.

'And so it went on. We were stuck, never touching, like steel rails running side by side. We had set so much store on love being the way of salvation. But it seemed, in the end, the pathway to hell.

'So the pattern was set. Two years after we married, you would never have known there had been any passion between us at all. Sometimes it made me so weary, I packed some possessions and went to stay with Mrs Selby. She always made me go back in the end. For better, for worse, Mary, she'd say. For better, for worse.'

William waited. And then Mary began talking again.

'They were cold izemorey days. Another wet summer lingered in the air so that everything smelled of damp. The rain fell in soft splinters or hung in a fog, like low cloud. Washing never dried. At dusk, when the lamps were lit, the Ship looked like its namesake, bobbing about in a sea of mist.

'One night the inn was almost deserted. Just a few old boys nursing their half-pints. I went out to the garden to lock away the chickens, and when I got back to the scullery, I heard the front door slam. And then I heard Mr Hobbs say, Well, will you look at the ghost the night brought in. I remember feeling afraid. I walked through to the front room.

'And there was Arthur.

'He was the same, of course, but so different. Broader,

stronger, older – still Arthur, but a boy no more. I saw him and I wanted to cry. I wanted to slide to the floor and tell him all about John, and the baby, and how our love hung raw and bleeding like the carcass of a butchered pig. But the inn was full of noise and shouting and the old boys cracking jokes, and all I could do was stare, as if Arthur were still a long way distant, far out of reach.

'And then he looked at me, with his bright blue eyes, and it was as if we were the only people in the room.

'He'd been living in London, working on the Royal Courts of Justice. He described a world from a fairy tale – electric lights, double-deck omnibuses, a stone plinth from Egypt brought to the River Thames and set on end, straight to the sky, like the rock of Old Harry.

'And then somebody said, So what brought you home? And Arthur looked at me. I caught my breath. He said, The sky. You stand in London and look up, and there's nothing but walls all around you.

'And so the talk went on, and the gossip about this and that, and it got later and later, and John said, So will you stay here tonight? And my heart missed a beat. And that night as I lay in the dark next to John, I thought of Arthur sleeping in the room next door.

'He was meant to stay only a few days. But the days length-ened into weeks. He found work as a stonemason here and there, and helped out at the Ship. His presence eased our lives. He balanced us, like the third leg of a milking stool.

'Mrs Selby said, How long is he staying?

'I said, I don't know.

'She shook her head. It will end in tears, Mary. I'm warning you now, no good will come of this.

'But she was wrong. We needed each other. Arthur had a home. John was calmer. I was happier. We told each other tales from our childhood. We remembered long summer days

75

on Dancing Ledge, fighting off pirates and French invaders, freeing missionaries in Abyssinia. We forgot the squabbles and the fights. We remembered only the sunlight. Sometimes I looked at John and felt truly sorry for all that I'd said and done. With Arthur at the Ship, the bickering stopped. We were kind to each other. I felt the great wound in our marriage knitting together underneath, bringing the edges closer bit by bit.

'Once I said to Arthur, Will you go to London again?

'He said, Why? Do you want me to?

'And I said, No, I don't want you to go to London.

'He said, What if I did? What would you do then?

'I said, I'd come and find you. And make you come home.'

———

It was a fog of rot – smoke and the stink of broken sewers. Steam was rising from burned brick blasted with hoses, the puddles oily and red-hot. Goering's Blitzkrieg, London bombed night after night. The civilians' Dunkirk, the papers said. Homes shattered, but not their hearts.

It was nearly a year since he'd first seen her, in her red coat, pushing the pram round the village green.

'All right, soldier?'

William stared. Here was the November morning, the new day, the sun. But nothing was real.

'Lost someone?'

William started stumbling through the rubble. The night before, when he'd first got to London – sirens, fires, explosions, continual bombardment – he had thought only of shelter. Underground in the station with the others, breathing in the fetid smell of old sweat, he had slept between the cold tracks in the draught from the tunnel. When he woke, watching grey mice streaming between the humped bodies, he remembered why he had come. No answer to his letters. He had to know if she was safe. So he stood up, found a dark corner to piss in, and climbed the stairs to the street.

Outside, on the opposite side of the road, the building had its windows blown out, like a mouth with missing teeth.

There were kids playing on the bomb sites.

An open-topped car drove by with metal milk churns in the back.

If he had known his way round the city, he might have found Silvertown sooner. He could have gone to the docks and followed the river. But he spent all morning wandering aimlessly, increasingly disoriented, stopping for men carrying ladders or women pushing prams. Once, his way was blocked by the carcass of a horse with no head. Another time he turned the corner, and there was the cinema with a slice taken from it, so it just said DEON in big letters.

He was aware that he was thirsty, and that his legs were tired. He nearly stopped for a cup of tea in a café with a sagging roof ('Business As Usual'), but a dog ran up and licked his fingers as if it knew him, which made him feel he had to press on while the going was good.

Under the arches, with a train running overhead, it was so dark he fell over a pile of rags, which moved and split apart and there was a huge white breast, gleaming, like the knuckle bone in a plate of stew, and a woman said, 'Coming home with me, love?'

His eyes were gritty with dust and tiredness. His head hurt. The sky was yellow with old burning.

It was late morning when he found it – an East End terrace, one of many that looked exactly the same, with front doors opening straight on to the street. He counted the houses as he passed. Then he stopped. In front of him was a heap of wood, finely splintered, like a pile of giant matches. Beyond that, two rows of huge empty matchboxes, one on top of the other, trailing twisted metal, ribbons of fabric, and spirals of grey dust.

Beneath his feet was powdered glass.

Stella's house had gone. There was nothing left.

———

She was watching him. 'I wish I knew.'

William stared, his eyes empty.

'I wish I knew what you were remembering.'

He took a deep breath.

Mary said, 'I sometimes wonder if that's how God punishes us. You don't look out and see the sky and the sea, taste the salt in the air, smell the meadowsweet and hawthorn blossom. All you see are the pictures in your head. You see nothing but memory.'

'Do you want to go on?'

'What do they do, Sergeant Mills and the others, when you stare into space like that?'

He said nothing.

'It must happen to a lot of soldiers.'

For a while, there was silence in the room. Then William said, 'So Arthur has returned and is living at the Ship.'

'Not until you're listening.'

'I am listening.'

Still she waited, carefully examining his face.

He said, 'Miss Holmes, I'm ready.'

'Arthur came back from London. I was twenty years old, an orphan, the mother of a stillborn child, an unhappy wife. But Arthur made the days easy again. In his company, John and I were civil to each other. Some of the drinkers at the Ship were wary, because you never knew what Arthur was thinking, with that empty expression in his eyes. But he was calm and polite, and quick to lend a hand, so people forgave his reserve. By the time of the shipwreck, he was so much a part of Langton, it felt as if he'd never been away.

'So the storm passed, and the bodies were brought up from the rocks, and the scavenging was hidden up chimneys, and in priest holes, and down the back of secret drawers. But the destruction in the village was terrible. Sagging roofs, broken windows, carts overturned. There was mud splashed everywhere, as if a giant had lumpered hurdle-footed through the fields. We heard stories of whole cottages flattened on Norden Heath. At Stoborough, the river flooded and boats went floating off over the fields. They said the winds had been so strong that the great ruins of Corfe Castle trembled.

'By seven o'clock the next morning, everyone had left. The survivors had gone to the vicarage to wait for the ship's agent, and we'd sent with them tattered bundles of flotsam to make it look as if we'd handed over everything we'd found. Arthur had gone to Durnford House to help Mrs Serrell with her fallen trees. The Ship was empty. I was so tired, I could hardly speak. But John seemed happy enough, whistling as he stoked the fire.

'Before he left for the smithy, he said, They say the ship was bound for Australia.

'I said, Well, it's not going anywhere now.

'There are others. Going to America. God's own country. Land of opportunity.

'There was something in his voice that made me look up. I said, What are you talking about?

'He laughed. He said, A man can dream, can't he?

'At church on Sunday, Mr Lester said he still hoped that some of the poor souls' belongings would come in on the tide, and asked us to keep careful watch. We looked down at our boots. Most of it was hidden away in our houses.

'A month after the storm, we risked a meeting in the Ship. Everyone gave a list of what they'd taken. A value was placed on each thing – tea, brandy, leather gloves, wine, books, boots, candles. Some of it was ship's cargo. Some of it belonged to the dead victims. Most of it was scuffed and battered, stained by salt and water. We agreed how it would be shared. And then we crept back home.

'One night, when the last drinker had left, and Arthur had shot the bolt across the door, John said, I need to talk to you both. It was more an order than a request. He fetched a bottle of brandy and three glasses. And we sat down and he told us about diving down the night of the storm, and the dead woman, and the cabin, and the key in the corner cupboard.'

Outside, in the main office, someone shouted, 'Hello?'

Mary looked at William. With difficulty, because his outstretched leg had pinned him in position, William turned to face the open doorway behind him. He was about to push himself upright when the tall young soldier, the colonel's driver, came into view. The energy of his arrival snapped the distant past back into dusty corners. The charge room seemed full of light.

Mary – who had been hunched forward, close to William's ear, to tell her story – sat up straight, as if guilty of some kind of breach of etiquette.

There was a ragged silence, full of strange ellipses.

The soldier said, 'Is Sergeant Mills here? I want to leave something for the lady I spoke to earlier.'

William just stared at him.

'Mrs Bascombe,' said Mary. 'She told me all about your conversation. How to use up offal. Hog's pudding, they call it in Devon. A lot of garlic. Nutmeg and black pepper.' She smiled. 'Mary Holmes. I don't believe we've met.'

The soldier strode over to the table, holding out his hand. 'Tom Lawrence. Pleased to meet you, ma'am.'

Mary opened her eyes wide. 'Well, what a coincidence! Like the famous T.E. Lawrence, or Lawrence of Arabia as we call him. You might have seen his effigy in St Martin's. I knew him well. He was so kind to the children at the school. Used to come and talk to them about archaeology and the secrets of the past. And of course the crash that killed him was because he swerved to avoid two boys on bicycles.'

William said nothing.

The soldier, uncertain, looked from one to the other.

Mary said, 'Something for Mrs Bascombe?'

'Yes, ma'am.' The soldier held out a brown envelope. 'It's my mother's recipe for scrapple. I thought your friend might like it. I hope I've remembered it right. It's a while since I've seen her make it.'

'How kind.' Mary smiled.

'If she needs any more help, Sergeant Mills knows how to find me.'

'You must come to tea one day, if you can spare the time. I live in North Street. Just five minutes away.'

'I'd like that, ma'am.' The soldier turned to William. 'I'm sorry for the intrusion.'

After the soldier had left, striding back through the main office, Mary said, 'Although I'm sure he'd much rather have tea with Dora Bascombe. With her four daughters between sixteen and twenty-two.'

The intense, intimate atmosphere had been lost. After the soldier's interruption, they were just two mismatched strangers facing each other in a stuffy office that smelled of old bacon.

William said, 'Miss Holmes, can we get back to your statement?'

'I suppose we should.'

'If you're too tired—'

'No, I want to go on.'

William took a deep breath. 'So John sat you down in the Ship, you and Arthur. Bolted the door after everyone had left. He had something to tell you.'

'No.'

William frowned.

'He had something to show us.'

William waited.

'He went upstairs. We heard his footsteps overhead.' Mary stopped, staring into space.

'Miss Holmes?'

'The more I tell you, the harder it becomes. I like to pretend it's an old story. Something that took place so long ago it doesn't hurt any more. But that's not true. It's as clear as if it happened yesterday. I can feel it, and smell it, and see it. I close my eyes, and I'm standing there in the Ship, youth running through my veins. That's what happens to memory. The present is dull. The days blur together. But the past is bright and shiny. That's why the old become children. Because they play with the memories that give them most pleasure.'

After a while, William said, 'So John went upstairs.'

She articulated the words with great care. 'And then he came back down, each tread creaking, and emptied a bag on the table.' She hesitated. 'For a moment, I just stared. A heap of gold.' Her expression was almost fearful, full of wonderment and awe. 'Then I reached out and pulled it into shape. It was a necklace, set with rubies. There were earrings, too, each with a single stone. I had never seen anything so beautiful – the whole thing heavy but finely worked, the earrings with tiny screw fastenings, the necklace with a strong clasp and safety chain.

'When I finally raised my eyes, John and Arthur were staring at each other. And when they talked it was as if each already knew what the other was thinking. I swear they were reading each other's minds.

'Arthur said, I could take it to London and sell it for you.

'John said, The problem is not the selling, it's the money – I can't explain away the money, so I could never spend it.

'Arthur said, Leave here, start a new life.

'But there's always a chance, said John, that someone is looking

82

for it. The dead woman's family. They hear the landlord sold up and left soon after the wreck, and they'll come looking for me. I don't want to spend my life looking over my shoulder, waiting for a knife in my back.

'I stared at him. I said, This isn't yours to sell. It belongs to the village. You know that. It won't just be grieving relatives coming after you. If they find out what you've done, it will be one of our neighbours with a knife to your throat.

'They ignored me. Both of them. I might as well not have spoken.

'Arthur said, You have a plan.

'John said, Yes, I have a plan. And shining from his eyes was the wicked devilment he'd had as a boy, an excitement I hadn't seen for years. He said, They won't come after me if I'm dead.

'I looked at Arthur. But all his attention was on John. He was listening as if every word mattered.

'And then John told us a story. Imagine, he said, a night like tonight. Everyone drinking. Then it's time to leave. They all go home. Just as they shut their doors, they hear a shot. They run back. And what do they find? They find me dead on the floor, covered in blood, a shotgun in my hand. I've killed myself.

'There was silence. John got impatient. Come on, come on, he said. Maiden's Grave Gate, up by Tyneham. The last resting place of a young girl who died by her own hand. And because she killed herself, she couldn't have a Christian burial. They took her as far away from the church as possible. Right up to the parish boundary. Buried her at dead of night with a stake through her heart so her ghost couldn't haunt them.

'I couldn't make head nor tail of what he was saying.

'They'll want me out, said John. They'll want me gone. They won't want my spirit roaming around making mischief, souring the milk, killing the lambs before they're born. Rotting the straw. Putting mildew in the sacks of grain.

'Arthur laughed. They'll want you buried so far from the village, he said, that no one will see you rise from the dead.

'And no one will ever suspect, said John. Because a dead landlord can't sell gold.

'I found my tongue. You'll fake your own death?

'That's right, said John.

'It's very clever, said Arthur.

'I lost patience. The villagers aren't stupid, I said. They know what a corpse looks like. They won't put a living man in a coffin.

'You're right, said John. They won't. But you will. As long as I stay still as stone, they'll let the grieving widow take charge. No one wants to bury a suicide. No one wants anything to do with it. When Arthur offers, they'll agree. They'll let him put me in a coffin and take me out of the village, far from spying eyes. And when he's ready, when he knows it's safe, I'll make my escape.

'I said, We'd never be able to come back.

'Why would you want to?

'All our friends are here.

'John smiled. We'll make new friends. Better friends.

'It's a mad plan.

'Arthur said, That's why it might work.

'But you'd be risking everything – for what? Would it even make that much money?

'Look at it, Mary. Look at it.

'So I did. I looked at the heavy mass of gold. And the blood-red rubies glowed.

'We split it three ways, said John. For Arthur, it's easy. They're used to the idea of him travelling. So he says he's going back to London. For Mary it's harder. So you say you can't stand living in the Ship any more, now that I'm dead. You sell up. By then, I'll be settled, with the money. And you come and find me.

'I said, But where will you be?

'And John said, Wherever you want.

'And he looked at me, and I saw in his eyes that this was a gift. Handing to me what I'd always wanted – a chance to escape, to see the world.

'I said, We'll never get away with it.

'Arthur said, I think it will work.

'And they looked at each other, and I could see the decision had been taken. Nothing I said would make any difference.'

As she spoke the last words, Mary fixed her eyes on William's face. A shaft of sunlight had sneaked its way past the brick wall outside and shone through the open window on to the table in front of them, turning William's hands bright white.

He said, 'So what happened?'

'That's it?'

'What do you mean?'

'I thought you'd want to ask me questions.'

William considered this. 'The year, perhaps. The year it happened.'

'The storm was in 1878. November. I was twenty.'

William sat back in his chair.

'You don't look happy.'

'There's something you're not telling me, Miss Holmes.'

'You sound quite cross.'

'Because you're holding something back.'

'I told you. It's a long story. You have to wait.'

'I have to be patient.'

Mary looked beyond him to the open door. 'I don't want to be rude, but I can't see anyone queuing up to talk to you.'

'This could take weeks.'

'I've told you, every detail matters.'

'To you, or to me?'

'That's unfair, Constable.'

William looked at her, exasperated.

'Shall we have some tea?'

He didn't argue, just pushed himself to his feet and made the slow journey across the room. She watched his every move. When the tea had been made and the brown teapot was on the table with the cups and saucers, milk jug and sugar bowl, she said, 'How long have you been in Wareham?'

'Not long.'

She smiled. 'Four months?'

'Five.'

'Where were you before?'

'I told you. Dorchester. Police headquarters.'

'You don't come from Dorchester, though, do you? That's not where you grew up.'

His face was expressionless. 'You know I won't answer personal questions, Miss Holmes. I don't know why you keep trying.'

'Why won't you?'

'Because it's not relevant.'

'If we only ever told each other the things that were relevant, nothing would ever get said.'

After a while, William said, 'Are you happy to go on? Or are you tired?'

'Tired?'

'I thought you might need to rest.'

'I'll save that for when I'm dead.'

William waited, his eyes on her face.

Mary said, 'After that first night, John didn't mention the plan again. Not to me. Neither did Arthur. But I knew they were talking about it. Working out every last step. In the village, I couldn't meet people's eyes. I felt like a child on the edge of sleep, struggling with shapes and shadows I didn't understand.

'In the weeks before Christmas, the village was in the grip of a hard frost, an iron cold that froze the soul. Carts slithered on ice and skidded into drifts of snow. The Isle of Purbeck was completely white. A world of silence.

'One night I said to John and Arthur, Tell me again from the very beginning.

'So we sat down when the drinkers had gone, and John went through it all, answering every question. After the fake burial, Arthur would come back to the village, and strengthen the lie by telling the story of the unmarked grave. John meanwhile would make his way to Poole harbour and then to Southampton where he'd book his passage. He would send word as soon as he could. But he would have to be careful. There could be no letter written by a dead man.

'On the night itself, the plan was simple. John would pick a fight with me. I would turn my back on him and sit with Arthur. John would get jealous. He would drink too much. When the inn was full, he would bring out a shotgun. I would scream and run out of the inn, up the road to Mrs Selby's house. John would chase after me, fire the gun in the air, and return to the Ship, slamming the door shut. At midnight, another shot would ring out. Arthur would discover the body.'

Mary paused.

William said, 'But he's not really dead.'

'No. He's pretending.'

William nodded.

'You do understand this? It's not real. He's tricking the village.'

'Yes,' said William, 'I understand.'

Mary continued to stare at him. William dropped his gaze, drew the cups and saucers closer and poured out the tea. After a while, she picked up her cup, took a sip, and said, 'They even decided the date. The week before Christmas. Saturday, 18 December.'

When she didn't go on, William said, 'What happened next?'

'I think you're humouring me,' said Mary. 'I don't think you understand at all.'

William didn't say anything for a moment. Then he said, 'It seems a very elaborate plan. Just to get rid of a necklace.'

'It was.'

'There would have been simpler ways.'

'Yes. I'll come back to that.'

Mary took another sip of tea, and then set down her cup, placing it in the saucer with great precision.

William said, 'Miss Holmes—'

'That Sunday, inside the church, the air was so cold that every breath hung like a cloud. When we all stood to sing the first hymn, there was a sound as if our clothes were cracking with ice. Mr Lester preached from Ephesians. *Let all bitterness, and wrath, and anger, and clamour, and evil speaking, be put away from you, with all malice. And be ye kind one to another, tender-hearted, forgiving one another, even as God for Christ's sake hath forgiven you.* And it turned in my heart like a knife the way we planned to deceive our neighbours, our friends, the people who had loved me all my life. I looked up at John, and he glanced down, and his whole face was lit up with excitement. And I thought, To him this is nothing but a glorious adventure. A feat of daring. I haven't seen him look this alive since he shinned up the bell tower as a boy.

'That night, when I came upstairs, John was already in bed. The ruby necklace and earrings were laid out on my pillow.

'I said, You won't persuade me that way.

'He said, I don't want to persuade you. I just want to see you wear them.

'I moved to pick them up, but he stopped me. He said I had to take off my dress. He wanted to see them against my skin.

'I don't know why the wickedness of stealing brought us back together. But it did. The fire was lit again. We were hungry for each other. Arthur saw it. He couldn't help but see it, living in the Ship. I remember he came across us one day in the scullery. There we were, breathless, buttons undone, ties loosened, hands everywhere. His eyes had no expression. Just that blank stare he'd had as a child.

'Later I said to him, Arthur, I'm sorry, that was foolish of us.

'He said, It's your house. I'm just a lodger.

'I said, But there are some things that should be private.

'He smiled. He said, He's your husband, Mary. Why wouldn't he want you?

'And that made it so much worse. I stood there in front of him, fingering the folds of my dress, burning with shame.

'I said to John, We must be careful. Poor Arthur has no one for himself. We don't want to make him feel lonely.

'John laughed. He said, Don't you worry about Arthur. Once we sell the gold he'll have enough money to buy any woman he wants.

'The following Sunday, Mrs Selby stopped me at the lych gate. She said, Come by later, Mary. It's so long since we've talked.

'Back at the Ship, I paced and fretted. I said to John, She knows me so well. She'll guess what we plan to do.

'She's a midwife, he said, not a witch.

'In Mrs Selby's front parlour, the best tea service had been laid out on a white lace cloth. She said she had thought for a long time about what she was going to say, but it was only what my mother would have said if she were still alive, God rest her soul. She said the whole village was talking about Arthur still living at the Ship. It wasn't right, when they all knew that he'd wanted to marry me, and had gone to London to try to forget me. Some say, she said, that you and Arthur are carrying on right under John's nose.

'That made me angry. They can say what they like, I said. It's not true.

'Mrs Selby shook her head. Those of us who love you, she said, can see that you and John are reconciled. You smile at each other. His eyes follow you round the room. You lean your head on his shoulder and his face lights up with joy. We are happy for you. But we are also afraid. The time has come for Arthur to leave you in peace. He must leave the Ship and find his own wife. I'm saying this for your own good, Mary. You know what John is like. He has a temper. If he hears what people are saying, he might do something he'll regret. He'll do something rash. And there would be many who wouldn't blame him.

'Later, back at the Ship, I thought over what she'd said. And I realised, with sudden understanding, that it all played into our hands. When John threatened me with a gun, and I ran up the street screaming, Mrs Selby would take me in. She would listen to my story. She would believe that John was jealous of Arthur. And at midnight, when the shot rang out, she would understand that my husband, in a moment of drunken folly, had turned the gun upon himself. I could almost hear her saying, I warned her. Just days before. I warned her.

'Christmas drew near. On the Wednesday, the pig-sticker came. And the next day, I was up before dawn, salting the sides of bacon, drying the lard, washing the guts. I made up parcels of chitterlings and trotters, cheeks and ears, as gifts to our neighbours. The bucket of blood I put in the scullery.

'On Friday afternoon I went into the back room and found John cleaning his gun. A single-barrel shotgun with a walnut stock and a brass-lipped rammer. We looked at each other. Even then, I could have stopped it. I could have said, This is madness. I won't join in. But I didn't. I looked away.

'Saturday dawned cold and clear. The snow was beginning to melt. I fetched water, swept and scrubbed, polished and cleaned. I beat the rugs, washed the windows, brushed the ashes from the fireplace. I worked all day. But in the end, there was nothing more to do, so I sat and waited. At four o'clock the light began to fade. Mr Hobbs came in, with that stiff little peg-legged gait he had, because he'd fought with the Duke of Wellington years ago and lost the use of his leg, and then Mr Dicker arrived, mumbling into his beard, followed by Mr Wade and Mr Driffen, and so I lit the lamps and fetched their beer, and poked the fire to make it blaze. Then I picked up my sewing, and sat by the open door to the scullery.

'John came in, black with soot and grease. I took a deep breath. I said, You don't sit down like that. I haven't spent all day cleaning for you to make the place filthy again.

'He said, You mind your tongue.

'And the old boys looked up, delight on their faces. Back to the old game. Punch and Judy for their evening's entertainment.

'So I needled John, and he gave as good as he got, and we bickered and sniped and argued. Mr Dicker said, Typical woman, sweet one minute, sour the next, and Mr Hobbs said, Where's that young Mr Corben? He always puts a smile on her face. And they carried on for the next hour, writing the lines of a perfect script, and John's face set like thunder, and I turned my back, pretending I was sick of the sight of him.

'At seven o'clock, Arthur appeared, and I smiled, and pulled out a chair for him, and fetched him his beer. Look, see, said Mr Dicker, just like I said, the sun's come out. And I hung around Arthur like a bee round a rose. I gave him knowing looks. I patted his shoulder and touched his face. And all the while John glared from the corner like a cold east wind. By late evening, his fury was thick in the air. But the drinkers stayed. I thought, they've taken bets on a fight. They're waiting for it to begin.

'When I judged the time had come, I sat down opposite Arthur. I bent my head and whispered, Lean forward. Lean forward so our heads are close. I was going to pretend we were as thick as thieves, telling each other secrets. But Arthur bent forward and kissed me on the mouth.

'Before we knew what was happening, John was upon us both. He threw Arthur to the floor. He pulled me up by my arm, wrenching my shoulder, shouting that I was a whore. Arthur got to his feet. John let go of me, turned, and punched him so hard I heard bone crack. I cried out. Arthur fell back against one of the tables.

'I shouted, That's enough, that's enough.

'John stood there, breathing hard, looking as if he hated me. That's enough? he said. And he turned and left.

'There was blood all over Arthur's face. He looked as if his nose was broken. People were helping him up. I felt sick. The violence had shocked me.

'And then John was back in the room, this time holding a gun.

'I screamed and rushed for the door, and the crowd parted, letting me through. Outside, I ran up the street, skidding on the snow. A shot rang out. I didn't stop. At Mrs Selby's house, I hammered on the door. I heard footsteps behind me. The door opened, and Mrs Selby grabbed me and pulled me inside. We stood there in the dark. My heart was beating fit to burst. Outside John was shouting my name. Mrs Selby hugged me tightly. We waited for a long time. And then we heard Arthur's voice. He said, He's gone. He's gone. You can open the door.

'I was shaking. Arthur said, You're cold. Mrs Selby found me a shawl. Then she fetched water and a cloth, and did her best to clean the blood from Arthur's face. Already it was swelling up, his eye half closing.

'And then there was the sound of a single shot.'

———

'So what will it be?'

When he'd first seen the bombed-out terrace, and the space where Stella's house no longer stood, he couldn't move. The shock of it pinned him to the earth like a tree. Then he started walking, covering the ground with long strides. A few streets away, he found a pub with dark green tiles round the door, and pushed his way inside. It was crowded. A soldier in khaki with his arm in a sling was shouting for two pints of best. Cigarette smoke spiralled upwards in grey clouds. There was a faint smell of old sweat and the sharp, ever pervasive smell of rotting meat from the soap factory nearby.

'Bitter,' said William.

'Right you are.' The landlord was wearing a brown waistcoat looped with a silver watch chain. His shirtsleeves were rolled up. His black hair was greased back.

'I'm looking for someone,' said William.

'Aren't we all,' said the landlord. He pulled the pump handle towards him. 'Got a name?'

'Stella Allen.'

From the end of the bar the bell of the cash register rang out.

The landlord frowned, searching his memory. 'Allen.' He finished the pint with a final short pull and set the glass on the counter. 'Lives round here?'

William nodded.

'Joan!' shouted the landlord.

'Hello.' The barmaid glanced over her shoulder.

'Young man looking for someone called . . .' He hesitated, stopped and looked at William, his eyes screwed up.

'Stella Allen.' William took a sip of his pint. It was warm and weak. As it hit his empty stomach, he almost threw up, right there, at his feet.

The barmaid handed change to a fireman with streaks of dirt down his cheeks, and walked over to William's end of the bar. 'Mum works at Silvertown Rubber?'

William shook his head. 'I don't know. I've never met her.'

'Where are you from, then?' The barmaid smiled. Her teeth were stained and crooked.

'Dorset.'

'That's a long way to come for someone you've never met.'

A fat man in brown overalls banged the bar for service.

'No,' said William, head swimming, 'I know Stella. I just don't know her mother.'

'Well, there was a family called Allen got bombed out a few weeks ago. Direct hit. And if it's the same one, they've gone to live in Knight's Road. By Lyle Park. About ten minutes' walk.'

'Was anyone killed?'

Her face went soft. She put out her hand and touched his arm. 'The truth is, I don't know, love. Bloody war. Get yourself over there. I'll be thinking of you.'

She turned away. William gripped the bar with both hands. He closed his eyes, fighting the nausea that rose up in waves.

———

'Arthur and I looked at each other. Mrs Selby's eyes were huge. She tried to stop me, but I pulled away from her.

'Outside, people had left their houses half-dressed, some in their nightshirts. As I ran down the street in the snow, white faces turned and looked after me.

'At the Ship, I burst through the door. There was a great spreading pool of blood on the floor. John lay in the middle, the shotgun in his hand, eyes tightly closed. I stood there, unable to move. And then, from behind me, came Arthur. He flung his coat over John's head, shouting, Don't look! Don't look! Still, I stood there. Arthur pushed me, and I remembered the plan, and fell to my knees, my body covering John's. And now I heard running footsteps and the door banging open and a clamour of voices, and Arthur said, He's blown his brains out. And I heard gasps and screams, and then Mrs Selby calling my name, but Arthur was somehow guarding me, stopping people from coming closer.

'What he did allow them, though, was a long look at the body and the huge pool of blood glistening in the lamplight.

'I began to sob, wailing John's name.

'Mr Lester arrived, roused from his bed. The crowd parted to allow him through. Mr Corben, said the rector, Mr Corben, what happened?

'Arthur said, He turned the gun on himself.

'The rector said, And is he dead?

'Yes, said Arthur, his skull is shattered.

There was a murmur of horror around the room. Terrible. The poor man.

'The rector said, Should we call a doctor?

'Arthur said, It's too late. A doctor could do nothing.

'It went exactly as we'd planned. No one could be summoned until the morning. Arthur would bandage John's wounds. Then he would sit with the corpse.

'You will come home with me, Mary, Mrs Selby said.

'No, I said, still on my knees, my arms hugging John's body, I will stay here with my husband.

'I was immovable. In the end, one by one, the villagers left. Even Mrs Selby was persuaded to go.

'The rector said, You will look after her, Mr Corben.

'Yes, said Arthur, I will look after her.

'And then, finally, the door of the Ship was closed.

'Arthur pulled the curtains. We waited until we were sure that everyone had gone. Then I poked John in the ribs.

'He opened his eyes. I can't talk, he said, I'm dead.

'I fetched an old sheet I'd put by for the purpose, and tore it into strips, and Arthur soaked them in the blood and bandaged John's head so that it was impossible to tell whether bits of his brain and skull were missing or not.

'Can I have a pillow? said John.

'You can stop complaining, I said, or I'll bandage your mouth, too.

'Arthur and I splashed a bit more of the sticky pig's blood on John's face and clothes, and then we wiped the floor and set the furniture to rights. We left the gun where it was, near John's hand.

'Now we wait, said Arthur.

'It was a long night. Arthur and I sat together at one of the

95

tables and rested our heads on our arms. But we stayed awake, on guard. Once I sat up straight, disturbed by a sound. But it was only John, fast asleep, snoring.

'Just before dawn, there was a knock at the door. I kicked John awake and put my finger to my lips to warn him. Arthur opened the door and let the rector in. Mr Lester's eyes took in the body on the floor with its head all wrapped in bloody bandages. He said, I've sent word to the coroner. He may want to conduct an inquest.

'After he'd gone, I said, An inquest? We never thought about an inquest.

'John said, Don't panic. This is Purbeck. They won't make a fuss like they do up north. They'll see the body and give their verdict.

'You'll never stay still that long, I said.

'Watch me, said John.

'At first light, Arthur went to ask Thomas Bennett about a coffin.

'I said to John, We should never have started this.

'John said, If it all goes wrong, I'll take the blame. I'll say I was angry with you for carrying on with Arthur and wanted to teach you a lesson. It's not a crime to pretend to be dead.

'I said, They'll hate you.

'He said, They already do.

'Arthur returned. The coffin would be ready early afternoon. I said to him, Does your face hurt? One of his eyes was shut, and the other had an eyebrow split in two by a gash of dried blood.

'Arthur said, I'll live.

'Your nose is straight again, I said.

'That will be Jem Bennett, said Arthur. He cracked it back in line.

'At nine o'clock, Mr Lester came back with the coroner. As John had thought, the coroner glanced at the body on the floor, but made no comment. He was a Purbeck man. He said the inquest would be held at noon, and he would ask the constable to convene a jury.

'Arthur went with him outside and I was left alone with the rector. Mrs Ball, he said, we need to talk. His eyes were sad. He told me that anyone who took his own life could not have a Christian burial. He said he thought it was cruel and wrong. But as the law stood, anyone who committed suicide had to be buried after sunset, between nine in the evening and midnight, and could not have the benefit of a church service.

'I hung my head. I said, So where will he be buried?

'He can be buried at St George's, Mrs Ball. There is a small patch of unconsecrated ground just outside the churchyard. He will be buried with grace and dignity.

'I couldn't believe my ears.

'I am truly sorry I cannot do more, Mrs Ball, said the rector. I will pray for your husband's soul.

'When Arthur came back, I motioned to him to bolt the door. I was finding it hard to breathe. Mr Lester says that John can be buried here in Langton, I said, clutching his arm.

'That's not the Purbeck way, said the corpse from the floor.

'I thought, I said bitterly to my dead husband, that you had planned everything.

'Keep calm, said Arthur. Leave it to me.

'When Arthur had gone, John kept trying to reassure me. In the end I told him that if he didn't keep quiet I would take a knife to him and finish the job properly.

'An hour later, Arthur came back to say that a small deputation of villagers had gone to explain to the rector that it was not fair to put Mrs Ball through the shame of seeing her husband publicly buried at St George's without the benefit of a Christian service. Far better for all concerned, given the law as it stood, for Mr Ball to be quietly buried outside the village by his old friend Arthur Corben. Mr Lester had reluctantly agreed.

'The corpse laughed. I told you they wouldn't stand for it, he said.

'Shame on them, I said. Frightened a ghost will haunt them in their beds.

'Be thankful for their cowardice, said Arthur.

'At noon, the coroner arrived with a constable from Swanage. Gradually the inn filled up. The jury was made up of local men, most of them regulars at the Ship. There was Thomas Bennett and his brother Jem, Tom Pushman, Jack Driffen from Scoles Farm, Daniel Thorne, Samuel Thompson, and William Bower from Scratch Arse quarry. The last four were the old boys who drank their half-pints night after night – Samuel Hobbs, George Dicker, David Hibbs and Arthur Wade. They all stood in a ragged circle, hats in hand, heads bowed. None of them looked at me. None of them looked at the corpse.

'The inquest took eight and a half minutes. The facts were clear. John Ball had died by his own hand. The coroner wanted his lunch. He said, Constable, you will supervise this man's interment tonight.

'Mr Lester coughed. The widow of the deceased, he said, has requested that her husband be buried by his friend Mr Corben.

'The coroner said, The law states only that the body shall be buried after sunset without benefit of church service. The choice of officiate is immaterial. It shall be as you wish.

'When everyone had left, and the door was shut and bolted, the corpse was allowed to sit up and have a tot of brandy.

'The coffin arrived early afternoon. It was large, as it had to be, to fit John's frame. Tom Bennett asked if Arthur would like help to lift John's body. I gave a little cry. Arthur said, No, we will manage by ourselves.

'When the light began to fade, I fetched a blanket and tucked it inside the coffin. John climbed in. Then he said, Go and fetch it.

'So I went upstairs and lifted the mattress and pulled out the soft bag with the ruby necklace and the earrings safely inside, and took it back down.

'John opened his shirt and put the bag next to his heart. He said, Don't look so sad. It will be a few weeks, that's all. A steamship across the Atlantic. I'll send word as soon as I can.

'I knelt down next to the coffin. The blood on the white bandages round his head had darkened to deep brown. I said, I won't rest till I hear from you.

'John smiled. I promise, he said. As soon as I can.

'Arthur took the coffin lid and chiselled in tiny air holes that couldn't be seen. But when he placed it over John's body and started hammering in the nails, I felt sick to my stomach. I called out. Arthur turned round. His swollen eye was beginning to open, but the skin around it was vivid yellow edged with purple, the scab across his eyebrow a dirty black. He said, You heard what John said. You'll see him again in a few weeks. This is nothing, Mary. Nothing. Just a bit of play-acting. And he smiled in that calm way he had, and I took a deep breath, and nodded, and he turned back and finished hammering in the last few nails.

'We opened the inn door. Outside, the villagers were already lining the street. The men had removed their hats. The women were weeping. Arthur had left the handcart, with its two huge wheels and solid wooden base, just outside. The Bennett brothers came forward, with Daniel Thorne and Jack Driffen, and the four of them lifted the coffin while Arthur held the cart level. Then Jem Bennett roped the coffin down securely, front and back, so that it couldn't slide off. Mr Hobbs held out a shovel, and Arthur tied it to the top of the coffin.

'Mrs Selby came to stand by my side. Arthur looked at me. I nodded. He bent over and pushed. He needed all his strength. John made a heavy corpse.

'We watched until Arthur and the cart disappeared from view in the gathering gloom.

'I thought, We did it. We hoodwinked them all.'

—————

For a long time after she'd finished speaking, the room was silent. Then William said, 'Is it all true?'

'True?'

'Is that what happened?'

'Yes.'

'Including the inquest?'

Mary shrugged. 'Purbeck justice.'

'An elaborate charade.'

'If you like.'

'There would have been easier ways.'

'They didn't want easier ways. Either of them.'

'What do you mean?'

'Just that. It was more exciting this way.'

'More dangerous?'

'Yes.'

William nodded. 'But something went wrong.'

'Why do you say that?'

'Something must have gone wrong. You say that both John and Arthur have been dead and buried for years.'

She bowed her head.

'Someone saw them that night? Robbed them and killed them?'

'I want to tell you in my own way.'

'We haven't got long. Sergeant Mills will be back soon.'

But she just looked at him. Eventually he raised both hands in a gesture of defeat.

'I waited. I stood by the window, watching everyone who passed. My heart jumped each time there was a knock at the door. Any day, I thought, any day now there will be a letter.

Not a telegram. That would be too public. But a letter in a disguised hand. Or some kind of parcel with a secret message tucked away inside. Or someone will come to the door and give me a book, and there on the flyleaf will be a strange address. But nothing happened. I kept thinking of excuses. Perhaps he'd given the message to someone who'd come home, got drunk, and clean forgotten. Or to a sailor who had drowned at sea. Perhaps he'd been followed on board ship and was even now hiding under a pile of rags, waiting until he reached port before it was safe enough to disappear into a crowd. I tried not to think about accidents, or a raging fever, or a gang of thieves beating him half to death. I tried not to think about storms at sea, or hurricanes, or shipwreck. Sometimes in the night I would wake suddenly as if I heard him calling. My dreams turned to nightmares, full of suffocating darkness. Again and again, I said to Arthur, Why hasn't he sent word?

'Arthur was always calm. Remember, he has to be careful. Be patient. It's early days.

'But the days stretched to weeks and then to months, and still I heard nothing. Mr Lester came to visit, just as he'd done in the days after my father's death. We sat there in the Ship, and he tried to comfort me, talking about our earthly bodies, and the promise of resurrection and eternal life. Once he said, I should never have listened to what people said. We should have buried your husband at St George's. Your grief would be easier now if you could visit your husband's grave. My eyes filled with tears. The thought of John dead and buried in some distant land was almost more than I could bear. But I could say nothing. I had to pretend to grieve for something that hadn't happened, while at the same time turning my back on something that was real and true and twisting my heart. I looked up. We had rehearsed it again and again, Arthur and I, in the long empty days after John left – a crafted answer to stop the wagging tongues.

'I said, Because he took his own life, my husband was denied a Christian burial. And I have to live with that, though it gives me pain every day.

'And Mr Lester stared back, his face full of sadness.

'Mrs Selby said, Come, Mary, this sorrow is making you ill. John would not want to see you like this.

'But it wasn't just that my mind was full of pictures of John injured or dead or dying. I remembered how strong he was. How brave. How I had never known him beaten in a fight. Had never known him weak from sickness. I began to face the unthinkable. In the dead of night, when I couldn't sleep, I began to wonder if John had betrayed me, betrayed us both. Left us and taken the gold for himself. And I would turn my face into my pillow and weep.

'I said nothing to Arthur. Keeping silent contained it, made the thought untrue.

'But it gnawed away at me, like a dog working marrow from a bone. It sucked the life out of me. I became as dry and useless as dust.

'Now that John was gone, Arthur could no longer stay at the Ship. He found lodgings near the rectory. I didn't reopen the inn. Who would want to drink where the landlord had blown his brains out? The smithy stayed shut, too. The anvil was cold. The great fireplace was empty. John's tools hung unused.

'Again and again Arthur said, Don't give up hope, Mary. Don't give up hope.

'But I stopped believing him. It was empty comfort. John had gone.'

———•———

'You could have knocked me down with a feather, turning up like that.'

'I had to know you were all right.'

'Oh, I'm all right. I'm always all right.'

Stella leaned back in the chair. She was wearing a grey dress with red piping round the collar, and a short crimson cardigan. In the faint light from the window, her skin looked as white as chalk. 'So how's the army treating you?'

He shrugged.

'That good?' The air in the room was cold. It smelled of brick dust. In the grate, last night's fire was a heap of ash and bleached coal. She took a cigarette out of the packet and spent a long time lighting it. 'How did you find me?'

'I went to your old address.'

She laughed. 'That must have been a shock.'

'Then I wandered about for a bit. Found a pub. Asked in there.'

She inhaled sharply, held her breath and let the smoke out, very slowly. 'This is my aunt's place. Two to a bed and people sleeping on the floor. Like Piccadilly Circus at night.'

'I wasn't going to stay.'

She raised an eyebrow. 'Did anyone ask you?'

He swallowed. 'How's the baby?'

'Not a baby any more. He's two. Getting up to all sorts.'

Outside on the street, there were people shouting.

'Mum has him while I'm at Tate's.'

'Tate's?'

'Sugar factory. Just down the road.' She screwed up her eyes against the smoke. 'You should have seen it the first night. A wall of fire. That's all you could smell for days. Burned caramel.'

They sat for a while listening to the clock on the sideboard. Stella finished her cigarette and stubbed it out in the ashtray. Outside the window, someone stopped – headless, legless – and moved on.

He said, 'Was anyone killed?'

'What do you think?'

'I meant – anyone you know.'

'You have no idea, do you?'

The room was so cold that the air touched his fingers like ice.

'They even got the church a few weeks ago. Direct hit. Broke through in the morning and found all these bodies lined up against the wall with children on their laps. Just sitting there, hair all dusty, staring straight ahead. Like dolls.'

He looked at her helplessly.

'Most nights they covered them up, the dead people. With coats. Or blankets. But they couldn't get round them all quick enough. Our Tommy was on messenger duty one night, on his bike. A bomb exploded and threw him into a crater. When he came to, he was lying on an arm. Just an arm – nothing else. With the glove still on.' She shifted in her chair. 'You get these black bits floating round in the morning, just floating round in the air, and you think, It's rubber. Or paint. And then it lands on your hand and you look at it and think, Maybe not. Maybe it's someone's skin.'

He leaned forward. 'I couldn't get leave.'

'It wouldn't have made any difference.'

'I kept reading about it in the papers. Weeks of bombing, night after night.'

'The Queen came, you know.'

There was shouting outside on the street again, and then a yell of laughter so close it sounded like someone else was in the room.

He said, 'You didn't answer my letters. Not after the first one.'

'Stood there in the rubble in her posh coat and hat. Four strands of pearls.'

William's voice was desperate. 'I don't understand why you're so angry.'

Her face was pinched and white. 'Because I don't know why you're here, that's why.'

He opened his mouth to speak but shut it again.

She said, 'You can't just turn up. From nowhere. After a whole year.'

'Stella—'

'And whatever you're thinking, it isn't going to happen.'

'I wasn't thinking anything.'

'You must be the only soldier that isn't.'

'I've been worried about you. I wanted to see you were all right. That's all.' He was pleading with her. 'To see if you needed help.'

She leaned back in her chair and the grey light from outside fell on the gold of her hair. Her eyes were less hostile. 'Like a boy scout.'

They sat, watching each other. When she spoke, she sounded tired. 'Why did you join up, anyway? You could have stayed in the police.'

'I'll go back when it's all over.'

'You wanted to be like your brother.'

He took a deep breath.

'Or fancied a few medals.'

He said, 'My father was in the army.'

Her glance flicked back to his face.

'The Somme. They all volunteered. To fight the bullies. Make a crooked world straight and decent again. It's the same now. Since Dunkirk. You have to do it. You don't have a choice.'

After a while, she said, in a kinder voice, 'I'm not good at writing letters.'

He nodded.

'Never any time anyway. What with work and looking after Peter.'

The ticking of the clock marked the seconds.

'I don't know why you sent me that bloody nappy. It was full of holes. And it stank of bleach.'

'Mrs Poyton wanted you to have it.'

'Probably hoped the smell would kill me.' She sat up, straightening her shoulders. 'So are you taking me out, or what?'

He looked surprised.

'We could go to the pub. Or get something to eat.' She raised her eyebrows. 'What is it? Cat got your tongue?'

'I thought—'

'You don't want to eat here. Everything's filthy. Dust everywhere, even now. The kitchen's the worst. I found bits of broken glass in a packet of flour the other day. Imagine that. Slicing your insides to ribbons with a jam tart.'

'You shouldn't stay here.'

'Where else would I go?'

'Somewhere safe.'

'I tried that. Remember? Like being buried alive.'

He was silenced.

'This is my home, war or no war.' She gave him a long look. 'And I don't know what you're complaining about. You should be glad I stuck to Silvertown. Or you might never have found me.'

'I don't imagine you're eating properly. Three single men on their own.' Mary looked round the charge room. 'I expect the cupboards are bare. Of course there's always the Granary on the Quay. Three courses for eightpence.'

William frowned.

'I worry about you. As white as whey. I keep thinking you're going to faint.'

He took a deep breath.

'Although I suppose it might be nothing to do with lack of food. It might be all those difficult memories.'

'Miss Holmes—'

'Rushing in when you least expect them.'

'We need to get back to your statement.'

'They make it so hard to concentrate, don't they, all those pictures in your head?'

'What makes it hard to concentrate, Miss Holmes, is that your story is long and rambling, and I can't tell what's important, and what's unnecessary detail.'

·'Oh dear,' said Mary. 'You sound quite cross.'

He stared at her across the wooden table.

'Shall I go back a little?' Mary's voice was kind and helpful. 'It might remind you where we'd got to.'

'There's no need.' William sounded weary.

'You're sure? You want me to carry on?'

He nodded.

'So John had been gone for nearly a year,' said Mary, 'when Mr Lester stopped us after the Sunday service. We stood by the lych gate and he said, Mr Corben, do you remember where you buried Mr Ball? His words rang out in the bright October morning. Mrs Selby stopped to listen, as did Samuel Hobbs and George Dicker. My heart was banging so hard in my chest I thought it would break my ribs.

'Yes, said Arthur. Why?

'The rector said, Because I believe we should try to change the law.

'No one said anything. We just stood there in the sunshine, staring at him.

'Then Mr Lester turned to me and said, If the law was changed, Mrs Ball, we could bring your husband back to the churchyard and bury him with a proper Christian service.

'I caught Mrs Selby's eye. I could see in her face what she thought. The village was sad that John was dead. Some of them still felt guilty. They had goaded him into violence by taking bets on a fight. But even so, they didn't want him in St George's. They wanted the body of a suicide kept at a safe distance so that his spirit couldn't vex them. Purbeck is full of ghosts. You can still hear the screams of a smuggler stoned to death at Worbarrow Bay, there's a headless coachman who drives his horses through Swanage, and Mrs Serrell always swore that Durnford House was haunted. A woman in a flowing black veil used to drift along the gallery and disappear into the stone wall at the head of the stairs.

'But Mr Lester was a foreigner. He didn't understand any of this. He thought it was a good idea to dig up John's bones and put them in the churchyard. I felt sick with fear. If they dug up the coffin, they would feel how light it was. And they would look at me and say, What happened, Mary? Why is the coffin empty? How did a dead man walk?

'Arthur said, Could the law be changed?

'I believe so, said Mr Lester. I intend to talk to those who can help us. Then he turned to me. But it will be a long, slow struggle, Mrs Ball. And there is no guarantee of success.

'I found my voice. I said, Why now? After all these months?

'He looked at me with sad eyes. Because I haven't had a moment's peace, Mrs Ball, since we banished your husband's body from the village.

'Later, Arthur came to the Ship and we sat in the dusty room full of empty tables. Arthur said, Nothing will come of it. He's all talk.

'But I remembered the earnestness in the Mr Lester's eyes.

'A few weeks later, a letter from the rector appeared in the local paper. He said that John Ball, late of the Ship Inn in Langton, had been buried like a dog at 9.30 p.m. on a wintry December night. Life had appeared so black to him that he'd shot himself. Because of that, he'd been denied a Christian burial. For charity's sake, said Mr Lester, we must protest against this. It is time to reform the law.

'Mrs Selby said, From what I hear, he's writing letters to everyone he can think of. Friends, family, the bishop. Mr Garland, of course. Spends hours at Leeson House looking at old books.

'Arthur was still calm. It means nothing, he said. We'll be gone from here soon anyway. As soon as we get word from John.

'But the winter came and went, and then the spring, and still there was no news.

'They were dark days. Without Arthur, I would have gone under. He was always calm, always patient. I remember one afternoon up on the cliffs by Encombe House. The wet grass was thick with wild flowers – blackamoor and bluebells, may-blobs and giddy ganders – and the sky was a brilliant clear blue. It was too lovely for the misery in my heart. I said, We should have stopped him. And then he would still be safe.

'Arthur said, You forget. Nothing could have stopped him.

'I said, I wish I knew where he was. I wish I knew he was alive and well.

'Arthur said, Have faith, Mary. It will all work out for the best.

'Mrs Selby lost patience in the end. We understand you're still in mourning, Mary. And we're the same. All of us. Every day we wish we could turn back the clock. Mr Hobbs and Mr Wade and Mr Dicker wish they hadn't teased him that night at the Ship. Mr Thorne wishes he'd taken your husband aside and talked to him man to man. And I wish I'd followed my heart and insisted that Mr Corben lodge elsewhere. We live with your husband's death on our conscience. It shocked us to the core. But what's done is done. It's time to face the future. And you must be brave, Mary. The village misses the Ship. It's time to start again. And you wouldn't have to do it all yourself. Jem Bennett could run it for you, just like he did before.

'I said, You would have the village drink in the room where John died?

'Of course not. Sell the old premises. Buy somewhere new.

'But I shrank away from the idea. What if John tried to send for me? I wanted to stay in the same place, looking out from the same window, in case there was a chance that he sent someone to find me.

'One afternoon in May, Mr Lester came to see me, his face all smiles. The tide is turning, Mrs Ball, he said. Parliament has passed an amendment to the law on burial.

'I was so shocked, I just stared at him with my mouth open.

'I know, he said, I feel the same – so full of joy I can hardly speak. It doesn't go far enough. It doesn't allow those who have committed suicide to be buried in consecrated ground. But a minister of the Church may now say prayers over the deceased – not the burial service itself, but comforting words from Holy Scripture and the Book of Common Prayer.

'I found my voice. I said, What use is that? It means nothing. It doesn't help us at all.

'Mr Lester took my hands in his. It does help us, Mrs Ball, he said. Because those with the power to change the law are beginning to see the iniquity of denying a proper Christian burial to those who have taken their own lives. God is with us. There is every hope that one day your husband will be buried in the churchyard at St George's.

'When I told Arthur, he just shrugged. Nothing will happen. It's the same as before. A lot of fuss and chatter.

'I'm tired of it, I said. All this talk of John's final resting place. I want to know he's safe. I want to know he's alive and well.

'There was a strange expression in Arthur's eyes.

'But I stopped him before he could speak. I said, I know what you're going to say. Be patient. Have faith. But it's hard to be that strong when your heart is breaking.

'And then he gave me a look I couldn't fathom. Almost as if he hated me, which made no sense at all. But later on, when I was alone, I realised I'd been selfish. The uncertainty was wretched for Arthur, too. And I was asking him to shoulder all my misery, as if John's disappearance was somehow his fault. I resolved to be more moderate in future – or at least to think before I spoke.

'But it was hard. Life without John was empty. The world was cold and dark, as if the sun had disappeared. We had fought every day since we were children, like two cats in a locked room, purring one minute, hissing the next. But now that he'd gone, I had only to think of him and my eyes filled with tears. I needed him to come home. I needed him by my side.

'One evening in August, we were walking home from the market in Swanage when Arthur stopped still in the middle of the road. I turned round and there he was, rooted to the spot. What is it? I said. Are you ill? He looked different somehow – bent over, defeated, like a man who's been dragging stone for miles and can finally go no further.

'He said, I can't go on like this.

'I was afraid. I took his arm and pulled him to the side of the road, and we sat down in the dirt, out of the way of horses and carts.

'Arthur turned to look at me. His eyes were full of despair. He said, I have to tell you the truth.

'I shook my head. I didn't want to hear it.

'But he reached out and took my hand. Every day I tell you not to worry. Every day I tell you that all will be well. But I'm lying to you, Mary.

'It felt like a knife in my heart. I tried to stand up. But he held my hand more tightly. He said, I can't pretend any more. The last thing I want is to cause you more pain. But John would never have left you worrying and waiting like this. Something terrible has happened to him. I am sure of this. There is no new life in America. No riches and grand houses and new friends. He has gone forever.

'No, I said. You're wrong. That's not true. I started to weep.

'Mary, he said. Please don't cry.

'Then don't say such terrible things.

'I have to. For both our sakes. The waiting has to stop.

'And he put his arms round me, and held me tightly, as if gathering up my terrible grief, and we sat there together in the ruts of mud as the light began to fade.

'After that, Arthur stopped telling me to have faith.

'And I didn't talk any more about missing John. It wasn't fair on Arthur. I carried my fear and longing alone.

'As the days grew shorter and the nights got colder, Mrs Selby persuaded me that the time had come to employ a blacksmith. I needed the money, and the village needed a forge. We settled on Harry Brown, the youngest of five brothers from a farm near Wareham, who had just finished his apprenticeship at Newbery & Sons. You won't have any trouble with him, said Mrs Selby. He's got an honest face.

'I don't think Harry knew how to lie. He spoke as he felt. On his first day, he said how sorry he'd been to hear of John's suicide. His mother had remembered John taking on the prize fighter at the fair in Swanage and couldn't believe such a fine man had taken his own life. My eyes filled with tears, and Harry found me a handkerchief, and said, I beg your pardon, Mrs Ball, I hadn't meant to upset you.

'No, I said, I like hearing John's name. It's worse when people don't mention him at all.

'Later I asked Harry why he hadn't wanted to stay on at Newbery's. He said he would have stayed if he'd been asked. But time marched on and nothing was said. So when he heard about the job at Langton, and mentioned he was making enquiries, Mr Newbery said, Well if that's the case, good riddance.

'Which made the choice very easy, said Harry.

'I laughed. I liked the way Harry saw the world.

'At the end of November, nearly two years after John had disappeared, Mr Lester went to London.

'I said to Mrs Selby, What's he gone there for? To find himself a wife?

'No, she said. Charles Garland at Leeson House has introduced him to his cousin, who's a Member of Parliament. They're all behind it now – bishops, lords, dissenters, everyone.

'Mr Lester, she said, has gone to London to change the law.'

———

'You got into bad habits, that's your problem.'

'Bad habits?'

'Your lawless days as a village bobby.' They were sitting in a pub at Waterloo station. Girls kept staring past William to get a better look at his brother. They might have been impressed by the pips on his shoulder. But it was probably the blond hair, blue eyes and wide, film-star smile. 'You made up the rules as you went along.'

William reached for his pint. It was his third, on an empty stomach.

'You didn't even charge that farmer who said he'd seen German parachutists landing in the woods.'

William looked up. 'You can't arrest people for making a mistake.'

'Spreading baseless rumours. Alarm and despondency. What was it in the end? Swans? Puffs of white smoke?'

William laughed.

'That's why you find it so difficult. You're used to making your own decisions. Working out for yourself what's important. And you can't do that. Your commanding officer's always right.'

'Always?'

'Always.'

William slumped so far forward he seemed to be mumbling at the table. 'It's just so pointless. The other day they had us mending fences. On a farm. Any dirty job and they call in the army.'

'All part of the war effort.'

113

'Inspections. Bloody inspections. Kit. Feet. Teeth.'

His brother smiled. 'You're drunk, Will.'

'No live ammunition. No equipment. I joined up to fight. Not to rub Brasso on buckles.'

The people at the next table were leaving, gathering coats and bags.

William examined his glass. 'And if you say to anyone, why are we doing it like this, the answer's always the same. It's the army. That's how we do it.'

'Have you thought about officer training?'

William looked up, his eyes sleepy. 'They wouldn't want me.'

'Yes, they would. You're just the kind of person they need. You're used to taking control. I can see you leading a platoon.'

'Would that make it any better?'

'It might.'

William focused on his brother with difficulty. 'What was it like?'

'What?'

'Dunkirk.'

His brother shook his head. 'You don't want to know.'

'They called you heroes.' The man at the next table lifted his suitcase and knocked over a chair. It fell backwards with a clatter. 'You fought. Even when you were surrounded. Right to the end.'

'With the French. Don't forget the French.'

'There were German Stukas dive-bombing. Firing at you while you waited on the beach. It was less than a year ago. But you never talk about it. It's like it never happened.'

His brother stood up. 'I should go, Will. If I sit here much longer, I'll miss my train. And you should get something to eat before you catch yours.' He hesitated. 'Look, take my advice. Stop worrying about it all so much. Keep your head down and do what you're told. Before you know it, you'll be back in your old police station, walking the beat, keeping the locals safe.' He picked up his bag. 'What happened to that girl?'

'What girl?'

'The evacuee. With the baby.'

'I don't know.'

His brother laughed. 'Liar.'

William, befuddled, was framing the appropriate response when he realised it was too late. His brother had gone.

———

From the passageway outside the police station came a yell, the sound of running footsteps, and then a muddle of loud voices. William, looking up, found Mary staring at him.

They heard the low rumble of a lorry's engine.

The door of the outer office banged open. Shortly afterwards, Sergeant Mills appeared at the threshold of the charge room. 'Still here, Miss Holmes? I thought you'd have gone by now. Told us everything you know, and gone back to put your feet up.'

'What was going on out there?' said Mary. 'We had to stop for a moment, didn't we, Constable? I was right in the middle of making my statement. But I couldn't hear myself think. What with all the shouting.'

Sergeant Mills laughed. 'I was coming back to the station and happened to glance down the passageway, and there he was. Young Vic Smith. He jumped out of his skin. Wasn't expecting a policeman.' He walked over to the sink and filled the kettle. 'They'd parked up a lorry with bits and pieces from the crash. The German bomber that came down near Stoborough. Of course, they'd just left it there while they had a cup of tea in Burgess's. Forgetting all these young lads are collecting whatever they can lay their hands on. Caught him red-handed, trying to twist a bit off the wing.' Sergeant Mills lit the gas. 'Not as bad as some of the things I see. They like emptying out the bullets. Quick flash of cordite. Or even worse. I was on the Common a couple of weeks ago and there was a young lad trying to pull an incendiary from the ground. He'd looped a bit of piano wire round the fin. I said, What are you trying to do? Set fire to yourself?'

William screwed up his eyes, as if he was finding it hard to hear.

'You'd think they'd learn, wouldn't you?' Sergeant Mills shook his head. 'I remember after they lit the decoy at Arne. Bombers pounding the village all night. Two hundred craters the next morning. Later that day, couple of lads out there playing where they shouldn't—' He blew out his cheeks, making a sound like a sudden explosion, and spread his arms wide.

William went white.

'There isn't the supervision, that's the problem. Half the schools are closed. Everyone busy fighting the war. In the forces. Manning the searchlights. There's no one around to stop them blowing themselves up.' Sergeant Mills, hunting round on the shelves for the brown teapot, looked at William properly for the first time. 'All right there, Constable?'

William's whole body was trembling.

'Cold, isn't it, for May? I should shut that window.' The sergeant glanced at Mary, and then back to William. 'Miss Holmes, might I ask if you could come back another time? It's been a busy morning, and I need a hand with the paperwork.' He checked his watch. 'And it's nearly lunchtime. You could probably do with a break.'

Mary looked at William. 'I was just about to tell the constable the next part of the story.'

'But you're probably near the end now, aren't you? Just one more session to wrap it all up.'

Mary stood up. 'Tomorrow?'

'Tomorrow it is.' The sergeant came to stand just behind her, edging her towards the door.

Mary adjusted her hat. 'Is there any more news?'

'News?'

'About the bodies.'

The sergeant frowned. 'What sort of news were you expecting?'

'Oh, I don't know.' Mary picked up her handbag. 'Cause of death?'

'I thought,' said the sergeant, 'that's why you were here. To tell us what happened.'

'Oh, I will,' said Mary. 'Possibly next time, if we don't have any more interruptions.'

William didn't turn his head as she left. He just sat there, pale and still, staring at nothing.

Wednesday

Outside Frisby's shoe shop in North Street, the jeep slowed down. An American pilot, the sun flashing off the brass badge of his peaked cap, leaned out to ask directions from Annie Mills, who was on her way to the factory. Their faces were bright with flirtation. The engine, idling, purred.

Constable Keyes, labouring to build up speed on his bicycle, wobbled past an army lorry on his way to Stoborough Farm. Richard Miden, the US warrant officer, waved at Marjorie Brewer, and then at a small boy, sent out on an errand, ducking back into the school run by Pinkie Skewes. Young Mrs Farwell lingered by Mrs Ford's dress shop, staring at a pair of white gloves in the window, and Lyle Brooks, one of the army cooks, was just leaving Worlds Stores.

Above the Rainbow Café, the clock showed ten minutes to eleven.

Inside the police station, William, sitting at his desk in the corner, sealed a brown envelope and put it on top of the pile. From time to time he glanced up at Mrs Bascombe in her green coat. Standing right in front of the high Victorian counter, holding tight to her basket – her hair escaping from a scarf twisted round in a turban, her cheeks bright pink – she appeared to be near to tears. 'Well, I thought it was lovely, going to all that trouble. His mother's recipe.'

Sergeant Mills raised an eyebrow.

'As far as I'm concerned,' said Mrs Bascombe, 'he's a young man far from home who's missing his mother. It's got nothing to do with Lilian. Or Rose, or Edie or Alice. And if I can make him feel a bit more comfortable by asking him round to tea, I will.' She caught her breath. 'What is he? Twenty-one? Twenty-two? Hardly more than a child. Any day now he might be going to war. Fighting side by side with our boys.'

Sergeant Mills opened his mouth.

'And before you start,' said Mrs Bascombe, 'if Bert were here, he'd say exactly the same thing.'

The main door opened. On the threshold, Mary paused, looking from Mrs Bascombe to Sergeant Mills and back again.

Vic Smith's dog shot through the open door.

'Oh, that dog!' said Mrs Bascombe, her voice high and angry.

Five minutes later, when they were sitting once again at the scrubbed wooden table in the charge office, Mary said, 'I think Dora's right. The poor boy's probably homesick.'

William said nothing.

'What the sergeant's really worried about, of course,' said Mary, 'is his daughter Annie. That's why he's so anxious about these American soldiers. In case she falls in love and ends up moving halfway round the world. They're so glamorous, these young men. Kind and attentive, handing out chocolate and cigarettes and nylons. So much more money to spend than our lot. Although that's the real problem, of course. Our young men just aren't here. They're off fighting in Africa or Italy or Burma. So it's the Yanks or nothing.' She sighed. 'And of course poor Dora is handling it all by herself, with Bert away. Something hush-hush. So she can't even say what he's up to. That must make it so much worse, don't you think? When you're not allowed to tell the truth. People can imagine all sorts of things are going on.'

'Like what?'

Mary opened her eyes wide. 'Oh, I don't think we should speculate.'

William reached for his notebook. 'Let's carry on, Miss Holmes. We must be near the end now, surely.'

She smiled. 'You know, I'm beginning to feel we know each other very well.'

William looked at her. 'Do you?'

'Well, we've spent so much time together. Although it's a little one-sided. You ask all the questions. So you know everything about me. But I know nothing about you at all.'

'It's a police interview, Miss Holmes.'

'Yes, I know that, Constable. But it's also a market town in Dorset where I've lived for sixty-two years. I know a lot about your sergeant. How he fought in France in the Great War. His late wife Elsie. His daughter Annie at the cordite factory. I know his favourite meal is liver and onions, he likes parsley on his new potatoes, and he's very partial to plum jam. But all I know about you is that you're twenty-four and last lived in Dorchester. That's it. I don't know where you were born. Nothing about your family, or your sweetheart. There must be someone. Good-looking boy like you. And you still haven't said where you got your injuries.'

His face was no longer the deathly white of the day before. He looked tired, but more his usual colour. 'I need to find out how they died, Miss Holmes.'

'Are you feeling better? That's the important thing. You didn't look well when I left yesterday. But he looks out for you, doesn't he, your Sergeant Mills. Where's he off to today?'

'He's busy.'

'Well, of course he is. He's always busy. I just wondered what he was doing?'

'Farm inspections. Checking on sheep dipping.'

'I didn't know the police were involved in livestock.'

'Our duties are many and various.'

'I don't know how you manage. I really don't. Pillars of the community.'

Today, Mary was wearing a crocheted scarf in a soft, silky beige. But the hat and coat were the same.

William said, 'So far you've told me about an elaborate plan to hide the theft of some jewellery. John Ball has faked his own suicide, Arthur Corben has pretended to bury his body, and he has gone off to the New World.'

'Texas was the plan. Although he also talked about Iowa and Wisconsin.'

'But I'm not sure how this links to John and Arthur being buried in the same grave. Or when it happened. Or how you managed to do it.'

'You're sounding very brisk today, Constable.'

'Sergeant Mills wants me to finish taking your statement.' William took out a pen from the breast pocket of his uniform jacket and laid it on the table.

'Yes, of course. We need to tie up all the loose ends, don't we?'

'I don't think we've got to the ends yet. I think we're still stuck in the middle.'

'When you look back, Constable, I think you'll find that I've told you much more than you realise.'

'This isn't Agatha Christie, Miss Holmes.'

'I would have told you yesterday, you know. If Sergeant Mills hadn't shooed me out. But then he's got a lot on his mind at the moment, hasn't he?'

William looked at her with irritation.

Mary smiled. 'Would you like me to go on?'

'Have you got any photographs?'

'Photographs?'

'Of John Ball? Or Arthur Corben?'

Mary looked at him as if he were stupid. 'You are a child of the present, aren't you? This was 1878. You think people like us were taking photographs?'

'It was a possibility.'

'Yes, well, Constable. Everything's a possibility. But it might save time if we stuck to what was likely.'

He clenched his jaw, as if clamping his mouth shut.

'So,' said Mary, after a pause, 'shall I continue?'

William nodded.

'I did re-open the Ship. Almost two years after John disappeared. Not in the same building, of course. No one in the village wanted to drink where the landlord had blown his brains out. We sold up to Tom Bennett. He wasn't put off by John's death. He made coffins, after all.'

'Is this relevant?'

'We bought Mrs Fry's old house. She'd been rattling around in it for a long time. I don't think she used half the rooms. She died quite suddenly. Ninety-two years old. And you know, Mrs Pushman's baby arrived on exactly the same day. Her ninth. Tom Pushman played the fiddle in Mrs Serrell's orchestra. Given the rate the children arrived, we thought he might be trying to set up a new one.'

'Miss Holmes—'

'And a few months after that, Arthur proposed again.'

William paused. 'Did you accept?'

'What do you think?'

'I don't know, Miss Holmes. I'm not sure I care. I just need to take your statement.'

'Have you looked up when the law changed on the burial of suicides?'

'No.'

'It was reported in the *Dorset Country Chronicle*. You'll find that everything I've said is true.'

'Miss Holmes—'

'Still no word on the bodies?'

'The investigations are continuing.'

'You'll find that one of them is six foot four. There aren't many men that tall.'

'Miss Holmes, tell me how John Ball died.'

'I intend to.'

He took a deep breath. 'You have half an hour.'

'It doesn't stop there, you know. His death is only the beginning.'

He said nothing.

'So the village was glad when the Ship opened again. The very first customer was Mr Hobbs. He headed straight for the table by the fire. Shortly afterwards, Mr Wade came in, followed by Mr Dicker. It felt like the old days. There they were, sitting in the corner, muttering into their long white beards. Then all the rest arrived – Tom Pushman, Jack Driffen, Daniel Thorne, Alfie Masters, David Hibbs. An hour later, the whole village was there. Laughing and singing. And then someone called for silence. The voices died away. Mr Hobbs pushed himself to his feet. A toast, he said. A toast to the late John Ball. And may God rest his soul.

'I couldn't bear it. I went outside to the garden at the back. And I stayed there until I was calm again.'

William shifted position, looking bored.

'Of course with two businesses to run, I had less time to brood. But I still thought of John every day. Sometimes it was like a dagger in my heart. I couldn't talk about it with Arthur any more. He didn't want me to have false hope. But I did hope, all the time. Miracles happen. I kept imagining that one day I'd turn round, and there would be a strange man I'd never seen before, a Spanish sailor, or a French Zouave from the mountains of Algeria with a sash and a rifle and flowing red trousers, and he'd step in close and say in a low voice, I have a message for Mrs Ball. And it would be the news I'd longed for all this time. News that John was safe. That he was waiting for me.

'But all the dreaming didn't make it happen. The days passed, and I watched and waited, but no news came.

'The forge was busy. Harry Brown was a good worker. Some days when I called by, and Harry was hammering away, dark hair falling over his face, he reminded me so much of John that

I caught my breath. For a moment, the whole wild plan had never happened and John was still by my side.'

Mary paused, staring into space.

'He was a kind young man. Easy manners. Always made me smile. I said to him one day, So you're happy here, Mr Brown?

'Very happy, he said. I like the village. I like the job. I like the people.

'Better than working for Mr Newbery?

'If you'll forgive me for saying so, Mrs Ball, that wouldn't be hard.

'I was still laughing when I looked up and saw Arthur in the doorway.

'Mary, he said, will you walk with me?

'I knew something was wrong. But it wasn't until we were some way from the village that Arthur said, What were you doing in the forge just now?

'I was talking to Harry Brown.

'You should be careful, he said, to keep your distance.

'I was very angry. What right have you, I said, to talk to me like that?

'He looked confused. I only want what's best for you.

'I'll be the judge of that.

'But the forge is a dangerous place, Mary. You hear of so many accidents. Burns and scalds and broken limbs.

'I laughed. I said, I misunderstood. I thought you meant we were carrying on, me and Harry Brown.

'Arthur opened his eyes wide. Of course not. I would never have thought that. He's just a young lad.

'You make it sound like I'm an old witch.

'You're his employer. He knows to treat you with respect.

'I said, I don't think we'll keep him for ever. He's ambitious. He'll go far.

'As it turned out, Arthur was right about the danger. A few

weeks later, there was an explosion at the forge. Sparks from the anvil set light to some powder that must have been sitting there for years, hidden in a dark corner unnoticed. Harry was lucky to get out alive. When I got back from the market in Swanage, people were still standing in the street, shocked. It had so nearly been a tragedy.

'I said to Mrs Selby, Poor Arthur. He spends his life worrying about me. And now he's more convinced than ever that I need protecting from trouble and misfortune.

'Mrs Selby said, Why does that surprise you? He wants to look after you. He worships the ground you walk on.'

'You know how to show a girl a good time.'

'I thought you were hungry.'

Stella stubbed out her cigarette on the pastry crust of the gooseberry tart. 'Not really.'

William swallowed a mouthful of custard and put down his spoon.

'It's all we ever do when you come to see me. Go out and eat. Next time we should go to the pictures. Or dancing. Make a night of it.'

He pushed away the bowl.

'If there is a next time.'

He looked up, his eyes full of alarm.

Stella laughed. 'Come on. Let's go to the pub.'

It was seven o'clock but still light. The spring air was warm, sweet with the Silvertown stink of sugar and decay. Stella was wearing a blue cotton frock, printed with daisies. The thin fabric showed the shape of her body beneath.

They left the restaurant ('For Your Tea To-Day We Recommend Fried Fillet of Codling 9d') and wandered off down dusty streets full of bombed-out buildings. Boys were playing on the rubble, slithering down piles of broken bricks. Bluebottles hovered over hidden rubbish.

Stella said, 'Uncle Ron was helping out when they bombed a pub in West Ham. Bodies. Bits of people. And then they found a baby. A few weeks old. Stone dead. And that finished them. Grown men just standing there, tears running down their faces. And Ron looked down, and there was half a bottle of whisky on its side in the ruins. So he picked it up and uncorked it and took a mouthful, and passed it on. And he was done for looting, up at the Old Bailey. Six months. Mum said, Can you believe it. They put you inside for helping people.'

'Which one's Uncle Ron?'

'You can't keep up, can you?' She sidestepped a ginger cat that shot through her legs and disappeared into a forest of tall green nettles. 'Dad's cousin. On his mum's side. Uncle Ron has a daughter in Bromley. That's where Peter is now. Just for a few weeks. Nice big house with a garden front and back. She's got a little boy the same age. Thick as thieves, they are. I'd rather he was here with me, but I didn't want to risk it after the last raid.'

'What about you?'

'What about me?'

'If it isn't safe for Peter, it isn't safe for you.'

She made a face. 'That's all you do, isn't it? Worry away.'

'It's hard not to.'

'You can't look at life like that. You've got to see the bright side of things. Live for today. Let tomorrow take care of itself.'

They passed a boarded-up church. The door was blackened and burned. Two soldiers, insolent, gave Stella a long hard stare as they passed. William glared back.

She said, 'What's your brother up to these days?'

'I don't know. I haven't heard from him for weeks.'

'Nice-looking boy.'

William shot her a quick glance. She laughed.

At the pub, they bought two whiskies and went to sit at a corner table. In the dying light of an April evening, Stella's hair seemed more fair than gold, her dress a washed-out grey.

'Go on, then.'

'What?' William was confused.

'You look like you've got something to say.'

He stared back, tongue-tied.

She shrugged and lit a cigarette. When he opened his mouth to speak, she mimed intense interest, as if she didn't want to miss a word.

He slumped, defeated.

'You're very strange, you know.' She took another long drag of her cigarette. 'Three times you've come all the way to London to see me. But when you get here, you just sit there, staring. And then rush off for the last train.'

'I wish . . .' But then he stopped again, saying nothing.

'What do you wish?'

He hung his head. They sat listening to the clink of glasses. In the corner next to the door, a red-faced man, finishing his story, slammed his fist on to the table. All around him, his friends broke into loud laughter.

She said, 'How did they die, your parents?'

The question startled him.

But she just waited, the smoke from her cigarette curling upwards.

After a while, he said, 'My father was never the same after the war. Left half of himself in France, my mother used to say. Just sat in a chair in the front room, looking out of the window. There was no money when he died. She didn't get a pension. One day I came back from school and found her on the floor. On her back, eyes closed, as if she were sleeping. Blue round the mouth. A heart attack, the doctor said.'

'How old were you?'

'Fourteen.'

Her eyes rested on his face. 'And then you left school and joined the police.'

'It seemed like a good idea. Safe. Steady income.'

There was a small silence. She shot him a quick glance. Then she said, studiedly casual, letting her gaze wander over the polished wood and etched glass, the row of hand pumps, the casks of spirits, 'Do you want to come back?'

'Come back?'

'There's no one there till ten.'

He swallowed.

She raised an eyebrow. 'Not if you have to think about it.'

'No,' he said, desperate, 'I didn't mean—'

She laughed. 'I bet you didn't.'

His eyes not leaving her face, he nodded.

'Drink up then.' She drained her glass. He did the same. She took a final mouthful of smoke, blew it out in a great cloud, and stubbed out her cigarette. 'Let's go before I change my mind.'

———

'Mrs Selby was right. All Arthur wanted was to look after me. One Sunday after church, as we wandered back past the old oak, he said, Why don't you sell the forge?

'Oh Arthur, I said, it was just an accident. No one was hurt. And Harry's looked in all the dark corners, and there's nothing else hiding away that might explode.

'But Arthur didn't seem to have heard. He said, You could sell the Ship, too, if you wanted. Start a new life. Leave here.

'I said, But Langton is my home. Why would I want to leave?

'He looked at me, his blue eyes puzzled. He said, I thought you wanted to see the world.

'It was just a dream, Arthur. Just a childish dream. Something I wanted a long time ago.

'We walked on. But he carried on frowning, as if he didn't really understand.

'Arthur still helped with all the heavy lifting at the Ship whenever he could. Sometimes he had to travel to Exeter, or Dorchester, or even to London. But he tried to find work close to home in case I needed him.

'One afternoon, we were down in the cellar, standing in a shaft of sunlight from the open trapdoor above, when he suddenly said, Marry me.

'I straightened up. What did you say?

'Marry me, Mary. Enough time has passed. Marry me.

'By now he had taken hold of my arm and turned me round to face him. He said, We don't know what's happened to John. But in the eyes of the world, you're a widow. You're free to take a husband.

'I told him I wasn't ready to marry again. He kept saying, why? Why aren't you ready? I couldn't think how to explain. Surely Arthur could see how wrong this was. For all we knew, John was still alive. I tried to keep calm. I said, I need time to think.

'He said, How much time? Five years? Ten years? I'm twenty-four, Mary. Most men my age have a wife and children by now.

'He wouldn't stop. I'd never seen him like this before. Words poured out of him like beer from a leaky barrel – when would I give him an answer, why was I hesitating, everybody expected it, it wasn't fair to keep him hanging on. Marrying him would make my life so much easier. Open up new choices. It wasn't too late to go to the New World. We could sell up, leave Dorset, go to America. He would find work. His skills were in high demand. It would be a new life for both of us, a new start, an end to all the misery and deceit. He was like a man possessed – hectoring me, bullying me, determined to beat me down. I felt almost afraid. He stood between me and the stairs, blocking my way out. I thought, He's never going to let me go. He's going to make me stay down here forever. He's going to keep me underground in the cellar until I promise to give in.

'In the end I said, Enough, Arthur. Enough. I can't marry you until I know for certain that John is dead.

'He said, And what will it take to convince you? His rotting corpse?

'It felt like he'd hit me. I was shocked he could be so cruel. He must have seen that he'd gone too far, because he shook his head and said, I'm sorry. I'm sorry. I don't know what came over me. I shouldn't have said that. But it's been two years now, Mary. He's gone forever. You can't spend your life wishing for something that isn't going to happen.

'In the end, I had to forgive him, because he looked so sad and his eyes were pleading with me to understand. I knew he only wanted the best for me. So we went upstairs and sat on the wooden bench outside in the sun and I told him I wasn't angry, and I promised to think about what he had said.

'But that night, alone in the bed I used to share with John, I couldn't sleep. I lay awake half the night worrying. He seemed so lonely and so desperate. I thought, I know this man. Arthur is kind. He is dependable. He has looked after me, helped me, comforted me all my life. Steady as a rock, as my father used to say. I can understand why he's impatient. He's waited a long time. He loves me.

'But that doesn't mean I'm going to marry him.'

Leaning on his forearms, eyes locked on hers, watching her every change of expression, smelling the sharp scent of her, feeling the heat of her body, moving together, slowly, slowly, her breath, then his, and then the same, breathing the same air.

The house was empty. It spread out around them, cold and

silent. Light filtered through the curtains on to her blond hair, fanned out on the pillow.

He bent down to kiss her, and she still tasted of whisky.

Beneath the window, someone was singing. He didn't hear it at first. He was deaf to it. It was only when Stella laughed, her eyes inviting him to listen, that he stopped, attentive. And then he heard it, too. The dirty song doing the rounds. 'The Deepest Shelter in Town'.

She said, 'And how are you finding mine?'

Loud, female and drunk, the voice outside was yelling about negligees and radios and alarm clocks.

He said, 'You need to ask?'

Her lips dark red against her white skin. 'All modern comforts.'

'Somewhere to put your hat,' shouted the voice. 'Somewhere to put your hat.'

He leaned forward and she gasped.

———

Mary, across the table, was watching him.

He hesitated. 'And then what happened?'

She shook her head.

'Miss Holmes, please go on.'

'Not unless you're listening. I looked up just now and you weren't there. Your eyes had gone blank again.'

William swallowed.

'Whatever it is, it keeps claiming you. Won't let you go. What happened to you, Constable? What is it that you don't want to remember?'

'You were telling me about Arthur. He was browbeating you. Pressing you to marry him. And the rector was in London trying to change the law.'

Mary's expression was stern. 'And you're listening now?'

He nodded.

'You're sure?'

'Yes.'

Still she waited. Then she said, 'So Mr Lester came back from London a month later. He called in at the Ship straightaway. He was normally so serious. Frowning all the time. But this time he was lit up with excitement. You may have heard, Mrs Ball, he said, that I went to London to see Mr Garland's cousin. He's a Member of Parliament, and supports a change in the law on burials. After all, it isn't just those who take their own lives who are denied the burial service. It's also babies who die before they can be baptised.

'Mr Lester said that while he'd been in London, there was talk of a bill being presented to the House. They had been hopeful. There was a lot of sympathy for their cause. Many rallied behind them. But, sadly, nothing had come of it.

'Well, you can imagine how confused I was. I thought, If it's all been a waste of time, how come he's looking so pleased with himself?

'Mr Lester bent down from his great height so that his eyes were level with mine. He said, But we mustn't lose heart, Mrs Ball. Because I've spoken to a number of very influential people, and they all believe it's only a matter of time. If we hold true to our course and lobby hard, we can introduce the bill next year.

'And the rector reached out and took my hand and crushed it in his so hard I thought the bones of my fingers would break. I won't give up, Mrs Ball, he said, I won't give up. I plan to return to London very soon.'

Up west, Stella had said. Let's meet in Leicester Square this time. Outside Dolcis. There's the Empire and the Ritz, so we can choose. But I don't want battleships and machine guns and officers with posh voices. I don't want to think about the bloody war. I want a bit of glamour. Bright lights. Music. Something to take me out of myself.

It was half past one. William was on time, but only just. He had run most of the way from the station, only slowing down when he hit Soho. From the other side of the road, he studied the queue. People were standing two abreast, an elongated crowd taking up the whole pavement, a mass of hats and jackets and shoulders and legs. The street was wet from recent rain, but the sun had come out again, shining on the shop façades.

Then he saw her. Someone stood back, and there she was, alone. Her hair was bright gold against the black of her jacket. He stared. She seemed to be waiting with no expectation of anything but solitude, her expression neutral, looking straight ahead. Her detachment was so complete that she looked like a picture in an art gallery, a studio shot of a Hollywood star.

She was so far away.

He started walking towards her, dodging the cars, increasing his pace. A man striding too close made her step back and swing round.

And then she saw him. There was a flash of recognition and her face lit up. She became flesh and blood, the Stella he knew.

People walked by, and a great curtain of hats and coats hid her from view.

When he next saw her, when the crowd parted, she was looking back at him with her usual air of cool indifference.

It was such a public reunion. They stood there, on the pavement in the thin May sunshine, surrounded by strangers. His hands hung useless by his side.

She said, 'You got here, then.'

'The train was late.'

'Good job one of us was on time. Or we'd be even further back.'

He couldn't take his eyes off her.

'*The Philadelphia Story*. Cary Grant and Katharine Hepburn.' Her lipstick was bright red. 'It's either that or *Gone with the Wind*. And I've already seen that. Three times.'

He found his voice. 'You should be kissed and often, by someone who knows how.'

She raised her eyebrows. 'Sounds like you've seen it too.'

All around them, people were chattering and laughing.

He dipped his head so that only she could hear. 'How long have we got?'

'You're very sure of yourself today.'

'Please. Tell me.'

'What's your rush?'

'I've missed you.'

She was so close he could feel her breath on his face. 'No one in the house all afternoon.'

For a long moment, they just stood there, almost touching.

William said, 'We don't have to see the film.'

She took his hand, turned her back and pulled him out of the queue.

'I don't know why Mr Lester was so obsessed with changing the law. It was wrong, of course, that some Englishmen could have a proper burial and some couldn't. But there were plenty who thought that a country parson shouldn't be meddling with Acts of Parliament – that he'd be better spending his time with the poor and sick. But he was a stubborn man, Mr Lester. Stubborn but mild, which is often the worst kind. You don't realise how determined they are until it's too late.

'After he'd left, I stood there, thinking over what he'd said. And the more I went through it in my mind, the more I realised that he was going to get his way. This giant, clumsy, unworldly man was going to persuade some of the most powerful people in the land to change the law. And once that happened, as sure as night follows day, the way we had tricked the village would come to light.

'I grabbed my shawl, ran round to Arthur's lodgings and hammered on the door until he let me in. I was so out of breath, I could hardly speak. The rector won't give up, I said. The bill failed this time. But they're going to try again. They'll keep on and on until they succeed. And then you'll have to show them the coffin. And it will be empty. And the whole village will know that John didn't shoot himself, and they went through all that grief and pain for nothing. And I couldn't bear that, Arthur. I couldn't bear it.

'Arthur said, I've told you before, it's all talk. Nothing will come of it.

'I couldn't believe he was being so calm. After I left him, I went to see Mrs Selby. I was ashamed of lying to her. The guilt was like a stone in my heart. But I had to find out if there was anything I could do to stop Mr Lester digging up the empty coffin.

'How lucky we are, I said, that the rector is so committed to changing the law. He's determined to see it through. He told me he's going back to London in the next few weeks.

'She laughed. I'm not surprised, she said. I hear the Member of Parliament has a daughter and Mr Lester is very taken with her.

'A daughter? I said.

'An unmarried daughter, said Mrs Selby, who has a passion for sketching seabirds and is keen to visit Dorset.

'That gave me hope. I remember feeling I could breathe again. Perhaps the rector's enthusiasm for London visits wasn't just because of my dead husband's bones.

'Early in the New Year, Mrs Selby came to see me, all smiles. What did I tell you? she said. Mr Lester is engaged to be married. It's all going to happen very quickly. Neither of them wants to wait.

'A spring wedding, I said.

'And what about you, Mary?

'Me? I said. Although I knew what she meant.

'You know Arthur is devoted to you. And he has waited such a long time.

'It's too soon, I said.

'Mrs Selby took my hand. She said, Listen to me. It may be a different kind of love to the one you had with John. But don't dismiss it. Arthur has looked after you every day since John died. I think sometimes that without him you would have lost your mind.

'My eyes filled with tears. I hated deceiving her.

'I felt less guilty when Mrs Selby insisted for the third time that month that Arthur Corben was a good man and would make a fine husband. I said, Has he asked you to nag me like this?

'And she blushed bright red, and said, Of course not, Mary. It's my own honest opinion. But I caught them in deep conversation under the old oak after church the next Sunday, so I didn't believe a word of it.

'A few weeks later, Mr Lester told me that Mr Corben had asked him how long a widow should wait before she took another husband. He is determined to marry you, Mary, he said.

'I was angry. Arthur knew I wasn't a widow. And it was wrong of him to use my friends to bully me. For a moment, my longing for John – my champion, my protector – was so strong that I almost fell to my knees in the dust and wept. But I lifted my chin and looked the rector straight in the eye.

'I said, Mr Corben can want to marry me all he likes. But that doesn't mean it's going to happen.'

—·—

'So you're glad I pushed you into it.'

William smiled. 'Maybe.'

'You look good, Will.'

'Thanks.'

'Second lieutenant.' His brother pulled a face. 'Catching up.'

They were having lunch near London Bridge. The Fishmongers' Banqueting Hall, with its ornate panelling and nineteenth-century carvings, was now a British Restaurant. There were at least a couple of hundred people in the vast, high-ceilinged room, all eating roast beef, mashed potatoes and boiled cabbage, all talking at top volume.

'So how have you been?' said William.

'What?'

'How have you been?'

The man next to them dropped his knife on to his plate, with a clang of metal on china. William screwed up his face to show that he hadn't heard.

'I said, this is probably my last leave for a while.'

William nodded. For nearly a minute, they chewed beef and drank tea, and listened to the high-pitched laughter of the woman at the end of the table. Then William said, 'Have you seen Aunty Ellen?'

'No. You?'

William shook his head. 'Too far.'

'What?'

William raised his voice, 'I need to ask your advice.'

'What?'

William half stood. 'Shall we get out of here?'

So they escaped.

They didn't discuss where they were going – just started walking along the river towards Cannon Street. It was a fine September afternoon, with a pale lemon sun in a clear blue sky. But you couldn't forget the war. All around them, everyone was in uniform – army, navy, air force, WVS, ARP. There was shrapnel damage from the recent blitz on the base of the stone balustrade.

William said, 'I want to ask you something.'

'Fire away.'

He took a deep breath. 'Is this a bad time to get married?'

'Get married? I didn't even know you were seeing anyone.'

'I haven't asked her yet.'

His brother laughed. 'You're full of surprises. Who is she?'

'But is it a bad time?'

'You're worried what would happen. If you had to go away.'

William nodded.

'One of my men asked me that once. In a trench, early in the morning. He was ten years older than me.'

'What did you say?'

'I told him to marry her. That's what he wanted to hear.'

'And did he?'

'Yes. Next leave. But everyone's different. Some people want to wait till it's all over. Others just seize the moment.'

'What would you do?'

'Is there any reason to hurry?'

'No.'

'That's a relief. Do you love her?'

'Yes.'

'So ask her. See what she says.' His brother stopped and turned round to look at him. 'You're very young to get married, Will. Only just twenty-one.'

'I worry about her. I want to look after her.'

'So what's she like?'

'You've met her. The girl in the village. The evacuee.'

They stood in the September sunshine staring at each other. His brother said, his voice flat, 'The one with the baby.'

'He's not a baby any more. Just had his third birthday. His name's Peter.'

'You didn't tell me you were still seeing her.'

'Because I knew what you'd say.'

His brother nodded, frowning, as if this was a fair point. Then he said, 'Why her, Will?'

'What do you mean?'

'I thought you wanted to go back into the police after the war.'

'She's not a criminal.'

'I didn't say she was. But can she be a policeman's wife?'

A man in a flat cap, white shirt and brown jacket looked at them with curiosity as he walked past. Two WAAFs, sitting on some stone steps, glanced up.

'What have you got against her?'

'Nothing.'

'You think she's unsuitable.'

'Keep your voice down. Everyone's staring.'

'I love her. I want to marry her.'

'But you know how it works. You told me yourself. She'd be as much a part of the force as you are. And if you marry her, and the chief constable doesn't think she's right, you'll have to leave.'

William's face was tense. 'If the police don't want her, I won't go back. I'll find something else to do.'

'You love your job. It's your whole life.'

'I love Stella.'

'Will, think about it. It's a big decision.'

William was white with anger. 'I can't believe you're judging her. You don't even know her. You have no idea what she's like.'

'I know she had a child without being married. They're not going to like that.'

'They won't have to know.'

'Oh, come on.'

'She's not the only one bringing up a child alone.'

'Think about it.'

'I have thought about it. I think about nothing else. She's in my head the whole time.'

'That doesn't mean you should marry her.'

William clenched his fists. 'Just sleep with her.'

'I didn't say that.'

'It's what you meant.'

'She's a pretty girl. I can see why you—'

'You're as bad as the rest of them.'

'I don't want to fight, Will.' His brother put up both hands as if warding off attack. 'You asked for my advice. I'm just telling you what I think. Marriage is a serious business. Don't rush into it. Make sure you choose the right girl.'

William looked at him with contempt. 'I know what's going on here.'

'Will—'

'Officer class. Posh accents. Pass the port after dinner. She embarrasses you, doesn't she? Makes you feel awkward. Because she reminds you where you came from. Poverty and fear and shame. You want to forget all that, don't you? A father who went mad. A mother who couldn't pay the rent. You want to pretend it never happened. That you're better than that. That you can mix with the people who really matter.'

'Will—'

'I've spent my whole life looking up to you. Thinking you were some kind of hero. And you know what? You're nothing. Nothing.'

'Stop. Please.'

'Prejudiced. A snob. A narrow-minded bigot.'

For one long moment, they stared at each other.

William turned and started striding towards Blackfriars.

He didn't look back.

———•———

A crash – so loud that even William heard it. Then the walls in the charge room seemed to shake. And then the glass in the lower sash window fell out as if someone had smashed a fist through it.

Mary's eyes widened in alarm.

Outside, people were shouting.

Mary said, 'What was that?'

William's hands were trembling so much his fingers were drumming the table.

For a while they heard nothing. Just some kind of disjointed argument outside. Then the door to the street banged open. There was a sudden clamour of voices in the outer office. Mary stood up.

'All right, all right.' Sergeant Mills was shouting over the racket. 'Calm down, calm down. Bloody truck hit the corner of the building. I'll be having words, I tell you. As if we haven't got enough to worry about. Constable?'

Mary called out, 'We're in here.'

Sergeant Mills appeared. 'Everything all right?'

William looked up, his eyes blank.

'No cause for alarm. An army truck, full of soldiers. Can't see any damage to the brickwork. But the telegraph pole's had it.'

Mary said, 'What happened?'

'They swerved to avoid a jeep. Which must have been driving at a fair lick.'

'Was anyone hurt?'

'Jim Carter fell off his bicycle. He's lucky it wasn't a tank. He might have been flattened. The roads are too full, that's the problem. Too many vehicles. It's a market town, not a military camp.' He looked down at the broken glass on the floor. 'Leave all this. I'll have a word with Constable Keyes on my way out. Get him to call Mr Puckett.'

Mary said, 'Do you want me to go? I can come back later.'

The sergeant shot a quick look at William. 'Why not make a cup of tea, Miss Holmes. Put some sugar in it. Must have been a bit of a shock.'

'It was very loud,' said Mary.

'If you ask me,' said Sergeant Mills, 'they're all driving too fast. Tearing round the countryside like Toad of Toad Hall. If they're not careful, they'll all be bloody killed before they've even been told where they're going.'

He went out, shutting the door.

'Do you have a dustpan and brush?' Mary had filled the kettle and set it on the stove, and was standing looking at the pile of broken glass. 'I could get the worst of it up at least.'

Through the shattered window, they heard an engine starting up. Then more voices, Sergeant Mills shouting, and the high-pitched scream of scraped metal.

'Poor Sergeant Mills. He's normally so calm. But he's not himself today.'

There was a thud as something outside fell against the wall. Moments later, the complete pane from the top sash pitched forward and smashed to the floor. Glass exploded across the room.

Mary said, 'Constable?'

There were tears on his cheeks. He knew this because the skin was cold.

'Shall I get someone?'

He heard himself moaning. To begin with, it was nothing much. Just a register of protest. But it got louder. He was bellowing like an animal in pain, gasping for air, his body jerking forward again and again. He tried to stop, pushing his palms down on the table, but the wailing was too strong. It hurled through him. It howled along his veins. He felt a hand on his back. There was a voice right in his ear saying, 'It's all right. It's all right.' Something warm was wrapped round him, and he felt his shoulders being rubbed up and down. And after a while, still shuddering, but the noise dying down, he returned to himself, slowly, coldly. He felt sick. His ears, his deaf ears, were ringing with a bell-like whine. He felt so tired he wanted only to sleep.

She said, 'Drink this.'

The hit of sweetness made him gulp with gratitude. He glanced up. Mary was looking at him with calm compassion.

His collar felt tight. He pushed in his fingers at the neck.

She said, 'You'll be all right now.'

William adjusted the blanket round his shoulders and pulled it in more tightly.

Mary said, 'Give yourself time.'

When his cup was empty, she picked up the teapot and refilled it, spooning in sugar as if rationing didn't exist. She said, 'Tea. It's what we miss most when we haven't got it. It was the same when I was a child.'

There were voices in the outer office, muted mumblings.

'It's hard to imagine England without tea, don't you think? Like imagining the sky without the sun.'

He sat, staring into space.

She said, 'Do you want to talk about it? What happened? Although you never quite know, do you? You think, where will it stop? Because you can't tell just one small part of it. It's like moving a pebble in a gwyle to let the water trickle through. Before you know it, there's a raging flood. I nearly told Mr Lester so many times. It would have been a relief. But I didn't want to lose his good opinion. Which I would have done, without a doubt. Because you can't take justice into your own hands, can you? It's for God to decide.'

He said nothing.

'It's even worse now, with the war on. We have to pretend things are normal. Because if you didn't, you'd start screaming. You know, when the bombs fell in Wareham, the ceiling fell down in one of the cottages. Chunks of plaster and great clouds of dust. And I was talking to one little boy afterwards, and I said, So what did you do? And he said, Well, my mum had just put lunch on the table. So we fished out the plaster and ate the stew. And you know what people are like with incendiary bombs these days. No panic at all. There they are, burning away, and people just kick dirt over them or cover them up with a bucket.'

The noise in the outer office had stopped.

She said, 'I think you're all right now. I'll go. Leave you to your reports.'

He focused on her face.

'The one thing I will say is that guilt is very heavy. And it gets worse with each year that passes. You might want to think about that, Constable. You can end up at my age feeling you're carrying Old Harry himself.' She stood up and started pulling on her gloves.

He swallowed. 'We haven't finished your statement.'

'I can come back tomorrow.'

'It's market day tomorrow. We'll be busy.'

'I'm sure we'll find some time at some point. You don't look well. You should go and lie down.'

'How many days did it take for God to create the world?'

Mary looked up, surprised.

William said, 'Six. At this rate your statement is going to take longer than creation itself.'

There was a small pause.

Mary said, 'I could tell you about the time I met the Prince of Wales.'

'I'd rather you told me the truth.'

'It is the truth.'

He sighed, looking weary. 'If you say so.'

Mary smiled. 'You're sure? You want me to go on?'

He nodded.

'Where were we?'

'I have no idea.'

Mary sat down. 'London, I think. Have you been to London?'

His mouth tightened.

'Mr Lester wanted me to meet Mr Garland. The Member of Parliament. I had to be persuaded. I said to the rector, What difference will it make?

'And Mr Lester said, I don't know. But he's asked to meet you.

'It was a long journey. A train to Southampton and another to Waterloo Bridge. And when you got there, you had to reset your pocket watch to London time. I couldn't believe the noise. Crowds and shouting and people pushing right up close to your face. Dogs barking. Children selling newspapers and flowers and beer and matches. Beggars on the pavement. And in those days you took your life in your hands whenever you crossed the street. Carriages and carts flying along, all going too fast. Great piles of horse shit. Smoke and dust and dirt, great clouds of it stirred up by the wheels and the hooves.' She paused, her eyes anxious. 'You're quite sure you're well enough? You don't need to rest?'

'Please continue, Miss Holmes.'

'We made our way to Piccadilly, and then to Green Park. Mr Garland lived in a huge white house with pillars either side of the front door. A mansion. Very tall windows, I remember. Mirrors, marble fireplace, Turkish tiles and a great big pot full of peacock feathers. The chair I sat on had springs in the seat. I felt like I was floating, as light as air. He was very attentive from the moment I arrived. Beady brown eyes like a robin. Not a tall man, but somehow you felt he was, because he held himself very straight, and you knew he wasn't frightened of anyone. Tell me the whole story, Mrs Ball, he said. Right from the beginning. I didn't see his wife. He said she wasn't well. She never came out of her room the whole time we were there. Although it might have been that she just didn't want to meet me. The woman whose husband had shot himself. So I talked to Mr Garland in his study, full of brown leather books from floor to ceiling. And then afterwards we had tea with his daughter and Mr Lester. She took against me straightaway. I think she thought I had designs on her fiancé.'

'Her fiancé?'

'Mr Lester. I thought I'd told you. He asked her to marry him. Of course she was getting on a bit by then. She was twenty-eight by the time she became his wife. But they managed six children. Two of the boys died in the Great War. Although they'd moved back to Surrey by then.' Mary paused. 'Are you sure you're all right, Constable? If you're feeling faint, I think we should stop.'

'Carry on, Miss Holmes.'

'She wasn't the best-looking woman in the world. Quite short, with thin brown hair and no eyebrows to speak of. Peculiar eyes. Light green, like a still pond with the sunlight on it. But she had a tiny waist. They say her wedding dress showed it off to perfection. Silk buttons all the way down from her neck to her arse. Mean little mouth, though. After we'd had tea, and we were standing in the great tiled hall ready to leave, I said, I hope I've been able to help your father.

'And she looked down her nose and said, On the contrary, Mrs Ball, I thought it was more a case of him helping you.

'Which I thought was unfriendly. And completely wrong. If I was helping anyone it was Mr Lester, because he was just obsessed with burial by then. He wrote to me right at the end of his life, in 1932, I think, or 1934. I hadn't heard from him for years, which was so sad, considering all the time we'd spent together. I remember so clearly the day he arrived in Purbeck. A Cambridge scholar, Latin and Greek, full of all the old stories. He took it upon himself to educate me. The *Odyssey*. Blinding the Cyclops, Scylla and Charybdis, Odysseus coming home and pretending he was a beggar, and even his old friend the pig-keeper taken in. So many tall tales. As Mr Lester said to me, Nothing is what it seems, Mary. Nothing is what it seems. I don't know why he left Surrey to come to Dorset. He never explained. I imagined some kind of family rift. Tea parties where he hid behind a giant aspidistra, a gaunt young man, the spectre at the feast.

'And then he came to Purbeck and he didn't fit in here either. Poor Mr Lester. But I made him welcome. And we became good friends. That's what he said in the letter. The one he sent me right at the end. I don't know how he found me. I didn't think anyone in Langton Matravers knew my address. But there it was. Miss Mary Holmes, Langton Cottage, North Street. He said he'd often thought of the time he'd spent with me in Purbeck and hoped my life had turned out well. So you can see why she was jealous, back then. Miss Garland, his intended. Because you might think, reading that letter, that he'd spent his whole life pining for me. Pining for all those times we sat either side of the fire in the Ship when I hung on his every word. But I think he just knew there was more to tell. An unfinished story. And the idea preyed on his mind for years. Kept nagging at him. Tap, tap, tap, like a thrush with a snail.' Mary paused, staring into space. 'I didn't answer the letter. I couldn't think what to say. And then I heard he'd died. Which made me very sad.

'So Miss Garland took against me and didn't want her fiancé thinking about me and the bones of my dead husband. To begin with, it was all right, because each time Mr Lester went to Westminster to lobby Members of Parliament, he spent time with her. So she was quite glad he had an excuse to come to London. But after they married, and she was living in the vicarage at Langton, she wanted him to forget all about it. It was bad enough being stuck in Purbeck with a whoreage of lawless stonecutters. But she didn't want to be here alone. She wanted her husband by her side. Especially once she was expecting her first child, which happened very quickly after the wedding. I think they realised they had to make up for lost time.

'It was while I was in London that Harry Brown packed up and left. Arthur said he'd been offered a job in Weymouth. He knew I'd be upset, so he'd found a replacement straightaway. Charlie Scadden from Stoborough. Well, it was clear he could shoe a horse and sharpen a paddle, but he was white and sweaty with a shiny bald head and a great pot belly. I said to Arthur, Did you have to employ someone with a face like a bladder of lard?' Mary paused, looking at William with sudden anxiety. 'I didn't tell you about meeting the Prince of Wales.'

William said, 'Let's come back to that.'

'So try as he might, Mr Lester couldn't do what his new wife wanted. He couldn't forget how John Ball had been buried like a dog at dead of night. By now he'd got it into his head that I wouldn't marry again until the body of my first husband had been given the respect it deserved. *Blessed are they that mourn: for they shall be comforted.* And he still felt guilty, more than two years later, about giving in to the village and not burying him at St George's.

'So he started thinking. And one day after church, he stopped me at the lych gate and asked if he could see me and Arthur that afternoon at the Ship. I thought he was going to talk again about the bill going through Parliament, and I said to Arthur, I wish he'd just let sleeping dogs lie.

'But when he came, he surprised us both.

'He said, I have been giving the whole matter a great deal of thought. Even if the second bill succeeds, we may not be allowed to move Mr Ball's remains to the churchyard. And so I have a proposal. It seems to me that what matters is not where Mr Ball lies, but that Mrs Ball can go to the grave and mourn his loss. Openly, in public. So what I propose, Mr Corben, is that you take us to the grave and then, in front of Mrs Ball's friends and neighbours, I will conduct the burial service over Mr Ball's final resting place. And Mrs Ball will feel that her poor husband can finally be at peace.

'We stared at him. Arthur said, But you told Mary it was against the law. That those who commit suicide are not allowed the burial service.

'You're right, Mr Corben, said Mr Lester. The amendment permits only comforting words from the Book of Common

Prayer and Holy Scripture. But I don't believe this is enough. Mrs Ball has suffered too long. She has told me many times that denying her husband the burial service has caused her great pain. So I am prepared to break the law.

'That afternoon, Arthur and I went for a long walk along the cliff path. It was a hot August day, with the grass full of chalk milkwort and horseshoe vetch. I was nearly in tears. The rector won't let this go, I said. He's determined that John should have a proper burial.

'I don't have to show him where the coffin is really buried, said Arthur. He can say prayers over a nice bit of turf with nothing underneath it but moles.

'I shook my head. The bill might go through, and the law might be changed, and the rector will want to dig up the coffin and rebury it in the churchyard. And it will be even worse if we've held the burial service over nothing but earth. Can you imagine how much they'd hate us?

'Arthur said, I could say I've forgotten where I dug the grave.

'No one would believe you.

'Arthur thought again. He said, What if you say you don't like the idea? You don't want the burial service unless it's in the churchyard.

'Why would I say that?

'So we went round and round in circles. In the end I started weeping. I said, I am tired of all this. I want it over. We shouldn't have done it. But we did. And now the lie is killing us.

'Arthur said, We can always leave, Mary. Leave Dorset. Go far away.

'I glared at him. I thought, Don't you dare start this again. Don't you dare start going on about marriage.

'My face must have shown what I felt because he just shrugged. He said, So we stay. And we put some bones in the coffin.

'I was puzzled.

'If that's what they want, he said, if that's what they need, a skeleton in a box, we'll give it to them.

'How?

'It needs to be a big skeleton, said Arthur. So that they believe it once belonged to John.

'I started shivering in the sunshine.

'So what I'll do, said Arthur, is dig up the skeleton of John's father, take it out to the fields, and bury it in the empty coffin.

'I cried out in horror. You can't do that, I said. You can't dig up a body from a churchyard.

'Oh, Mary, said Arthur. His spirit has long gone.

'God will strike you down.

'God has got more important things to do, said Arthur, than watch over a few old bones.

'We argued all the way past the quarries, and all the way back along the Priest's Way to Acton. Arthur kept laughing at me, treating the whole thing as a joke. And I thought, I hate the idea of digging up old bones. But at least the overbearing, bullying Arthur has disappeared. No more cornering me in cellars, or getting friends in the village to gang up on me. This is the Arthur I remember – calm and good-natured, certain that everything will turn out for the best.

'By the time we got back to the Ship, we had reached an uneasy agreement. Arthur would go out one night when there was no moon and see how easy it would be to dig up John's father's grave. Then we would decide what to do.

'Should I come with you? I said.

'It's better if I go alone.

'But I want to help.

'Arthur smiled. Stop worrying, Mary. Leave it to me.'

'No soap. That's what they're saying now. They're going to ration soap.'

'I'll find you some.'

She shifted on to her back, staring at the ceiling. 'And where are you going to get it from?'

'I don't know. But I'll find it somehow. Leave it to me.'

'No lipstick. No rouge. No mascara. No powder. No nail varnish.' She counted off the list on her fingers one by one. 'It gets you down. Takes all the fun out of life.'

'You don't need any of that stuff.'

'I want it, though. You get tired of doing without.'

They were lying side by side in Stella's narrow single bed at her aunt's house. It was late afternoon. The curtains – pale yellow, with pink rosebuds – had either shrunk in the wash or been taken from another window, as they hung six inches from the sill. The bleached February sunlight, creeping in underneath, showed up the dust on the chest of drawers.

It was the first time he'd ever seen her without red lipstick. She looked younger somehow. More fragile. 'You're beautiful, Stella Allen. Just as you are.'

'Liar.'

'It's true.' He studied her face. 'I don't know why you don't believe me.'

'I know what men are like, that's why.'

'Which men?'

'That would be telling.' She gave him a sideways glance, eyes laughing at him.

He turned his head into her shoulder, breathing in the warmth of her skin.

She said, after a while, 'I'd better get up.'

'Don't go yet. I've hardly seen you.'

'What do you call this, then?'

He didn't answer.

'Mum's on lates tonight. I've got to pick up Peter.'

He said, after a pause, 'Does she know about me?'

'Who?'

'Your mum.'

Outside in the street, children were shouting, playing some kind of war game.

'What's there to know?'

He said nothing. The silence got longer.

Stella stretched an arm towards the wooden chair by the side of the bed and picked up her cigarettes and matchbook. She wriggled backwards until she was half sitting against the pillows, the sheet wrapped round her. William watched as she lit a cigarette.

She said, blowing out smoke, 'Go on, then. If you've got something to say, say it.'

Now on the street came the sound of singing, high voices chanting.

'I don't know what you want. After all this time. I still don't understand.'

She shook her head as if he'd said something stupid.

He pulled himself up to sitting. 'Don't you see?'

'No.'

He stared at her, lost.

She drew on her cigarette with a sharp intake of breath, then relaxed her mouth, letting the smoke escape. 'I was your first, wasn't I?'

He looked away, his face reddening.

'It's nothing to be ashamed of. We've all got to start some-where.'

He said, anguished, 'That's got nothing to do with it.'

They sat side by side, miles apart.

She said, in a gentler voice, 'What about you, copper? What do you want?'

In a sudden movement, he kissed her hard on the mouth, pushing her back against the bed. The hand with the lit cigarette flopped backwards. As he turned his body into hers, there was a moment when she responded, soft and compliant, accommodating him. Then she jerked to one side, turning her face away. 'I've got to go.'

'Five minutes.' His voice was desperate.

'I told you. I've got to get Peter.'

He didn't move, collapsed over her, resting his forehead on the pillow. Then he rolled off, and she sat up, turning her back to him.

As she reached down to pick up clothes strewn on the floor, he could see her ribs, thin lines in white skin.

She said, 'You'd better get dressed. Aunty Lil will be back soon.'

He watched as she stubbed out her cigarette. 'Maybe next time we could go away somewhere. We could plan it. A couple of days.'

She put a pink silky slip over her head and stood up. 'Where?'

'Somewhere in the country. Surrey. Or Kent.'

For a moment, the pink slip stayed bunched round her waist, leaving her naked below. Then, like a curtain on stage, it fell.

'Mr and Mrs in a hotel? And you a policeman.' Stella picked up her dress and turned to face him while she did up the buttons at the front. 'You've got that look on your face again. Like there's something you want to say.'

He hesitated.

'Spit it out.'

'I won't be around for a few weeks. Battle school.'

Stella picked up her belt. 'You think you'd know how to fire a gun by now.'

'But I'll see you when I get back?'

Her eyes rested on his face as she fastened the buckle. Her voice, when she spoke, had no expression at all. 'It's like I said. It's the only thing left that isn't rationed.'

———

The door burst open.

'Constable,' said Sergeant Mills, 'may I have a word?'

William looked up, his eyes empty.

'Not bad news, I hope,' said Mary.

'Not at all,' said the sergeant. 'Not at all.'

'Everything all right at home?'

Sergeant Mills gave her a searching look. 'Why wouldn't it be?'

'Oh, no reason,' said Mary. 'No reason at all.'

Sergeant Mills looked as if he might be about to say something else, but thought better of it.

'Do you need to talk in private?' said Mary. 'Should I go?'

'I think that might be wise, Miss Holmes. If it's possible for you to come back tomorrow.' Looking beyond her to the window, he realised for the first time that the whole frame, top and bottom, was empty of glass. He said, startled, 'When did the other half go?'

'I think it was when the lorry reversed,' said Mary.

The sergeant shook his head. 'It's one thing after another round here.'

'What about Constable Meech's bicycle? Did you find it?'

'In the hedge. Minus the light. And with a puncture.' Sergeant Mills looked at Mary more closely. 'Is there something you're not telling me, Miss Holmes?'

Mary stood up. 'What time shall I come tomorrow?'

'It's market day, of course,' said Sergeant Mills. 'Which is always busy.'

They both looked at William. But he still had the dazed look of someone who's only just woken up.

'Come early, Miss Holmes,' said the sergeant. 'Nine o'clock. Then the constable can type it up and have it finished by the afternoon.'

Mary glanced at William. 'I'll see you tomorrow, then.'

As Mary left, Sergeant Mills peered after her until he was sure she'd left the building. Then he turned back to William. 'I've just been having a quick chat with the coroner.'

With great effort, William focused his attention.

The sergeant sat down heavily on the bench. 'Some doubt as to the age of the skeletons. But definitely not recent. At least sixty or seventy years old. So more of an archaeological find, you might say. Both male. One was very tall – six four, six five. No obvious cause of death. Some evidence of skull fractures on the shorter skeleton, but whether these occurred before or after death, it's impossible to say. If you ask me, it still fits with the idea of a quarrying accident. A tunnel collapsing, smothering them with stone dust, that kind of thing. Loose rocks could have caused the skull fractures.'

William waited. It was clear from the sergeant's gloomy expression that there was bad news to come.

'The coroner says that ordinarily, in the normal course of events, he would not have ordered an inquest. These are very old remains. We're in the middle of a war. Resources are limited and we must be clear about our priorities.'

'Although we might be quite near a conclusion,' said William. 'Miss Holmes's story is long and rambling, but she's given me two names. I could ask the vicar at Langton Matravers to look them up in the parish records.'

'Hold your horses, Constable.' Sergeant Mills looked weary. 'It gets complicated. The coroner found something else buried with the bodies.'

William stared, his face tense.

'Gold jewellery worth a small fortune.' The sergeant held up his hand. 'I know, I know exactly what you're thinking. We're already pushed to the limit. Hardly have time to breathe. But because of the gold, there has to be an inquest. Coroners' Act 1887. A jury will have to decide what happens next. Is this a treasure trove? Hidden or buried on purpose, owner unknown? In which case, it belongs to the Crown. Or was it just lost, or abandoned, or stolen? In which case, we have to find out who owns it and get it back to them.' He looked miserable. 'Either way, it means we have to mount a major investigation. Given we're so short-handed, I can't see what else we can do but ask Dorchester for help. God knows, I don't want them breathing down our necks. Once they start digging around, going through our files, examining our records, our lives won't be our own. And I can't imagine Inspector Pearce will be pleased to get back and find his station taken over by officers from headquarters. But what else can we do? I don't think we have a choice.'

The atmosphere in the charge room was thick and heavy.

William said, 'Did you tell the coroner about Miss Holmes?'

'I told him that an elderly lady claimed to know the identities of the bodies, but that she gets a bit muddled, and it's taking a long time to take her statement.'

William said, in an encouraging tone, 'She did know that one of the skeletons was six foot four. It wasn't in the newspaper report.'

'Don't forget she used to live in Langton. She might have talked to the quarrymen who found the grave.' The sergeant sighed. 'Anything else? Any other detail that gives you hope she might be able to shed some light on all this?'

William hesitated. 'Nothing I'm sure of yet.'

'So it might all be a pack of lies. One long work of fiction.'

'Or we might be lucky. Maybe Miss Holmes has the key to the whole mystery.'

'Well, all we can do is carry on. Get her statement. Check the parish records. We've got till the end of the week.' Deep gloom settled over the sergeant's features. 'And after that, we'll have to hand it over to headquarters. And I'm sure you'll say they're a pretty fair-minded lot. Aware of the pressure we're under, managing all this build-up of vehicles and weapons and troops, looking after the US army. But no good will come of it, you mark my words. If we get headquarters down here in Wareham, no good will come of it at all.'

Thursday

It was market day in Wareham. Already, at half past eight in the morning, the streets were full of delivery vans, cattle trucks, bicycles and the odd pony and trap. At Cottees, the auctioneers in East Street, cows were being herded into metal pens, lowing in a grumbling kind of way as if protesting at the inconvenience. Chickens were strutting about on stiff legs in the yard at the British Legion. At the Corn Exchange, fruit and vegetables had been set out on wooden trestle tables along with wild rabbit, pigeon and bloody piles of offal. One of the farmers' wives, wearing a wide-brimmed straw hat, was selling herbal medicines from a tray held in front of her – valerian for nerves, coltsfoot for coughs and autumn crocus for gout.

The sun was shining, glinting off the windscreens of an Austin 7 and two Fords parked in South Street.

Mary sat on a chair by the wall next to Sergeant Mills's high wooden desk. The police station was full, a crush of bodies standing elbow to elbow. Many of the farmers who lived in outlying hamlets – Swineham, Northport, Ridge, Worgret – visited Wareham only once a week, and this was their chance to make complaints, fill in forms and query regulations. The air was full of loud voices, laughing, the creak of wicker baskets and the faint smell of manure.

Mary, in her black coat and hat, looked like a mourner at a May Fair.

By nine o'clock everyone had gone.

'I'm sorry for the wait, Miss Holmes,' said Sergeant Mills. 'He won't be long. Just had to make a telephone call.'

Mary nodded.

'Complete mayhem on Thursdays. Always is. You can guarantee a few extra problems when everyone comes into town. We used to be able to bring in one or two constables from some of the villages. Just for the day. But we can't do that any more. Even with all the specials, there just aren't enough of us.' The sergeant hesitated. 'I'm glad you're early, Miss Holmes. Gives us a chance for a little chat, if that's all right with you.' He came out from behind his desk, picked up a wooden chair and set it down next to Mary's. 'In confidence, of course. Just between the two of us.'

Mary raised her eyebrows.

'I didn't say anything at the beginning, because I thought it would all be over quite quickly. I had no idea that taking your statement would be such a long job. You've been in every day this week, haven't you?'

'Every morning. But not for long. We never seem to have quite enough time.'

'Indeed.' The sergeant frowned. 'The thing is, Miss Holmes, I have to be quite careful. The constable's not himself.'

'I can see that.'

'All his injuries, obviously. Take their toll.'

Mary nodded.

'He had some bad news a while ago.'

'Did he?'

'There was a telegram. Not all telegrams are bad news, obviously. Mrs Thorner from Diffey's Farm got one last week and nearly fainted, but it was just her son in the navy saying he was coming home on leave. I don't think he'll be doing that again. She didn't know whether to hug him or hit him when she saw him.'

'What did the telegram say?'

'I don't know. I wasn't here when it came. But Constable Fripp saw the look on his face when he read it. We need to keep an eye on him, Miss Holmes. Make sure he doesn't overdo it. Now, I don't know what's taking so long with your story. And I do understand that it's an hour here, and an hour there, and that delays it all, of course. But given what's happened, I think we should try to wrap it up as quickly as possible, don't you? Let the constable write his report. And I'm sure you want to get it finished as much as I do, Miss Holmes. It will be a relief for both of us. I can get the constable back to his regular duties, and you can relax at home with a cup of tea, put your feet up, and forget all about it.'

The door opened, bringing in a rush of noise – shouting, car engines, boxes being loaded on to lorries. A young GI – the colonel's driver from Binnegar Hall – ducked underneath the doorframe.

Sergeant Mills stood up. 'Good morning. How can I help you?'

'The colonel's chief of staff wondered if you might be able to call in to see him at Binnegar Hall, sir.'

Sergeant Mills rubbed his forehead. 'When would he like to see me?'

'Immediately, sir, if that's possible. I can drive you there now.'

The sergeant sighed. 'I can see this is going to be a long day.'

The door to the charge room opened. William, white-faced, limped in. He looked at Mary and nodded.

'I have a letter the colonel might like to see,' said Sergeant Mills. 'If you can wait just one minute.'

As the sergeant rummaged through his papers, Mary looked up from her seat against the wall. 'Good morning, Tom.'

The soldier smiled. 'Nice to see you again, ma'am.'

'A lovely day, don't you think?'

'The sun always shines in Dorset.'

'You are all very charming, you Americans. But you know that's a lie.'

The soldier laughed. 'It just seems that way. I drive around the country, and the birds are singing, and there are flowers in the fields, and I think England is just the prettiest place I've ever seen.'

'What do you like best?'

He shrugged, as if the answer was simple. 'The people.'

Sergeant Mills straightened up, holding a small white envelope.

The soldier said, 'I could see the day we arrived that you'd had it tough. Bomb damage. Your men away fighting. No milk, no sugar, no gasoline, everything rationed, places you can't go, things you can't do. For more than three long years. You're tired. And you're hungry. But not one word of complaint. I don't know where that comes from. But it's what you Britishers do. You're just going to carry on. You're just going to keep on going until it's all over.'

There was a small silence.

Sergeant Mills cleared his throat. 'Constable, while I'm at Binnegar Hall, you're in charge.'

William nodded.

'Leave the door open until one of your fellow officers returns, will you? So that you can hear if anyone needs assistance. The rector is due here at eleven, but Constable Keyes can see him in my absence.' The sergeant frowned. 'I hope you and Miss Holmes can conclude your discussions today.' He turned to the American, narrowing his eyes as if the young man stood in bright sunlight. 'Let's make a move, shall we?'

William gestured to Mary to go through to the charge office. As they sat down at the scrubbed wooden table, she said, 'That was interesting. But completely wrong. I hear grumbling all the time. Don't you? Especially when you've been queuing for an hour and they run out before you get there.'

'I think he was just being polite.'

Mary put her head on one side. 'It's very strange.'

'What is?'

'You seem almost pleased to see me this morning.'

'I'm always pleased to see you, Miss Holmes.'

'For someone who's always going on about the importance of telling the truth, you set a very bad example.'

William smiled.

'You know, I think I prefer your normal miserable scowl.'

'Am I always that unpleasant?'

'Pain does terrible things, Constable. Turns us from angels to devils in a moment.'

'You were very kind to me yesterday.'

'I could see you were suffering.'

William opened his notebook. 'Shall we make a start?'

'It's dark in here, isn't it, with that window boarded up? Although you don't get the sun in here much anyway, looking out on to a brick wall.'

'It might be a while before we can get the glass.'

'And it smells of bacon fat,' said Mary. 'Is that what you have for breakfast every morning?'

'Would you rather we went somewhere else? I could talk to you at home if that's easier. It would give us more privacy.'

'Oh,' said Mary.

William looked up.

'You've had the results from the coroner's office.'

William's expression didn't change.

'That's why you're being so nice to me. You finally believe I might be telling the truth. They found the necklace, didn't they? And the earrings. I wonder what they look like after all those years underground. They could probably do with a bit of a clean.'

William took a deep breath. 'Are you ready to start, Miss Holmes?'

'It's suddenly more important now that money's involved, isn't it? It wasn't that interesting when it was two dried-up skeletons and a mad old woman going on about suicide. But now there's buried treasure, you're quite excited.'

'We don't have much time.'

'So you keep saying.'

'On Monday, the investigation is being taken over by a senior officer.'

She looked surprised. 'Why?'

'It's not my decision.'

'Your sergeant didn't mention anything about it just now.'

William said nothing.

'He seemed more concerned about you. Wanted me to hurry up so you could get back to your records on sheep dipping, or whatever it is you do.'

There was no sound from the outer office. Even with the door between the two rooms open, it was dark and stuffy.

William cleared his throat. 'Right at the beginning, you said you killed them both.'

'In a manner of speaking.'

'You did? Or you didn't?'

'I think you need to wait till the end, Constable.'

'Which could be today, Miss Holmes?'

'I hope so. If we're allowed to continue in peace. There are so many interruptions in a police station, aren't there?'

William took out his pen and carefully unscrewed the cap. 'So just to be sure I've understood, Arthur Corben has buried an empty coffin. Which could be a problem if anyone ever digs it up. But this never happened, did it?'

'It could have happened. That's what we were afraid of.'

'So because the empty coffin might be a problem if anyone ever finds it and digs it up, Arthur Corben is planning to put some bones inside. Bones belonging to John Ball's father.'

'Yes.'

William looked sceptical. 'That's a little far-fetched, isn't it? I can't imagine anyone thinking that was a sensible idea. Grave-robbing. He hadn't been dead that long, had he? John's father? Fifteen years?'

'It was Arthur's idea. Not mine.'

'In any case, you told me on the very first day that the skeletons belonged to Arthur Corben and John Ball.'

'Yes.'

'Not John Ball's father.'

'No.'

'So the coffin isn't empty. What we have is a coffin containing the bones of Arthur Corben and John Ball, together with an extremely valuable ruby and gold necklace.'

'And earrings.'

'Which the murderer left behind.'

'Yes.'

'Miss Holmes, you have told me stories about a lot of people who lived a long time ago. The gentry in big houses and the servants who looked after them. Vicars and midwives and pig-stickers and stonemasons. I'd like to forget all that now, please. I'd like to concentrate on just one important question. How did John Ball die?'

Mary looked sad. 'That's the problem.'

'What is?'

'It's not as straightforward as you think.'

'Why?'

'I don't know how he died.'

William stared.

'I'm sorry, was I speaking too quietly?'

His whole face tensed. 'I don't understand.'

'I don't know how John Ball died. I wasn't there.'

He looked at her with irritation. 'So why have I been sitting here every day this week listening to the story of your life?'

'Because I can guess.'

'You can guess what?'

'I can guess what happened.'

'That's not good enough, Miss Holmes.'

'It's the only explanation that makes sense.'

He held on tightly to the edge of the table, his knuckles white. 'I don't believe this.'

'You're angry.'

He shook his head.

'I can see you're angry. Your mouth has gone all thin.'

'So this whole week has been a waste of time.'

'That's quite rude, Constable.'

William shut his notebook. 'I was right all along. This is your idea of entertainment. Coming along to the police station and making up stories.'

'It's quite hard to keep up with your moods. One minute you're all smiles. The next, you've got a face like thunder.'

'You could have told me right at the beginning that you had no definite information.'

'I don't think it's wise to sound so irritable. Because I don't think you have much choice. I can tell you what I think happened, and why I believe I'm right. Or you can get someone to drive you all round Dorset until you find another eighty-six-year-old who might be able to shed some light on the whole thing.' She shrugged. 'I know what I'd do with an important case like this. All that money involved. A bird in the hand, as they say. But it's completely up to you. I could save it up for the senior officer on Monday if you like. I could explain that you didn't really have the time to listen. And in fact that you don't listen at all half the time. Even when you're sitting there, your mind's elsewhere. They'd be understanding, I think. A young policeman horribly wounded in action. Slightly deaf. Done his bit for his country. In the service of his King. Now a little confused about his priorities. Not quite sure what's going on. Ignoring a first-hand account because he doesn't really understand what's important.'

The room was white with silence.

She stood up. 'On reflection, I think that may be the best option. Talking to someone who can concentrate on what I've got to say.'

'Please sit down.'

'I'll come back on Monday. Talk to your senior officer.'

'Miss Holmes—'

'Sad for you. I understand that. You would have liked to get the credit. Especially in your position. Holding on to the job by your fingernails.' She picked up her brown leather handbag and looked past him, through the open door, to the main office. 'Ah, I can see Constable Keyes coming back. That's good, isn't it? He can man the desk while you tackle that all-important paperwork. Farm inspections. Missing bicycle lights. I expect you'd like to count all the tins in the basement again, wouldn't you? Check all the emergency stocks of food. You know, I had a lovely chat with Constable Keyes this morning when I was waiting for you. Brought me up to date with all his news. Did you know that he sings light opera? Very keen on Gilbert and Sullivan. And he was telling me all about the Wareham pig club. Even his six-year-old helps with collecting the vegetable peelings. All the neighbours are part of it. A real community enterprise.'

William pushed himself upright. Wincing, he limped to the door and leaned on it heavily so that it slammed shut. He switched on the light. When he turned round, his face was pinched and pale.

'Please don't stand in my way, Constable. I want to leave.'

'We haven't finished.'

'I told you, I'm going to talk to a senior officer on Monday.'

'Please continue. I want you to tell me what happened.'

'Why should I?'

'My brother was killed.'

They stood there, looking at each other.

'Six weeks ago. In Italy. Monte Cassino. Is that enough?'

'I don't quite understand.'

He made his way back to the table, dragging his stiff leg with each step. He was trembling. He lowered himself to the bench. 'Consider it a down payment. A deposit.'

Mary put her handbag on the table. She sat down. 'Constable, I'm very sorry to hear about your brother. But I don't know what you're talking about.'

'It's what you want, isn't it? You want to know all about me. So I'll make you a deal. Tell me how John Ball died. And then I'll answer any question you like.'

She looked at him for a long time.

Outside in the passageway, someone was whistling.

She said, 'All right.'

'On one condition.'

'Which is?'

'Now. Straightaway. I don't want to hear any more about vicars and bills in Parliament. I want you to tell me how John Ball died.'

They sat listening to the clock ticking. Then Mary said, 'The snow was beginning to melt. But it was still cold. Everyone was shivering, stamping their feet, pulling their coats and shawls tightly around them. Daylight was fading.

'We were all in a state of shock. The day had been full of police and coroners and what the law would and wouldn't allow. Mrs Selby in tears. Villagers searching their consciences, angry at themselves, horrified by the violence of John's death.

'And then Arthur picked up the handles of the cart. Suddenly everyone was still. All eyes were on the coffin, so hastily made. Mrs Selby came to stand by my side. We watched as Arthur began the long walk out of the village. No one moved, not a muscle, even though our fingers were turning to ice. We waited until Arthur was nothing but a speck on the brow of the hill, far away on the road towards the sea. And then we turned and shuffled indoors, sad and ashamed, heavy with guilt.'

Mary looked up.

'I wasn't there. But this is how John Ball died.'

Arthur needed all his strength. The cart was heavy. Before long, the last houses had been left behind. By now it was pitch black, but Arthur's feet knew the journey. They took him up the hill to where the road began to level off, and then left, on to the track to Acton. Either side of him, the fields spread out. The grinding of the cart wheels settled into a rhythm. His mind began to drift. It had been a long day. It was hard to believe the plan had worked. He was triumphant but tired. He wanted to finish the job and get back home. To sleep.

He heard knocking from inside the coffin. A signal that John wanted to know what was happening. So Arthur bent forward and whispered, 'Be patient. Still a long way to go.' The knocking stopped.

Eventually the track turned past a string of stone cottages. There was a faint glow from some of the windows, but most of them were blank, like blind eyes. Arthur heard a dog barking. He tensed, waiting to be challenged. But before long, those houses were behind them too, and Arthur was facing thick black darkness. There was no moon. It was lucky he knew his way. Here, in the fields, were the open-cast quarries. You could stumble on a stone buttress, fall over a capstan, and no one would know. You could roll down a mineshaft, break your neck, and not be discovered till morning. But Arthur wasn't afraid. He knew these mines. He had worked here all his life. So he kept moving, pushing the heavy cart. All around him, the air was ruffled. The bats were out hunting.

Once or twice, he stopped the cart and listened, his ears straining to pick up every sound. He felt eyes on his back, watching his every move. After another fifteen minutes, he stopped again, this time setting down the handles so that the bed of the cart slanted towards him. He put his mouth close to the holes he'd chiselled in the lid. 'I think someone's following us. Don't make a sound. This is a good place. I'm going to stop here and start digging. But don't move. Not until I tell you it's safe.' He lit a candle and set it on the ground. He untied the shovel from the cart. Using loose stones, he marked out a large rectangle behind it, slightly longer and wider than the coffin itself. Then he began to dig. The earth was like iron. A man less strong – less determined – would have found the job impossible. But Arthur was used to striking out hard clay compressed between layers of stone. He'd spent years as a child working in the dark with only a candle to help him. His body picked up the rhythm. He kept looking around him, constantly vigilant. He was covered in sweat. But he didn't stop. It had to be done.

Now he was a few feet down, digging from the inside. He smelled the clay. Sweat ran into his mouth. He worked for twenty minutes, thirty minutes, perhaps an hour, before he laid down the shovel. He climbed out of the hole. 'John,' he whispered, 'are you all right?'

There was a rap of assent.

'I think they've gone. But I want to be certain. I'm still digging.'

Back down inside the hole, Arthur set to once again. Now it was like being underground in the quarry shaft. His clothes and boots were covered in thick clay. When he tried to lift his feet, it felt as if strong hands were pulling at his ankles.

At long last it was done. Arthur climbed out of the hole. Now to one side was a mountain of wet earth, clay and stones. Arthur listened again, peering into the darkness, breathing hard. The sweat was cooling on his skin. He stamped his feet and clapped his hands to get the blood warm again. Then he went back to the cart and lifted the handles so that the coffin was once more level, jamming the shovel under one of the wheels to keep the cart steady. He untied all the ropes.

Then, with all his strength, he pushed both the handles upwards, lifting them high into the air. The coffin shot down, like a cart of stone sliding backwards into a quarry. There was a thud as the coffin hit the bottom of the hole.

John was shouting from inside. Arthur jumped into the grave, into the extra space he had dug, and manhandled the coffin until it lay flat. A thunder of noise accompanied his work – yelling and knocking and punching against wood. Then he climbed out once more. He leaned bodily on the pile of loose earth at the side of the grave so that an avalanche of clay thudded on to the lid of the coffin. He pushed again and again. Then he picked up the shovel and, working furiously, shifted the rest of the clay back into the pit he had dug.

After just a few minutes, the grave was so full of earth that Arthur could no longer hear John screaming.

Much later, when the earth was once more flat, and the turf had been bedded down so that not even the most inquisitive of eyes could have guessed that the field had ever been dug, Arthur retied the shovel to the cart and blew out the candle.

He lifted the handles of the cart. He felt quite calm. He began the long walk back to the village.

In the dark, musty room with the central electric light, there was silence. Mary had long ago stopped talking to William. All through her account, she had stared straight ahead, telling the story to some mid-point in the air.

William said, 'Miss Holmes, did anyone see this happen?'

She turned and looked somewhere in his general direction. 'What?'

William got up and limped across the room. He filled the kettle and set it on the stove. He opened the cupboard above the sink where the sergeant sometimes kept a packet of ginger nuts. But there was nothing there but the end of a stale loaf, half a pot of apricot jam and a packet of Oxo cubes.

When the teapot, cups, milk and sugar were on the table, William lowered himself down on to the bench. Mary hadn't moved.

'Miss Holmes, you've just told me that Arthur Corben buried John Ball alive.'

She looked up. For the first time in four days, he realised how old she was. She looked very tired. 'Yes.'

'But you didn't see it happen.'

'No.'

'You've just imagined it.'

'You're saying,' said Mary, 'that it sounded like a piece of fiction.'

'It was very polished.'

'It should be after sixty-two years.'

William considered this. 'The first day we met, you said the bodies belonged to John Ball and Arthur Corben and that you had killed them both. Now it appears that Arthur killed John. You weren't even there.'

'I was responsible.'

'In what way?'

'I allowed it to happen.'

William's hands began to tremble. 'What do you mean?'

'I wouldn't hang for it, Constable. But I'm still guilty. I could have stopped it, but I didn't.'

William clenched his fists to make the shaking stop.

She said, 'You can always make excuses afterwards. Try to convince yourself that you had no choice. But you know the truth. You know what you did was cowardly and wrong. And you can't forgive yourself.' She paused, looking at William's face. 'That's what doesn't go away. It grows stronger as the years pass. It becomes impossible to bear.'

William wouldn't meet her eyes.

Mary said, 'Shall we have our tea?'

He didn't move.

'Constable?'

The cups clattered on the saucers as William arranged the crockery. When he picked up the teapot, the lid rattled, china clinking against china. Tea splashed on to the table as he poured.

Mary, watching him, said, 'It takes it out of you. Coming to terms with things you don't want to remember.'

William lifted up a spoonful of sugar, but the shaking was now so violent it sprinkled itself across the table, a powder of sparkling snow.

They both sat there, looking at it.

In a quiet voice, Mary said, 'I've been watching you for weeks, you know. From the moment you arrived. People said, poor young man. Can you imagine what he's been through with injuries like that? His nerves must be shot to pieces. He needs rest, they said. Peace and quiet. Give him time. That's the best healer.' She leaned forward, dropping her voice still further as if telling him a very important secret. 'But they're wrong. All of them. Because time is your enemy. Time allows you to build a wall. And when you next look, you'll find you've built yourself a prison.'

William stared down at the table.

'Constable? Are you listening?'

The silence stretched out around them.

After a while, Mary said, 'You know, I'm almost too tired to drink my tea. It's been a long morning. '

William said nothing.

'I think I'll go home now. But I could come back later, if you like.'

The shrill ring of the telephone in the booth cut across the silence.

'Three o'clock?'

William pushed himself to his feet.

The main office was deserted. The door to the charge room was shut. Wareham seemed quiet and sleepy, enjoying an afternoon nap. Through the windows overlooking the street, Mary could see the last stragglers coming back from the market. Mrs Walbridge was heavily laden, evenly balanced by wicker baskets filled with spinach, cauliflower and asparagus. Mrs Legg was carrying rhubarb wrapped up in newspaper, with a bundle of spring cabbage under one arm. There was Miss Bussell from the sweet shop and Mr Beck from Worlds Stores. From time to time came the sound of a bicycle bell, or the rattle of a horse and cart. Once, a huge army lorry shook the building, oblite-rating the view entirely.

The clock above the high Victorian counter showed ten to three.

Then, from the distance, came the steady, rhythmic beat of boots. The sound grew louder and louder, building to a pounding roar, until a great wall of khaki blocked the light. It seemed huge, never-ending, a cacophonous apocalypse. Mary stood transfixed, her heart beating as the wave passed.

The front door of the police station opened.

'Ah, Miss Holmes,' said Sergeant Mills, coming in at great speed. 'Back again?'

'That felt like a whole army going by just then.'

'On their way to Bovington.'

'There seem to be so many soldiers in Wareham now.'

'With tanks, trucks and ammunition. So much weight on the island, it's surprising it doesn't sink.'

Mary looked up at him. 'Is this it, then? The second front?'

'Miss Holmes, I'm as much in the dark as you are. All I know is that everything's top secret. And that we'll be the last to know.'

The door of the charge room opened. William appeared, looking distracted.

'Everything all right, Constable?'

'Gentleman from Hethfelton House would like to speak to you, Sergeant.'

'On the telephone?'

'Yes. I asked him to wait.'

'If you'll excuse me, Miss Holmes.' The sergeant strode towards the charge room and shut the door.

'How are you?' said Mary.

William looked confused.

She said, 'I'm sorry I had to leave rather abruptly this morning. But you have to know your limitations at my age. You suddenly run out of energy. Like a car running out of petrol.' She frowned. 'Although of course there aren't many cars with petrol at all these days. Unless they're army jeeps.'

William said, 'I don't think Sergeant Mills will be very long. And then we can carry on where we left off.'

Mary went to sit by the far wall. William lowered himself into the chair by his usual desk and pulled the typewriter towards him. For a while there was no sound in the room but the shuffling of cardboard files, the hesitant tapping of keys and the ring of the carriage return.

Then Mary said, 'Of course, we could just carry on anyway. Given there's no one here. We can always stop if anyone comes in.'

William, who had been about to pull paper and carbon copies from the black rollers, looked up. A shaft of afternoon sunlight fell through the window, putting Mary in a bright spotlight.

'Unless your paperwork is very urgent.'

'It can wait.'

Mary stood up and came to sit by William's desk, holding her brown leather bag on her lap. 'You know, there's a dance tomorrow night. At the Corn Exchange. You should go.'

William shrugged.

'Dances aren't just for dancing, Constable. It's where you meet people. A nice young lady, for example.'

'Can you remind me where we got to this morning?'

'I was only thinking of you. They've been talking about it all

179

week, you know. All the girls in Wareham. What they're going to wear. How they're going to do their hair. I know the sergeant's daughter was nearly in tears when she thought she'd have to do the evening shift at the factory. But her friend's mum swapped with her.'

'Miss Holmes—'

'Between you and me, I think the sergeant's only just worked out what's going on. So hard for him bringing up a young girl on his own. Mrs Bascombe tried to warn him, of course. And she's been thinking up all these ways of keeping Annie busy. But she hasn't quite managed to distract her. You see, Annie's quite keen on that young American in the cookhouse. Lyle Brooks, he's called. From St Louis in Missouri. Not that there's anything going on, of course. He's engaged to a girl back home. But he's always so kind to her. Makes her feel special. She doesn't realise he's like that with everyone. Just being friendly, as most Americans are. But she hasn't understood that. So she's lost her heart to him. Mopes about at home. Then finds out where he's going and rushes off after him. I think that's why Constable Meech's bicycle keeps going missing. She's only borrowing it, of course. But it's a nuisance when he needs it the next morning and it's got a flat tyre. I think Sergeant Mills would like to take the young man to one side and tell him off for bothering his daughter. But that wouldn't really make sense, because it's more the other way round. And I think the sergeant might be worried about the dance tomorrow. Annie might make a fool of herself. Or realise once and for all that Lyle's not interested. Either way, it will all end in tears. It might be a kindness to the sergeant, Constable, to go along tomorrow and keep an eye on her. Just in a friendly way. In case there's any trouble.'

William opened his mouth to speak.

'And then there's the Congregational Chapel on Sunday. They're showing *Higher and Higher*. With Michèle Morgan. Poor

Annie won't see any of the film. She'll just be staring at the back of Lyle's head.'

William took a deep breath. 'Miss Holmes, I don't think any of this is relevant.'

'It's always the way, isn't it? There's one who loves, and the one who's loved. Romeo and Juliet. Lancelot and Guinevere. I'm not sure about Scarlett O'Hara and Rhett Butler. They seemed to take it in turns. Oh, that last line of his. Frankly, my dear. You want to cheer and weep at the same time.'

'Can we get back to—'

'Of course. And there's no reason at all why you should take an interest in the welfare of Sergeant Mills's daughter just because he's always looking out for you.' Mary paused. 'Although I have to say, the older I get, the more I believe that the only way to be truly happy is to put yourself last. Which goes against all natural instincts, of course. Not so much love thy neighbour as thyself as love thy neighbour much more than thyself. It's a daily struggle, I find. The drive to be selfish is so strong. You know where you are when you're fighting to be first.'

'Miss Holmes—'

'And with Arthur, it consumed him completely. I don't think he ever thought about it. He had to win. But you would never have known. That was what was so clever. He'd look at you with those clear blue eyes and you wouldn't think he had a selfish bone in his body. I trusted him. So did everyone else – Mr Lester, Mrs Selby, Mr Hobbs, Mrs Serrell at Durnford House. He did terrible things, but he was never punished. No one ever suspected him. No one ever found out. So he got away with it.' Mary paused. 'Are you cold, Constable? You're shivering.'

William shook his head.

'The guilty should be punished, don't you think? Whoever they are. Colossians three, verse twenty-five: *But he that doeth wrong shall receive for the wrong which he hath done: and there is no respect of persons.* There have to be some rules we live by. Otherwise we might as well give up.'

The door to the charge office opened. Sergeant Mills appeared, looking perplexed. 'Thank you, Constable. Do please use the room now if you need to.'

Mary said, 'Is everything all right?'

The sergeant stopped and turned round. 'What?'

'Is everything all right? With your phone call from Hethfelton House?'

'Fine, thank you, Miss Holmes.' He glanced at William. 'Constable, we'll have a chat when you're free.'

William hauled himself up, holding on to the desk for support.

'Shall we say in an hour's time?' The sergeant gave Mary a warning look. 'Miss Holmes? Do please remember that the constable is busy. As concise as you can. Let's get this finished.'

Mary lowered her eyes.

It was airless in the dark and gloomy charge office. The walls, normally a nondescript beige in daylight, had turned the colour of old mushrooms. Once the door was shut, it seemed like an underground bunker, an air-raid shelter dug into damp earth.

Mary said, 'Do we really have to have the window boarded up, Constable? It's hard to breathe.'

William let himself down on to the bench.

Mary sat down opposite him, but with evident reluctance. 'It wouldn't really matter if there was no glass. Not in May. It might be quite pleasant. The odd spring breeze.'

Once again they were facing each other across the table.

'You see,' said Mary, as if there had been no interruption at all, 'no one ever thought he could kill anyone. And afterwards everyone kept saying, poor Arthur, he's been through so much. I remember old Samuel Hobbs sat me down with tears in his eyes. He said, It was only meant to be the old teasing the young. There he was, the landlord, built like a bull, ready to charge at anyone who crossed him. Who'd have thought he would take a gun and blow his brains out? And then the next morning, the curtains of the Ship shut. And you inside, Mary Holmes, crying your eyes out, and young Mr Corben rushing here, there and everywhere, talking to the coroner, calming Mrs Selby, pleading with the rector to bury John Ball in the old way. And in the end Mr Lester agreed. But I will never forget, said Samuel Hobbs, the sight of Arthur Corben pushing the coffin out of the village, bent over, like a man with the weight of the world on his shoulders.

'And that's what they all thought. Arthur Corben had lost his best friend. And of course they knew he'd played his part that night. He'd let me flirt with him. He'd kissed me on the lips. But none of them thought he was guilty. Because they liked him. It was John Ball who took the blame, because he was stupid and rash and hot-headed. They'd never trusted him. And that's always the way, isn't it, Constable? If you like someone, you think well of them. You let them get away with murder.'

William's hands shook. 'Miss Holmes, I need you to tell me how Arthur Corben died.'

'I think you've forgotten our bargain.'

William tensed.

Mary said, 'You said if I told you how John died, you would answer any question I liked.'

He said nothing.

'You're not going to go back on your word, are you?'

William raised his eyes.

'Tell me about your brother.'

There was a long silence.

'If it helps,' said Mary, 'I can ask you questions. Although I don't think I'm very good at it. Not like you. I expect you've had a lot of experience of getting people to talk. Coaxing the information out of them. I imagine you have to step right inside their minds sometimes. Be one step ahead. So you ask them questions before they've worked out how to avoid the answers.

But you have to be careful, don't you? You can't bully someone. If you do, they'll just stay silent. Or they'll talk, but they won't tell the whole truth. They'll just give you enough so that you go away and stop bothering them. And then you don't know where you are, do you?'

'He didn't want to tell me.'

Mary put her head on one side. 'I don't quite follow, Constable.'

'Kept going on about holding the position.'

'Who was this?'

'The officer who came to see me. Someone from the regiment. He'd had his foot blown off, so he couldn't fight any more. He brought me a photograph. The two of us on the farm. My aunt's farm. Aunty Ellen.'

It's not much. But I thought you'd like to have it.

'It was just a brown wallet. Could have belonged to anyone.'

They would have sent it to you. But I wanted to hand it over myself.

'They used to go to Naples on leave. I think he would have picked it up there.'

Talked about you all the time.

'Is this your brother, Constable?' Mary moved closer. 'Are you talking about your brother?'

———

'It's not much. But I thought you'd like to have it.'

On the table was a brown leather wallet. William picked it up. There was very little inside – a twenty-lira note, a sprig of grey-green leaves, and a black-and-white photograph of two boys on a five-bar gate, smiling for the camera. William was in school uniform. His brother – taller, broader, hair combed back from his face – was wearing an open-necked shirt and a jacket. On the back was written *Abbotsbury, 1934*.

William swallowed. 'My aunt's farm. Just before he joined up.'

'They would have sent it to you. But I wanted to hand it over myself.'

They had a table in the corner at the Black Bear Inn, out of sight of prying eyes. Neither of them had drunk their tea. The grey-looking sandwiches, bread curling at the edges, were untouched.

William cleared his throat. 'How did you find me?'

'With difficulty. But I knew you'd had words, so it seemed important to come and tell you. He was very proud of you. Talked about you all the time. He was going to come and find you when he got home. When it was all over.'

William waited until he could speak. 'I want to know what happened.'

'I was proud to serve with your brother. He was a good officer. You should know that. Well liked. Always put his men first. They owed their lives to him, many of them.'

A waitress, passing, picked up William's napkin from the floor and handed it to him. William took it without looking and put it on top of his cup.

'We had to hold the position. Push through if we could. But conditions were bad. By the time we got there, they'd all had a go. Canadians. Indians. North Africans. We came after the Maoris. Before the Poles. It's a bloody great mountain. Bloody great rock, with a monastery right at the top. We all bombed it. Bombed the hell out of it. But the Germans are still there, hiding in the ruins. You can hear them sometimes. Singing "Lili Marlene".'

William was tense, listening.

'Your brother kept the whole thing going, kept morale high. They're only a hundred yards away, you see, and they have their guns trained on you the whole time. We're camped in a sort of crater right at the top. Down in the valley, there's white smoke from the shells. You have to keep shelling to hide what you're doing. Especially bringing up supplies. Because they can see everything from the monastery, looking down on you the whole time. During the day, you have to keep low. Can't stick your head up or they'll blow it off. So you move on your stomach. Or don't move at all. Try to sleep. Play cards. Write letters home. No tea, because there's no water. But your brother kept our spirits up. Kept thinking of ways to harass the enemy. Always trying to surprise them. Nothing happens until night. As soon as it's dark, you move. And that's when you bomb the hell out of each other. The shells are screaming all the time. Constant artillery. Everything under fire. The mules bring up supplies, three hours up the mountain tracks. But the Germans try to shell them before they reach us. Blow up the food. Blow up the water. Blow up the ammunition. And we do the same back to them. Blow it all up. It's still going on, of course. They'll carry on until they break through.'

Around them was the sound of silver spoons on saucers, tongs on sugar bowls, the gentle percussion of afternoon tea.

William said, 'How did he die?'

'Mortar bomb. No warning. Three of them, one after the other, out of nowhere. Five in the afternoon. Wrong time of day.'

William couldn't speak for a long time. Eventually he said, 'Where is he buried?'

'On the mountain. They worked hard on the grave. A wooden cross. A rectangle of stones. White stones.'

———

'Constable? Are you all right?'

'I'll go and find the grave one day. When the war's over. Get up the mountain somehow. He drew me a map. They're all buried up there. A whole cemetery. Gurkhas, Maoris, Moroccans.'

'I've got a handkerchief somewhere.' Mary opened her bag and rummaged inside.

William used his hands to wipe his face. 'He was blown up by a bomb. Just a random mortar attack. One afternoon, in broad daylight.'

'How old was he?'

'Twenty-eight.'

'Older than you.'

The muscles around William's mouth kept tightening, seemingly at random. 'The seventy-eighth Infantry. Battleaxe Division. Fought at Dunkirk. Then Tunisia and Sicily. Then Italy.'

'You were very proud of him.'

William looked up. His face shone with tears. 'He always wanted to be in the army. Joined up five years before the war started.'

'You should have taken time off, Constable.'

'They're still fighting on the mountain. They don't have a choice. They have to break through the Gustav Line, get to Rome.'

'You haven't told anyone.'

William shook his head.

'What about your parents?'

'They're both dead. I lived with my aunt for a while when my mother died. On a farm. But she lives in Wales now. Haven't seen her for years.'

'So it was just you and him.'

'Always.'

Mary's eyes were very sad. 'This is what you keep imagining, isn't it? You keep picturing it. The explosion that killed him.'

———

Behind the desk, through the bow window, William could see a crush of late-flowering roses in bloom – coral, mauve, cream and pink. The colours of Italian ice cream before the war, Rossi's on the esplanade in Weymouth. He felt behind him for the arms of the chair and sat down, smothering his small intake of breath by clearing his throat.

His leg stuck out in front of him, stiff and unyielding, like a thick-barrelled gun balanced against his groin.

'Still causing you difficulty?'

'Yes, sir.' He felt a trickle of sweat run down between his shoulder blades.

'Have they said any more?'

'They don't recommend surgery. They think it would do more harm than good.'

The major laced his fingers together and put his joined hands on the desk in front of him. It was a fine desk – polished mahogany with an inlaid leather top. Battalion headquarters was temporarily in a Georgian manor house in the lush green loveliness of southern England. 'Well, I'll come straight to the point. Was it your original intention to return to the police once you were released from the army?'

'Yes, sir.'

'I thought so. Well, our battalion commander has had a word with the Chief Constable of Dorset. This was his regiment, as you know. When he heard what had happened – a young and promising officer badly injured – he was most anxious to help. The chief constable believes he will be able to find you a suitable role in the force. Once you're fully fit, of course.'

William was finding it hard to breathe. Great waves of heat kept passing through him, interspersed by icy grips of pain. His collar was too tight. Every pore of his skin was prickling with sweat.

The major said, 'You look concerned.'

There was pressure in his ears as if someone had pushed his head underwater. 'It's just that I'm not sure how useful I'd be to the police now, sir.'

'He's thinking of an administrative role. Headquarters in Dorchester to start with. Then one of the smaller stations. Typing up crime reports, that sort of thing. They'd be very keen to have someone with practical experience of police work. And you're a grammar school boy, aren't you? You'd find the work very straightforward.' He paused. 'You may be lucky. Your mobility may improve. And indeed more of your hearing may return. So there's every chance that you could look forward to a more active role in time. The kind of policing you're used to.' He nodded, as if agreeing with something William had said. 'I've seen some remarkable recoveries in recent years. Always best to be optimistic, I feel, in these circumstances.' Frowning, he leaned forward. 'It was a terrible accident. We particularly regret the loss of life. But you were in no way to blame. Indeed, if you hadn't acted so swiftly, the outcome could have been far worse.'

The familiar trembling began.

'One more thing I should mention. The details of what happened must remain confidential. Your records will simply state wounded in action. And that should be your reply if anyone asks.'

William tried to speak, but his jaw locked as his whole body tensed to control the shaking.

'We do understand each other? Perfectly clear?'

With panic in his eyes in case the words never came, William said, 'Yes, sir.'

'Good man.' The major sat back, satisfied. 'I believe you're off to convalesce in Hastings. The country air should do you good. When you're given the all clear, we'll let you know about the new job.' He paused. 'I'm sure you'll do very well.'

———

The police station was quiet.

After a while, Mary said, 'I think the sun is shining outside. Shall we go for a walk?'

William cleared his throat. 'Are you doing this on purpose?'

'What?'

'Talking about things I can't do just to make me feel worse? I can't dance. I can't walk.'

'You can get as far as the Quay. We can sit on a bench and

watch the river. The swans have had cygnets. Five of them in a little line.'

William took a deep breath. 'We haven't finished your statement.'

'I think you ought to have a break. I don't think you're well enough to continue.'

'It's what we agreed, Miss Holmes. Your story in exchange for mine.'

'But you left something out, didn't you? When you were talking about your brother's death?'

He looked at her, his eyes dull.

'That's the problem, you see. Once you start, you can't stop. You have to keep digging. Do the job properly. Not bide and spuddle about, as Mr Hobbs used to say.'

I'm sure you'll do very well.

'Constable? You've disappeared again. Are you listening?'

William squeezed his eyes shut and opened them wide, focusing on the dingy beige walls of the charge room.

'Are you all right? Shall I get you a glass of water?'

He said, in a sudden rush, his voice unusually loud, 'Why are you asking me all these questions?'

'I just told you. Do the job properly. It's the only way.'

He wasn't listening. 'You didn't have to start all this. You could have stayed at home. You didn't have to come here and confess to murder. You hadn't talked about it for years. You could have kept quiet.'

'Not once they found the bodies.'

'That's not true. No one would have known you had anything to do with it.'

Mary smiled. 'I told you. I'm tired of it. Secrecy eats away at you.'

They stared at each other.

He said, 'I don't have a choice.'

'What do you mean?'

'I have to keep it secret.'

She looked surprised. 'I didn't know you were involved in that kind of war work.'

'I wasn't. I'm not.'

Mary lifted up her hands and took off her black hat. She put it on the table in front of her. Her hair was a rather beautiful soft grey, almost silver under the single electric light. It was the first time he'd seen her without a hat. She looked less formal, more approachable. 'I think it's time you told me what happened to you, Constable.'

'I can't.'

'Why?'

'I told you. I'm not allowed to talk about it.'

'Who am I going to tell?'

He shook his head. 'I can't.'

Mary said, 'I think you must. If you carry on like this, you won't survive the war. Even when the fighting's all over.'

He raised his eyes to her face.

'William,' she said, 'please. Tell me what happened.'

Time passed. There was no sound. They sat silently in the twilight of the charge room, far removed from the bright May afternoon outside. Then William said, 'The firing was continuous. Explosions all around us. Most of the houses were occupied. There were snipers on the roofs and in the bell tower of the church. Each time you raised your head above the stone wall, there was a burst of machine-gun fire. We'd been told the others were still in the woods to the south, unable to advance. But then wireless communication stopped. So our orders were the same. Take the village, secure it, and wait for reinforcements.'

'Where was this?' said Mary. 'France? Italy?'

'We were exhausted. The day before had been one long assault course – out of the boats, wading through water up to our waists, running up the beach, all the while under heavy bombardment. We'd had to negotiate minefields, barbed wire, thick undergrowth.

Men were falling all the time. Sometimes it felt like a bad dream, some kind of nightmare. And then the sound of shellfire would shock us awake.

'The village was right in front of us. It must have been pretty once. One of those ancient hamlets dating back to the Middle Ages. Now it was half in ruins, with pockmarked stone and burned-out buildings. I remember there was a tree by the stone well. It been blown up from the inside, split into stalks like a head of celery.

'Jack decided our first priority was the white farmhouse on the outskirts. It would give us a better view of the church, which seemed to be the enemy's HQ. As he outlined the attack, it started to rain. A heavy shower that pummelled the earth, splattering mud in all directions. We could hardly see the village any more.

'As soon as we began to move forward, the skies went black. Machine-gun fire intensified. Jack was out in front, with Abbott and the Prof on either side. Jack threw a grenade. It exploded a few feet from the front of the house. The blast took out the main door. But the firing continued. Jack was lying on his stomach, almost flat in the mud. He looked back over his shoulder and nodded towards the open door of the house. A bomb exploded to my left. I took out a grenade, twisted and pulled the pin, drew back my arm, and threw.

'It landed by Jack's head.

'I had almost reached him when it exploded.'

For a moment, William sat there, trembling, staring into the middle distance. Then he said, 'I woke up in hospital. They were very nice to me. A lot of my hearing had gone. But they were more bothered about the rest. They kept me doped up for weeks. It was touch and go with my leg. But they saved it in the end. Then I had to learn to walk again. They said I was doing very well. My CO visited once. He was very nice to me, too. And you know why?' William looked up. His eyes were dark and furious. 'Because none of them knew what happened. I threw the grenade. But they all thought it was Jack. That's what the others said. Abbott and the Prof. At the formal investigation. They thought Jack had pulled out the pin and dropped it. So when I came to, in hospital, I was a hero. They said I'd tried to run forward and pick it up. I ended up deaf, with a shattered leg, because I tried to save the life of a fellow officer, and shield the others from the blast.'

'Jack died?'

'Of course he died,' said William, his voice angry. 'And they thought he'd blown himself up because he'd been rash and stupid. Hadn't followed the rules. But it was me. My stupidity.'

Mary said, 'It was an accident.'

'I should have told the truth.'

'Why? What good would it have done?'

'It would have stopped me hating myself.'

Mary shook her head. 'It's war. It's terrible. It takes lives. It maims and kills. I should know. I remember all the young men killed the first time round. A whole generation slaughtered. And now I'm living through it again.'

William laughed.

Mary looked at him, astonished.

'It wasn't war,' said William. 'I never left Britain. It was a training exercise in north Wales.'

Mary put her hand to her mouth.

William seemed to collapse forward, as if he no longer had the strength to stay upright.

The room was silent.

After a while, Mary stood up. She went over to the sink and filled the kettle. She lit the gas. Then she turned round. 'You'd better start at the beginning.'

Something in her voice made him look up.

'I need to know,' said Mary, 'how something so terrible could have happened.'

He watched as she gathered up the teacups and saucers, found the milk jug and the sugar bowl, and put them all on the table. When the whistle on the kettle blew, she turned off the gas, warmed the pot, spooned in the black tea leaves, and poured in the boiling water so that the steam billowed in a great cloud. Her movements were brisk and purposeful.

He waited until she sat down. Then he said, 'The lesser of two evils.'

'You have to explain.'

He stared down at his thin white hands on the table. 'There's no point. What's done is done.'

'But it isn't, is it? For you, the past is alive. It's more real to you than the present.'

William carried on staring at the table, saying nothing. Then he looked up. 'How much do you know about army training?'

Mary shook her head. 'Nothing. Except watching them march up and down North Street. And hearing the guns at Lulworth.'

'When you join up, you start with the basics. How to clean your gun, how to polish your boots. Routine tasks, a lot of repetition. But what they're really doing is teaching you how to obey orders. You come in as a private citizen with a mind of your own – a teacher, an accountant, a policeman. You end up as part of the army. A cog in the machine. I found it hard. I was used to being in charge. I'd spent two years running a village police station before I joined up. My brother said, Why don't you apply for officer training? I said, I don't think they'd want me. But they did. First it was pre-OCTU. Bad accommodation, overflowing latrines, running up and down hills for eight weeks. A lot of soldiers returned to the ranks. Then it was OCTU itself. Officer Cadet Training Unit. I was there for four months. Came out in August 1941, just before my twenty-first birthday, a second lieutenant.'

Mary said, 'You must have been very proud.'

His face had a kind of feverish intensity. 'We were physically very fit. Fourteen-mile runs carrying rifle and full equipment, assault courses, route marches. We did map reading, basic signalling, learned how to drive lorries and tanks and carriers. I enjoyed it. I was good at it. But the training didn't go far enough. This was two years ago. Do you remember?' His eyes were fixed on hers. 'The Germans had taken the whole of western Europe. Greece. North Africa. Millions in the Red Army killed. A war machine more powerful than anything the world had ever known. It traded on fear. It understood psychological attack. And how were we preparing our troops?' His voice was bitter. 'Cross-country runs.'

Mary was very still, watching him.

William leaned forward. 'I wasn't the only one. There were a lot of young officers who felt the same. The worse the news across the world, the more anxious we became. Back then, no one understood the importance of the infantry. We were either polishing our buttons or planting potatoes. We were like some kind of national labour exchange. Anyone who needed manpower borrowed from the infantry – farmers, the RAF, even the NAAFI. It's true. Manning mobile canteens. Helping to set up concerts and picking up singers from the station. Or you might find your NCO was suddenly posted elsewhere. Personnel changed all the time. The minute you felt your battalion was some kind of fighting unit, it all fell apart, and you were back to square one.' William's whole face was set and tense, desperate for her to understand. 'We knew how to use weapons. Bren guns. Boys rifles. The Piat. But ammunition was rationed, carefully controlled. If they wanted to liven things up, they threw thunderflashes at you. Or smoke grenades. Or they exploded fourteen-pound cans of aminol to sound like shells. Fireworks, we called it. It was play-acting. A performance. Just something for the top brass to watch. Preparing right up to the point of battle, but not for the battle itself.'

For a while, they sat in silence. Then William took a deep

breath. 'Someone in the battalion heard about the new battle schools. They were just starting up – one for each division. The War Office still wasn't keen. They didn't like the idea of set battle drills. Said it hampered a soldier's initiative. But the more I heard, the more I wanted to go. I kept badgering my CO until he sent me. He said, You've done enough training. Any more and you'll be writing the bloody manuals. But he liked me. Said I was sound. A good man. So he gave in.'

This time the pause went on for so long that Mary said, 'So you went?'

'February 1942. To the top of a mountain in Wales. So cold your breath came out in a cloud, like smoke from a dragon.'

She waited.

'There were thirty of us altogether – all officers and NCOs. All hungry to learn. The first evening we arrived, they talked about the German army – how they operate, what tactics they prefer, how they're likely to react. We talked about the best use of weapons, battle psychology, the importance of morale. Then they filled us in on what the course was going to teach us. There were three basic principles: extreme physical fitness; battle drill; live fire. We had NCO instructors and a demonstration platoon. And it was all starting the next morning.

'They threw us in at the deep end. Shocked us to attention. A three-day exercise: two nights in the open, very little cover, hardly any food. Rough terrain over rocks, through rivers, across barbed wire, all the time carrying heavy equipment. Under fire the whole time. We'd been pretty cocky when we arrived. We all thought we were fit and able to get through anything. But this was different. There were ambulances standing by. One man got three fingers blown off on the first morning. Another had a .303 bullet through his backside. It was brutal. The reasoning was that it was better to get a few killed in training than to lose hundreds in action. Because these were the officers who would be leading their men into battle. Responsible for the safety and well-being of hundreds of others.'

Mary looked shocked. 'They were expecting people to die?'

'The school I went to didn't even have the worst record. There were rumours that some of them had a quota of deaths for every course.'

Mary stared at him.

'I told you before.' William's expression was agitated. 'The lesser of two evils.'

For a while, they sat there saying nothing. The ghosts of young soldiers marched behind them, pounding across the stone floor before passing through the walls into the spring air outside.

William said, 'It was so cold. That first night I fell asleep the minute I lay down, on a rock, fully clothed. I woke wet through. I thought it must have rained overnight. And then I moved, my jacket cracking like glass, and saw it was snow. Snowing for hours, and we hadn't even noticed.

'To begin with, we were stupid with fear. But as the week went on, it got interesting. Every day we trained with live ammunition. We knew everything there was to know about the limitations of our equipment, what to use, what to hold on to at all costs, what to dump if we were up against it. All of us could correct any fault in a Bren gun with our eyes shut. You worked out which instincts were useful, and which ones weren't. You found ways to think when your mind was frozen with panic. You got so used to being under fire that you could judge how near a bomb was going to land from the sound it made as it fell.

'We were pushed to the limit. So you got to know each other very quickly. Most of us had nicknames. I was Copper, of course. There was a Welshman called Taffy, Legs, who was six foot four, and the Prof, who was an Oxford academic. Jack was Frost, as he was always complaining about the cold.

'By the second week, the weather had got worse. We were

either in icy mists that reduced visibility to zero or in blizzards of swirling snow. We were bone tired. But we still had the final part of the course to go. This was to put into action everything we'd learned about tactics and battle drill in lectures and in the field. It was an exercise. Play-acting, still. But as real as they could make it. And we'd seen enough – the ambulances, the stretchers, the injuries – to know they meant business. We had to think fast and act decisively or we'd get our heads blown off.

'We came down the mountain to an army training area on the coast. Barbed wire everywhere to keep out civilians. You didn't want to kill a postman or blow up a school bus full of children. It was a perfect setting for invasion manoeuvres – sea, beach, cliffs, hedges, open countryside. There was a small Welsh farming village right in the middle. Evacuated some weeks before. It was an eerie sight – the church, the school, the long terrace of stone cottages where people had lived for generations. There were even curtains at some of the windows.

'The first day was hell. We fought our way in from the beach. They threw everything they had at us. Legs broke his shoulder and had to be taken out by stretcher. The Prof was in pain from a twisted ankle. Jack was in charge that day, and had a hard time keeping up morale. Just before the attack on the village, sitting with our backs against a stone wall at the edge of a field, Jack said, The only way to get through it is to think of something you really want at the end of it. He said, I'm imagining a large whisky in front of a log fire. He said he wanted it so much, he could almost feel the heat.

'Twenty minutes later, I blew him up.'

The hot, dingy charge room was silent for a long time after William had stopped speaking. You could hear nothing from outside. Wareham had disappeared.

Mary said, 'Are you all right?'

William looked up, dark eyes in a white face.

'It's a shock hearing you say so much. I've never heard you speak more than two words before. You couldn't stop, could you, once you started? Like a flood. A river bursting its banks. All pouring out in a great big torrent.'

He had been calm throughout the whole narrative. Now he began to tremble.

'And there's more, isn't there? There's more to come.'

Under the single electric bulb, a light sheen of sweat shone on his forehead.

'You might as well get it over with.'

He looked at her, his eyes desperate.

'William?'

With a sudden movement, William stood up. He said, almost shouting, 'We have to stop. I promised Sergeant Mills I'd only be an hour.'

Mary, looking up at him, said nothing.

William's whole body was shaking, as if he were standing outside in a cold wind. 'What I told you just now, about what happened two years ago – it was confidential. It mustn't go any further.'

Mary picked up her brown leather handbag.

'Miss Holmes? If army exercises fail, it remains secret. It has to. For reasons of national security. Especially now, with the second front coming. You must promise not to pass on anything I just told you. You must promise.' His voice was rising.

Mary looked at him as if he were a small child panicking about goblins. 'Constable, I am eighty-six years old. Nobody believes a word I say. Even if I said anything, they'd ignore me. You have absolutely nothing to worry about.'

'But you promise.'

'I promise.' She paused, examining his expression. 'You're sure you want to stop?'

'Yes. We have to.'

She nodded towards the door. 'After you.'

It was a relief to get out of the dark, airless room.

Outside in the main office, Sergeant Mills was leafing through a pile of War Office driving permits. On his left hand, the little finger and ring finger were nothing but stubby knuckles. He glanced up. 'Ah, Constable. All finished?'

'I felt we'd done enough for today,' said William. He was a sort of grey-white colour, like a gravestone.

Sergeant Mills nodded. 'Very wise.' He turned to Mary. 'You have been very generous with your time, Miss Holmes.'

'I'll call by tomorrow on my way to the fish shop. Just in case the constable has any final questions.'

'We'll look forward to it,' said Sergeant Mills. He came out from behind his desk and went ahead of her to the main door to the street. When he opened it, noise from outside rushed in – shouting, an army motorbike, a bicycle bell.

They both watched as Mary walked away, a small but purposeful figure moving off through the afternoon sunlight.

Sergeant Mills shut the door. 'I think you deserve a medal. I've never known anyone spend so long with Mary Holmes without requiring medical attention.'

William, swaying, held on to the edge of his desk for support. 'I need to check my notes. To make sure I've covered everything.'

'Before you do, there's something we need to discuss.' Sergeant Mills leaned forward and lowered his voice. 'While your fellow constables aren't here. I'm having a private word with each of you in turn.'

William cast about for a likely subject. 'About the bicycle that keeps going missing?'

'What?' The sergeant looked surprised. 'No, we dealt with that first thing. Young Tommy Cornick. I had my eye on him for a while. I knew he was finding it hard to get to the station in the mornings. He's not the brightest button in the jar. As I said to him, Tommy, if you're going to steal a bicycle, make sure it doesn't belong to a policeman.' Sergeant Mills rubbed his forehead. 'No, it's something quite different. A delicate matter. Do you remember some time ago, a gentleman from East Stoke dropped in to say thank you? We'd rescued his dog, a fine Irish setter. He was anxious to show his gratitude and offered me a bottle of whisky.'

William struggled to concentrate.

'Of course,' said the sergeant, 'I couldn't accept. No policeman can accept gratuities. It lays you open to accusations of bribery. Upsets the whole relationship between a police officer and the general public. So what I had to say was, It's a very kind offer, sir. I'm very grateful. But I'm afraid I must refuse. Perhaps you could consider making a donation to the Dorset Police Benevolent Fund instead.'

'I don't—'

Sergeant Mills fixed William with a pointed stare. 'Is there anything you'd like to tell me, Constable? Anything you'd like to get off your chest?'

William, stunned, stared back.

'Because I always think it's better to tell the truth. Don't you?'

The world began to slip away. Darkness shot backwards, into the distance, a long grey tunnel. William, losing his balance, felt hands on his shoulders.

'I've got you,' said Sergeant Mills in his ear. 'I've got you.'

Friday

As Mary walked into the police station, she nearly collided with a broad-shouldered, solidly built US soldier, who apologised, smiled – white teeth against black skin – and held the door for her. Once inside, she turned and watched through the window as he hoisted himself with one athletic movement into a waiting jeep.

'Always so polite,' she said to Sergeant Mills, who was standing at his desk, staring into space.

'I beg your pardon?'

'American soldiers.'

'Aren't they,' said the sergeant.

'Young Lyle Brooks, for example. You know? The cook from Missouri? I just stopped for a moment on North Street yesterday to catch my breath, and he insisted on giving me his arm. Walked me right back to my front door.'

'How kind.'

'You sound very tired this morning.'

'I've just had some rather bad news.'

'Oh dear,' said Mary, interested.

Sergeant Mills gave a loud and dramatic sigh. 'I try my best. I really do. But there are some things beyond my control.'

'What's happened?'

'A disaster, Miss Holmes. No US soldiers are allowed evening passes tonight, including those billeted in the town. Orders from Binnegar Hall.'

Mary's eyes opened wide. 'But what about the dance?'

'Exactly.'

'But that's terrible,' said Mary.

'A catastrophe,' said the sergeant. 'And it's my job to spread the news. There'll be young women weeping from here to Tolpuddle.'

'I expect Annie will be disappointed.'

'Oh, she'll be fine.' The sergeant's voice was suddenly casual. 'She's got her eye on the young man in charge of the Tetryl department at the factory. Says he looks like Trevor Howard.'

Mary frowned.

The door to the charge room opened. William limped out.

'Good morning,' said Mary. 'I was about to go and pick up my salt cod. But I thought I'd call in first to see if you had any more questions.'

'That's very kind,' said William. 'I've just been going over my notes and, yes, I do have a few more queries. Could you spare half an hour?'

Sergeant Mills looked as if he were about to object, but the main door opened and Mrs Bascombe appeared, followed shortly afterwards by the brown streak of Vic Smith's dog.

The charge room smelled of damp tea leaves, sour milk and old socks.

'Thank you,' said William.

'For what?'

'For not telling Sergeant Mills that we're nowhere near finishing the report.'

'We got a little sidetracked yesterday,' said Mary. 'And you were very tired after all that talking. But here we are, a brand-new day, ready to start all over again.'

William nodded.

'Although it's getting quite hard to breathe in here,' said Mary.

'Mr Puckett should be able to replace the glass tomorrow.'

'Well, that's a relief.' Mary sat down. 'Why was Sergeant Mills pulling faces at you?'

'I didn't notice.'

'I wondered if it was something to do with Annie. And the young man in the Tetryl department. Was that true, what he said?'

'I've got no idea.'

Mary sighed. 'I was thinking about Sergeant Mills yesterday, and how distracted he seems all the time. And I suddenly wondered if there was more to it than worrying about Annie disappearing to America. I started thinking about that phone call from Hethfelton House. The farm next door belongs to Constable Fripp's uncle, doesn't it? On his mother's side. And you know, they've had such a run of bad luck there. The fox has got into the chicken run so many times, I've lost count of the number of birds they've found mauled to death. And now, to cap it all, I hear one of the pigs has died. Fine animal, by all accounts. A Berkshire sow. From what I've heard, the death is a complete mystery – frisky and healthy one minute, keeled over the next. So worrying in wartime when slaughter is so strictly regulated. The last thing you want is a farmer accused of dealing on the black market. I expect that's why Constable Fripp is round there so often. He's probably trying to think of a way to help. Given the farm belongs to a member of his family. I expect he's working very hard to find out why they have such a problem with their livestock. That would explain why his bicycle is there so often. Mrs Bascombe said she saw it in the yard twice last week.'

William cleared his throat. 'Miss Holmes, you know I can't discuss police business.'

'Of course not. I was only thinking aloud. It's what happens, you see, when you get to my age. You have a lot of time to mull things over. Has Constable Fripp mentioned it at all?'

'Miss Holmes—'

'As your sergeant has said so many times, policing in wartime is so complicated. No end of new regulations. And there will always be someone trying to bend the rules and make money out of it.

They say you never go hungry in the countryside, as long as you're willing to turn a blind eye. A box of eggs on your doorstep. A shoulder of pork wrapped in newspaper. A parcel of bacon.'

William pushed his fingers into his forehead, massaging the skin, as if he had a headache. 'Miss Holmes, we do need to carry on.'

'He's very distinctive, Constable Fripp, isn't he? With that bright red hair. It must be quite a disadvantage for a police officer. I know he's got the helmet on most of the time. But the minute he takes it off, everyone recognises him. So he can never hide what he's doing. Not that he'd want to, of course. You're policemen. So everything you do is open and above board.' She paused. 'Are you all right, Constable? You don't look well.'

You look all in. 'Before we start, Miss Holmes, I want to be sure that you'll keep what I said yesterday confidential.'

'I don't know why you keep going on about it. I really don't. Look at my record. I've kept quiet about John Ball and Arthur Corben for sixty-two years. I think that makes me the soul of discretion.'

William fumbled in his pocket for his notebook. 'So where were we?'

'One more thing before we begin.'

William looked up.

'What was it you didn't tell me about your brother's death?'

I hope nothing bad has happened.

Mary kept her eyes fixed on his face. 'I've told you before, you can't pick and choose. Once you start, you must go on. It's like swimming out to a rock in a storm. The shore's way behind, so you can't go back. And if you don't keep going, you'll drown.'

Are you sure you're up to it?

'Constable, you've gone very white. I know you're anxious to finish this, but I don't think we should carry on if you're feeling unwell. Should I come back this afternoon? I live only a few minutes' walk away.'

They stared at each other.

William's face was expressionless.

Mary sighed. 'As you wish.' She paused. 'So you know about Arthur killing John. That was in 1878. December. And then there were all those months when Arthur was telling me to be patient. And then Mr Lester starting talking to people in high places about changing the law, and went off to London, and came back with a wife. And then in the summer of 1881, Mr Lester wouldn't stop going on and on about having a burial service where John lay, in the fields at Acton, so that I would finally be at peace. And we couldn't think what to do. Because once we'd shown them where the empty coffin was buried, we weren't safe any more. The secret would come out eventually. And so Arthur said, if they want bones in the coffin, I'll put bones in the coffin. And he said he'd dig up John's father, and take him up to Acton and put him in the empty box.'

William nodded.

'Constable, are you sure you're ready? You've got your note-book open, but you don't have anything to write with.'

———•———

William stood outside the house in Silvertown. The streets looked the same – bombed-out houses where kids scaled rafters and threw spears made from sharpened lathes. It smelled the same, too, that Silvertown stink of chemicals, rotting carcasses and sugar. His heart was beating fast.

The door opened. A woman in her forties in a pale yellow dress – tired face, hair tied up in a turban, eyes wary – stared at him.

'Is Stella in?'

'Who wants to know?'

'My name's William.'

'She doesn't live here any more.'

He hesitated. 'Do you know where's she gone?'

'Why?'

William couldn't think what to say.

Something about his expression made her kinder. 'You'd better come in.'

The front room was as cold as ever. There was no fire in the grate. The chair where Stella had sat, smoking, had disappeared, replaced by a round table covered with a white cloth. The room was crowded, full of furniture. Otherwise nothing had changed in two years.

The woman went over to the wooden sideboard and picked up a pile of letters next to the clock. 'She wrote it down for me somewhere. Just before she left.'

'When did she go?'

'Have a seat. If it's not here, it'll be in the box upstairs.'

William limped over to one of the upright chairs by the table, pulled it out further and sat down.

She glanced up, watching him. 'So what happened to you, then? Far East? Breaks your heart seeing all the boys coming home like this. If they come home at all. Alf next door just got the telegram. Son killed in Burma.' She shook her head. 'Light of his life. His whole world. I don't know how he's going to manage without him, I really don't.'

William cleared his throat. 'Where's Stella gone?'

'Kent. One of her dad's cousins lives down there now. She brought Peter back here for a while. But when all the raids started up again she thought better of it. It gets to you, doesn't it? Pall Mall, last week. Westminster. Number Ten. God knows what Mr Churchill thinks. We've only just finished clearing up after the last lot. Especially round here. The Mannings have got Stella's room now. Their house was only held up by number six, and once that went, the whole lot fell down.' She held up a small sheet of paper with a flourish of triumph. 'There, you see? I knew I had it somewhere.'

He recognised the handwriting. Stella wrote like a child – each letter a different size, all of them leaning in haphazard directions, like pins splayed out in a game of skittles. As William copied down the address, his hand shook.

'So when did you last see Stella, then?'

'It's been a while.'

'How long?' She looked puzzled. Then her face cleared. 'You're that friend of hers, aren't you? The one she met in Dorset, right at the start of it all. They said there'd be gas attacks, didn't they? So all the children left London. Stella thought Peter would be safer in the country. So she took him away, too. Well, well.' She leaned back against the sideboard, looking at him with more interest. 'She never told me a thing about you. Where you lived. What you did as a job. Your name, even. I always teased her. I said, He's not real, is he? You just made him up. She said, Oh he's real all right. So I said, Go on then, bring him round for tea. But she never did. I think she wanted you all to herself.'

William swallowed.

'I remember the day you took her to Greenwich. It was Peter's birthday, wasn't it? I was there when she made the cake. Begged sugar from all the neighbours. She couldn't get candles for love nor money, so she stuck in three little twists of paper and dyed the tips with cochineal. You had a picnic in the park, she said. Sandwiches and jam tarts. I can see Stella's face now. Coming back with her eyes all shining. Peter liked you, didn't he? Nice little boy. And I thought, It's about time she had some luck. After all she's had to put up with.' She shook her head. 'Bloody war, tearing people apart. She was getting worried, you know.'

'I was in hospital for six months.'

'Hadn't heard from you for such a long time. It must have been two years, at least. Peter's five now. Six in September.'

'And then a convalescent home in Hastings.'

'She said, I hope nothing bad has happened. It's never been

this long before. He comes to see me every time he's on leave. Every few months. Regular as clockwork.'

'And after that I was in Dorchester. I was there for a year.' He looked down at his leg, sticking out like a plank of wood.

'I knew there'd be a good reason. Stella said, He wouldn't leave me in the dark like this. I know him. He always does the right thing. He wouldn't leave me hanging on, waiting and worrying. And I said to her, No news is good news. It'll turn out all right in the end, you'll see. And I was right, wasn't I? Here you are, after all this time.'

William stared at the floor, his eyes blurring with tears.

'She'll be so pleased to see you. I haven't heard from her much lately. But then she's never one for writing letters. And when she's quiet, she's happy. She always liked Kent. Used to go down with her dad, hop-picking. September, every year. Had the time of our lives, she said. Outside on the farm in the sunshine. You can breathe out there. Feel it clean in your lungs.' She paused, glancing at his stiff unbending leg. 'It's a long way, though. Right across London. The train goes from Victoria.'

He nodded.

'Are you sure you're up to it? You look all in.'

Mary took a deep breath. 'I killed him with a shovel.'

He looked up, shocked. 'What did you say?'

'You might need to write it down, Constable.'

'You killed him?'

'Yes.'

'You're admitting that you murdered Arthur Corben?'

'I don't know why you're looking so surprised. It's what I told you right at the beginning. Nothing's changed. I just filled you in on all the background.'

William groped for his pen. 'So what happened?'

She looked bored. 'Do you really want me to go through the whole thing? I killed Arthur Corben. Isn't that enough?'

'No. I need the whole story.'

'Why?'

'I need to be sure you're telling the truth.'

'I should have thought you'd be pleased. You've found the murderer. Solved the case. That'll make you look good, won't it? When the top brass comes down from Dorchester.'

For a moment, William shut his eyes tight shut as if trying to clear his mind. He waited, marshalling his thoughts. Then he said, 'What happened, Miss Holmes?'

'I probably shouldn't say this, Constable, but I don't feel it was wrong to kill Arthur Corben.'

'Miss Holmes—'

'I know a judge might take a different view. But I believe he was an evil man.'

'Can we—'

'I think he killed his uncle all those years before. I can't prove it. The old man was lazy and slapdash. Perhaps he didn't tie the knot properly. Perhaps he was using rope so old it frayed and broke. But I think it's more likely that Arthur did something to make the cart hurtle back down the slide and crush the life out of him. It must have broken every bone in his body. The cart was full of stone. And I think he probably killed Harry Brown, too. I didn't tell you that part, did I? After I moved to Wareham and bought the forge, I thought I'd find out how Harry was. Just in case I could persuade him to come and work for me again. So I went to see his mother. She lived on a farm at East Stoke. She said that Harry hadn't gone to Weymouth. He'd left England altogether. Arthur had found him a job in America. Texas, she thought. She hadn't heard from him since he left. She said she prayed for him every day, and hoped he was well and happy and enjoying his new life.'

'People do emigrate, Miss Holmes. Perhaps Harry Brown did go to Texas.'

'And never wrote to his mother?'

William looked distracted. 'Some people aren't very good at writing letters.'

'You're taking Arthur's side.'

'I'm just saying you might be wrong. There might be an innocent explanation.'

Mary's face was set and determined. 'No, I'm not wrong. I know what I'm talking about. Arthur Corben was an evil man. And he got what was coming to him.'

The wind was so strong that the white smoke billowing past the window seemed to change direction mid-air. But inside the carriage, it was cramped and hot. All the seats were taken. Two of the women had babies on their laps. William was pinned between a large man in a brown fedora and a woman clutching a basket of cabbages. Faint smells mixed together – camphor from a mothballed coat, a pungent nappy, hot Bovril from an open flask.

'Could you open the window?' said William. He could feel the sweat in a damp film on his face.

'Wait till we get through the next tunnel, love,' said the woman by the door. 'Or we'll get all the smoke blown back in.'

William tried to steady his breathing. He looked above the heads of the passengers at a framed picture of London: majestic buildings and smiling people bathed in brilliant sunshine. Nothing like the city he'd travelled through on his way from Silvertown – grey skies, bomb damage, faces lined with exhaustion.

A blast of cold air rushed into the carriage. The train hooted like an owl. William looked up in panic.

'That better, love?' said the woman by the door. 'Horrible when you're not feeling well, isn't it? I'd close my eyes if I were you.'

The large round baby opposite was grizzling. His mother – young and pretty, with her fair hair tied up with a white ribbon – held him more firmly on her lap and jiggled her knees up and down. But the baby just cried harder, tears spilling down his red cheeks. Glancing up, she caught William staring.

She said, sharp and defensive, 'He doesn't like it when things are different.'

William smiled. 'I don't blame him.'

She gave a quick surreptitious glance at William's stiff leg – splayed to one side, taking up far too much room – and turned away.

Through the window William could see that the rows of London terraced houses were giving way to wide green fields.

———

'So you want the whole story?'

William narrowed his eyes, as if blinded by sunlight.

'Because I'm not sure I want to tell you now that you've taken to defending Arthur.'

William tried to concentrate, but most of him was still on a train speeding through the Kent countryside.

'I do wonder sometimes how he had the patience to wait so long. It was two years after he killed John before he asked me to marry him. And he would have gone through the whole rigmarole of the burial service and getting the coffin reburied if it would have helped to change my mind. I sometimes think he would have waited for me his whole life if need be. With the odd flash of irritation, of course. But that was only natural.'

'Miss Holmes—'

'And that's been my lesson in life, I think. I never had that kind of steadfastness. I married John on a whim. Some months I wanted him. Some months I didn't. I spent more time wishing him different than enjoying the time we had. And it was only when he was taken from me that I realised he was the only man I could ever love.'

William was silent.

'You regret many things when you're my age, Constable. And most of the time, you think, what's done is done. I did my best, and there's no point grieving over what can't be changed. But this I regret every day.' She looked up. 'The last time I saw him, I didn't tell him I loved him. I didn't even kiss him goodbye.'

It was dark by the time the train reached Bromley South. It had stopped for an hour outside London. There was no point moaning about it. Troops and freight took priority, so ordinary passengers had to wait.

The baby's screams were still ringing in his ears.

Because he walked so slowly, all the other passengers had disappeared by the time William had negotiated the stairs and made his way through the ticket office. So he found himself standing outside on the road in the dark with no idea of which way to go. It was cold. He put his hands in his pockets. His fingers touched the bar of soap, begged from a nurse at the convalescent home in Hastings. The plan to see Stella had been alive even then. Day after day he had sat in his chair on the rolled green lawn under the weeping willow and imagined their first meeting after months of separation. Sometimes she was pleased to see him. Sometimes she couldn't work out why he'd bothered to come.

He'd kept the soap safe the whole year he was in Dorchester. It lay wrapped in a clean handkerchief in the drawer of his desk, hard and pink, smelling faintly of tar.

As he stood there hesitating, a policeman loomed out of the blackness. William asked for directions. The policeman shone his torch on his face, searching for signs of criminal intent. William didn't introduce himself as a fellow copper. He didn't say he had a desk job typing crime reports in a police station in Dorset. It seemed easier to say as little as possible.

The streets were very quiet. Once he startled a cat, which turned to him full face, eyes shining like car headlamps. But there were no people around. There were few bicycles either. No one could get the batteries for lights any more.

William nearly tripped on an uneven flagstone, and righted himself by grabbing hold of a wooden gatepost. He stayed there for a moment, letting his breathing return to normal, and looked up towards the house to his left. There was enough moonlight to see a gravel path and the dark blob of a squat yew tree. Stella must feel like a fish out of water round here. It couldn't be more different from Silvertown.

His leg was so painful that walking was an act of will.

Ten minutes later, his body damp with sweat, William limped round the last corner. He counted the houses as he passed. Outside number twelve, he stopped. The blackout here, as everywhere else, was so complete it was impossible to tell whether anyone was home or not.

William took a deep breath. Shivering from the effort, he dragged himself up the path to the front door.

———

'Constable? Can I have a word?'

Sergeant Mills was standing in front of him. William's heart pounded. He hadn't even heard him come into the room.

Sergeant Mills looked down at Mary with a solemn expression. 'I'm so sorry to interrupt, Miss Holmes. I do realise you're trying to go through the outstanding queries on your statement. But

I'm going to be out now until later this afternoon, and I wanted to make sure the constable was fully informed about police business.'

Mary stood up. 'I quite understand. I'll go outside, shall I?'

'If you wouldn't mind, Miss Holmes.' The sergeant stood back with extreme courtesy. 'That would be very kind.'

They waited while she picked up her bag and, with her usual brisk efficiency, made her way out to the main office.

Once the door was shut, the sergeant sat down. 'Are you feeling all right? No more faintness?'

William shook his head.

'I should have stuck to my guns and insisted you stayed in bed today.'

'It was nothing. Just tiredness.'

'I still think you should see Dr Barton.'

'There's no need.'

Sergeant Mills sighed. 'When I have more time, I will insist that you take your health more seriously. In the meantime, I owe you an apology.'

'For what?'

'I've been trying to find a moment to talk to you all morning. There have been further developments since we talked yesterday.'

'From the coroner's office?'

Sergeant Mills looked surprised. 'Were we expecting anything?'

'I thought there might be more news.'

'No, Constable. We're just waiting for your report. Revelations from Miss Holmes.' He paused. 'I'm talking about bacon.'

'Because of Constable Fripp's uncle? The dead pig?'

Sergeant Mills frowned. 'What dead pig?'

William said, floundering, 'Just something Miss Holmes said.'

Sergeant Mills looked up at the clock on the opposite wall. 'I must get a move on. I promised to call in and have another word with the rector.' His face became serious. 'No, it's about what we were discussing yesterday, just before you were taken ill. I jumped to conclusions, and I'm sorry. I should have known that none of my officers would ever buy anything on the black market, or get involved in shady dealings. It does go on – terrible trouble in Folkestone last year. But I should have realised there was a perfectly innocent explanation. After we'd taken you upstairs and got you to bed, I sat down with Constable Meech, and he told me what had been going on – every detail. I understand that all you young constables were involved – you, Constable Meech and Constable Fripp – and that you're all equally responsible. Now I don't want to make this into something bigger than it is. There's nothing like a bit of bacon to set you up for the day, and I know it's not easy living here at the police station. No home comforts. Fending for yourselves. But it has to stop. Do you understand?

'The next time that nice young Lyle Brooks offers you handouts from the army kitchen, I'd like you to refuse. Politely, of course, and with grateful thanks. But a firm no. It looks wrong, you see. It's just an act of generosity and friendliness – of course it is. I know these Americans are always throwing tea parties and giving out sweets to the children. But this is different. And it could be interpreted in the wrong way by those intent on seeing evil where none exists. I'm sure you know what I'm talking about. Special favours. That kind of thing.' Sergeant Mills paused to add weight to his words. 'I need to be completely sure, particularly while Inspector Pearce is away, that we are above reproach. Not the whisper of a rumour of anything untoward. Everything honest and above board. I want the inspector to see, on his return, that he left the station in safe hands.'

When Mary knocked on the door, William was still sitting at the wooden table, staring into space.

'May I come in?'

He said nothing.

'I must say, there's an air of mystery round here today. All very cloak and dagger. The sergeant taking you aside for private conversations.'

William frowned.

Mary opened her eyes wide. 'I wasn't suggesting you tell me what's going on.' She sat down opposite him. 'Although I did wonder if it was to do with Constable Fripp.'

He took out his notebook.

'And the pig.'

Silence settled over the room like a grey blanket.

Mary sighed. 'It's not a story that puts me in a good light.'

He looked up, startled.

'You do want me to go on, don't you? You said you wanted all the details.'

Slowly, refocusing his attention, he nodded.

'I'm not sorry I killed him. Not sorry at all. But none of it would have happened if I'd refused to go along with it. I should never have listened to John. I could see how excited he was. The wickedness, the brilliance of a fake suicide, all the plotting and planning. But I knew something was wrong. Each time we talked, the three of us, there were shadows beneath the surface. Like fish underwater, slithering out of reach. But I ignored it all. I closed my eyes to it. And all the while, of course, Arthur was astonished by his good fortune. Everything comes to he who waits. All those years planning the murder of his uncle. His long apprenticeship as a stonecutter. Then two years in London until he heard that my marriage to John was broken. And now, at last, he could claim his reward. James five, verse seven: *Behold, the husbandman waiteth for the precious fruit of the earth, and hath long patience for it, until he receive the early and latter rain.*'

William was still, his eyes on her face.

'I followed him. October 1881. He'd already told me he was

waiting for a night with no moon. And then he'd go to the churchyard and see how easy it was to dig up the body of John's father. He said, Leave it to me, Mary, leave it to me. But in my mind Arthur was still the scarecrow in flapping clothes – a little boy, boots way too big, falling over his own feet. I thought I could help him. Hold the lamp. Act as a lookout. So in September, on the night of the new moon when the sky was as black as a crow, I kept watch. I sat there by the window, shivering in my shawl, until first light. But I saw nothing. I wanted to ask Arthur what had happened. Why hadn't he gone to the churchyard to dig up the bones? But I'd promised to leave it all to him. So I bit my lip, and didn't question him.

'But the next month, at the new moon, staring into the black night from an upstairs window, I saw him escape from the shadows. It was just after midnight. I grabbed my shawl and followed him.

'Then came my first surprise. I could see he was holding a shovel in his hand, and he had a bag slung over his shoulder. But he walked straight past the churchyard. He carried on, all the way up the road, past the cottages, past the smithy, and turned left towards Acton. I was surprised. But I turned it over in my mind, and I thought, He must be farther along than I thought. He must have dug up the bones of John's father already and hidden them somewhere safe. It never occurred to me that it was all a lie. Why would it? I trusted him. I'd always trusted him.

'So we passed all the cottages in the hamlet. There were no lights. And then we got to common land. In the distance I could hear the sea, so I knew we were near the quarries. He kept turning round to check he wasn't being followed. But the night was so black he saw nothing.

'We came in sight of a long stone wall. The ground underfoot was soft and claggy, pulling at my boots. He turned, and walked next to the wall for several minutes until he came to a stile.

Then he set down his bag and his shovel. He stretched his neck either side, easing his muscles. I waited. Then he started digging. Quite quickly he built up a rhythm, though the earth must have been as hard as iron. It was so cold. But I pulled my shawl tightly around me, and crouched down low against the wall to keep watch.

'After a long while, I saw a faint glow on the surface of the field. So I crept closer. He was way down inside a deep hole. He'd set a lamp on a shelf he'd cut in the mud. You could smell the clay, heavy and wet. I watched as he dug deeper. I couldn't see a coffin. I could see nothing but blackness. He paused, and reached inside his pocket and brought out something long and thin. A chisel. He poked about, picking and gouging at different points in the floor of the hole. I guessed it had all gone rotten, the wood in the wet soil, and he couldn't see how to lift the lid. And of course he had to disturb it all as little as possible, in case anyone ever dug it up. It had to look as if it hadn't been touched for years.

'He stopped, and stared down. Then he bent low and started pulling with his hands. He lifted a great slice of darkness. And he reached inside. And now he had something in his fist and was holding it up against the lamp. I remember staring, puzzled, trying to understand what I saw. And then, with two hands, he stretched it out.

'The necklace settled in a graceful curve, dirty but beautiful, the loops and swags like a spider's web against the light.

'Arthur moved. And now I could see, in the ground, a body on its side. White ribcage, long leg bones, libbets of skin. Black hair. The white jawbone of the skull wide open.

'I heard myself screaming.

'Arthur's hands were on my shoulders. He was shouting my name, shaking me. When the screaming didn't stop, he hit me. He slapped me across the face. For a moment I couldn't breathe. Then I started clawing at him, dragging my nails down his cheeks, trying to reach my fingers into his eyes. He grabbed both my wrists. I was still fighting and shouting and swearing and crying. He pushed me to the ground and sat astride me, pinning my arms to the ground above my head. So I lay still. His face was covered in blood where I'd scratched him.

'And I spat at him.

'For a moment, I thought he might hit me again. But he rolled off. He sat some distance away, folded in on himself, legs drawn up, arms round his knees.

'I dragged myself to the grave and looked down. I could smell it now, the stink of decay. The wood had rotted, and mud and water seeped in, so he lay in a shiny slurry of soil. I could see the teeth in his open mouth. Black hair against white bone. His arms were stretched out to the side. One of his hands was separate, a pale grey glove, sloughed off from the bones of his fingers. As if the skin had crawled off by itself.

'No face. No eyes. Just the silent scream.

'I turned away and retched in the earth, but the smell seemed to billow up from the grave, great clouds of cloying rot filling my eyes and throat and stomach. I was sick again and again until there was nothing left.

'The wind began to blow in from the sea.

'He said, I didn't want it to happen.

'I shuffled back from the edge. I wanted my shawl, but it was long gone. I hugged my arms to my body, tense against the cold.

'He said, I brought the coffin out of the village. I kept leaning over, saying, Be patient, John, be patient. When we got here, I started digging. I had to be sure it was safe. I had to carry on until I knew for certain that no one was watching. When I let John out, he was grumbling. Said I'd taken too long. I told him he should go. I said, The sooner you leave, the safer you'll be. The hours of darkness will cover your tracks. I bent down to pick up my tools, and as I stood up he hit me. Punched me to the ground. My head was swimming. I could hardly hear. He said, I've been thinking it over, and the one flaw in the plan is you, Arthur Corben. You've always wanted Mary. You'll betray me. You'll tell the village what I've done so they come after me and kill me. And then you'll have Mary for yourself.

'John kept on and on. I couldn't persuade him he was wrong. And when he started towards me, I was afraid. You remember John's temper, Mary. Once his blood was up, he had no control. He would batter me to death. So I picked up a rock. John said, You think that will stop me? And he came at me with a roar, and I threw it at him, as hard as I could. It hit him on the forehead, and he fell. Just crumpled and fell. I stood there, waiting for him to get up. I thought, Any minute now he'll move again. He'll sit up, shaking his head, and then he'll be after me again, even angrier than before. But he lay there, as still as stone. I called his name. I crept closer. I thought that as soon as I got near enough, he'd have his hands round my throat and throttle me. It was only when I knelt beside him that I realised he was dead. I listened to his heart. I checked his breathing. But he had gone.

'I said to Arthur, You killed him?

'He said, Yes.

'You killed John?

'If I hadn't, he would have killed me.

'I looked down into the grave, at the body on its side, legs bent, the arms out straight. The jaw of the skull was wide open. I said, So how did he end up like that?

'Arthur said, When it was over, I dragged the coffin into the hole. Then I pulled John's body to the edge and let it fall.

'I said, It fell like that?

'Arthur said, I had to move the arms and legs.

'Why?

'So it would fit inside.

'I put my hand to my mouth.

'Arthur said, I'm sorry.

'I said, Why didn't you take the gold?

'Arthur said, I didn't want it. It was John's plan, not mine. I never set my heart on being rich, Mary. I'm happy here in Langton. I always have been.

'I said, You lied to me. For years.

'What else could I do? If I'd told you the truth, you never would have spoken to me again.

'I thought about this. I said, Tell me again.

'The whole thing?

'From the beginning. I want to hear it again.

'And I knelt by the grave, my head bowed, just as I'd done years before with the little maid with the missing jaw, and Arthur told me the whole story once more. As he talked, he picked at the sharp end of his shovel, pulling off the wet clods of clay that hung to the metal tip. A good workman always cleans his tools.

'I wept. I said, Couldn't you have defended yourself without killing him?

'He said, Mary, you remember what John was like. He was much stronger than me.

'And that was true. John was as strong as an ox.

'Arthur said, I'm sorry. I'm so sorry. I never wanted to cause you pain.

'I put out my hand and took the shovel from him. I said, Let me bury my husband.

'Arthur nodded.

'I swung it round my head with such force that the metal, side on, lodged in his skull. He fell backwards. I stood up and pulled the shovel out of his forehead and brought it down again, flat this time, so that his whole face collapsed in a crush of bone and blood. I wanted to be sure, so I lifted the spade and smashed it down one more time.

'You couldn't recognise Arthur Corben any more.

'In the distance, above the sea, the sky was getting lighter.

'I put down the shovel. I said, to what remained of Arthur's face, You are lying. You would never have stood up to John. And he would never have let you kill him. You buried him alive.

'Then I picked up his legs and dragged his body to the hole he had dug. When his feet were at the edge, I went back to his shoulders, to his bloody head, and pushed. I used all my strength. But he wouldn't move. Stubborn even in death. So I lay on my back and kicked with my legs, bit by bit, until his body edged over into the pit and finally fell inside. He landed in a slithering heap at my husband's back, his limbs tangled up, his face in the filth.

'I couldn't see the necklace or the earrings. Arthur had dug them up to destroy them, so that I would never know the truth. But he had failed. I left them there in the dirt and decay. I hoped they would give John comfort in the dark.

'It took more than an hour to fill the hole. I kept batting down the earth. When the hole was full and the ground was flat, I put back the turf. I stamped it down with my feet. Just as I was finishing, the first light of dawn began to appear, and it started to rain, softly at first, but then harder and harder.

'I wiped the shovel clean with a handful of grass. Then I turned my back and walked towards the sea. On the cliffs, I stood with the wind and the rain whipping my dress, and I lifted the shovel high above my head, and I threw it down to the sea below.

'Then I turned and walked back to the village.'

———

The house was semi-detached – the left-hand one, set back from the road. In the darkness, William could make out the front path, its surface pale and uneven. He opened the gate. The thin bare branch of a tree brushed his face like a skeleton arm.

There were two steps leading up to the porch. The glass in the door gleamed like black water. William felt around for the bell. Eventually he knocked. But there was no answer. He heard rustling in the fleshy leaves of a plant nearby. But then all was silent.

The sweat was cooling on his face. He was suddenly very tired. It felt as if he'd been travelling for weeks. Dorset to London, London to Kent. The desire to see Stella, when he finally gave in to it, had been so strong that he hadn't even thought about what he'd do if he didn't find her. So here he was, in Bromley, on a Tuesday evening in March. He knew no one. He had nowhere to stay.

There was the noise of a latch being unfastened.

The door opened.

In the darkness, her pale face was smudged and ghostly.

After a while, she said, 'What are you doing here?'

There was a long, empty silence.

'You'd better come in.' She stood back and opened the door.

The air inside was cold. It was pitch black. She said, 'Wait a minute.' Behind him, she pulled a curtain across the stained glass. Then she turned on the light. He stood there, his back against the wall, looking down at her. Her hair was longer, pulled back from her face. But otherwise she looked exactly the same. She was wearing red lipstick. Her hair was bright gold. 'Well,' she said. 'This is a surprise.'

He shifted his weight. The pain shot through him, so sharp he almost cried out.

'How did you find me?'

'Your aunt. She had your address.'

From a room off the hall, a man's voice called out, 'Stella? Who is it?'

'Here,' said Stella, 'give me your coat.' He shuffled out of his long wool overcoat and she hung it on the rack. Then she turned, pushed open the door behind her, and announced in a loud voice, 'It's an old friend of mine.'

William followed her inside. It was a big room, painted cream, with a pinky-beige sofa and a matching armchair. By the fireplace, in another armchair, was a man in shirtsleeves just visible behind an open newspaper. As William walked in, he shook out his newspaper, refolded it, and put it on the table next to him. He looked up. One side of his face had collapsed, dragged down by a long red scar from eye to mouth. The lower eyelid had been pulled too far, red-rimmed and watering.

'Someone I haven't seen for years,' said Stella. 'His name's William.'

William limped forward.

'Frank,' said the man, as they shook hands. He had shiny black hair and a neat black moustache.

Stella sat down on the sofa. William, after a small hesitation, made his way over to the remaining armchair.

Above the fireplace was a bucolic painting of green fields and a thatched cottage.

'He's a copper,' said Stella.

'Better watch myself, then,' said Frank.

After a pause, William said, 'How's Peter?'

'He's asleep. Upstairs. Tired out from playing in the garden.'

William narrowed his eyes, remembering. 'There was another little boy, wasn't there?'

Stella laughed. 'Not that I know of.'

William swallowed. 'Your cousin.'

'Oh,' said Stella, 'he's thinking about Kath's little boy.'

'Ah,' said Frank.

'They live just down the road,' said Stella. 'He's six now. Stan. As thick as thieves, the pair of them.'

William looked from Stella to Frank, and back again.

'That's how we met, wasn't it?' said Stella. 'Round at Kath's house. Christmas just gone. A whirlwind romance, you might say. That's what happens these days. No time to waste.'

William tightened his grip on the arms of the chair.

'So where do you live, then, William?' said Frank.

'Dorset born and bred,' said Stella. 'He was the village bobby, where I was evacuated in 1939. When Peter was just a baby. Such a pretty village. And everyone so friendly. Really made you feel at home.'

William half rose from his chair. 'I should go.'

'You've only just got here,' said Frank.

'I've got a train to catch.'

'You should have a cup of tea at least,' said Frank. 'You never know what's going to be open these days.'

'I tell you what, Frank,' said Stella. 'Why don't you go and put the kettle on? I want to ask William about Mrs Poyton. She was the woman I stayed with all those years ago. Her kitchen was so clean you could eat your dinner off the floor. Scrubbed everything to within an inch of its life. How's she doing these days? She had a cat, didn't she? Great big black thing. It used to go out hunting every night. Came back with a rabbit once. Only a baby rabbit, but I couldn't believe my eyes. I thought cats only caught mice.'

Frank stood up. 'How do you like your tea, then, William? Strong or weak?'

'As it comes.'

They heard his footsteps going off down the hall.

Stella reached for the packet of cigarettes on the arm of the sofa. When she tapped it upside down on the palm of her hand, he could see her fingernails were painted red.

'So,' she said, picking up her matchbook, 'what happened to you?'

He said nothing.

'Back to being a copper?'

He nodded.

The match flared. 'Where?'

'Dorset.'

'I should have guessed. You've got roots there. Like a tree.'

She lit her cigarette and inhaled deeply, blowing out the smoke in a great cloud. 'I did wonder, from time to time, where you'd gone. You used to write letters. Remember? Just to tell me when you were next on leave. So I'd know to expect you.' She shrugged. 'Then it all stopped. My aunt said, It's the war, Stella. These things happen. And I said, I suppose they do.'

'I was in hospital.'

'For two years?'

He stared at her, his eyes hopeless.

She flicked the end of the cigarette towards the ashtray. 'You just disappeared. There one minute, gone the next. Like you'd thought better of it.'

He couldn't speak.

'Water under the bridge now, though. Time moves on.'

He swallowed. 'You said you'd never leave Silvertown.'

She took another deep drag. 'I changed my mind.'

'What about Frank?'

'What about him?'

He couldn't take his eyes off her face.

'Like I said, it happened very quickly. We met at Kath's on Christmas Eve. A bit of a last-minute party. His wife had just packed up and left. He got back from the front, blind in one eye, and she took one look at his face and scarpered. He was all over the place.' She paused, watching the smoke spiral up. 'I haven't told Mum yet. Or Aunty Lil. I'm not sure they'd approve. His divorce won't come through for months.'

He opened his mouth to speak, but said nothing.

'There's a lot of it about. They come home and their wives don't recognise them. Arguments. Tears. It doesn't always make the heart grow fonder. You just end up strangers.' She looked up. 'What about you?'

He shook his head.

'I thought that's why you stopped writing. Found another girl.'

'No.'

Her face showed no emotion, as if the conversation bored her.

He leaned forward. 'Would you have . . .?'

'Would I have what?'

But he couldn't finish.

She stubbed out her cigarette, pressing it hard into the ashtray. 'Some things don't change, do they?'

His mouth trembled.

'All those times you came to see me. And you just couldn't say it.'

His hands were shaking.

'Couldn't spit it out.'

His eyes were pleading with her.

'So we'll never know, will we? What might have happened?'

He said, in a voice that was much too loud, 'He was killed.'

She stared at him.

'My brother. Last week. In Italy.'

She looked shocked. 'What happened?'

'I thought, I'll go and see Stella. It made sense. I thought you'd want to know. As soon as I heard. I thought, I'll go and see Stella.' He rubbed his face with his hand, like a child dazed by sleep.

'I remember him, from the village. Good-looking boy.'

William said, 'He never knew you the way I know you. He didn't know you at all.'

She looked confused.

'You must believe me. I wanted to come before. So many times.'

They heard footsteps in the hall, and then Frank appeared in the doorway carrying a tray. 'I brought a bit of carrot cake. Just in case you hadn't eaten, William.'

William was still staring at Stella. He didn't appear to have heard.

Frank set down the tray on the table by the armchair. 'You don't want to be starting a long journey feeling hungry.'

Out of the silence came the long, slow crescendo of an air-raid siren.

'I don't believe it,' said Stella. 'That's all we bloody need.'

William stood up, a look of panic in his eyes.

'Frank,' said Stella, scrambling to her feet, 'get Peter, will you?'

William was already blundering out to the hall, plunging towards the front door.

On his way to the stairs, Frank shouted, 'You're safer here, William. In the shelter. Tell him, Stella. It's just out the back. At the bottom of the garden.'

William was moving forward with such purpose that Stella had to hang bodily on to his arm to stop him. He stumbled, and she pinned him against the wall. They stood there, swaying, like a drunken couple trying to dance.

In the distance, they could hear the ack-ack guns.

Frank was already coming back down the stairs, carrying a sleeping Peter.

'It's his leg,' said Stella. 'He tripped. You go ahead. We'll come on behind.'

'Mind yourself on the steps outside the back door, William. They're slippery at night.'

Frank disappeared down the hall, Peter's head on his shoulder. Stella turned out the light. In the sudden darkness, William said, 'Do you love him?'

'What do you care?'

The siren was one continuous, urgent call.

She said, 'You shouldn't have come.'

'I had to see you.'

'Well, now you have. And it's time to go.'

He said, 'Don't marry him. Marry me.'

'You think that's how it happens, do you? Just like that?'

'It's not too late.'

'Really?' Her voice was angry.

William bent down to kiss her but she turned her face away. The sound of the siren filled the air.

He said, 'I wanted to come before.'

'So you say.'

'So many times.'

'Don't forget your coat.'

He turned, unseeing, felt for the dark wool and lifted it down from the hook. As he struggled into the sleeves, the bar of soap in the pocket banged against his leg. 'Stella—'

'Goodbye, copper.'

He fumbled for the latch and opened the door. Outside the searchlights were sweeping the sky in huge brilliant arcs. He said, his voice urgent, 'It's not too late. There's still time.'

She said, 'I've got to go. Peter needs me.'

But when he got to the road, and looked back down the path to the front door, she hadn't moved. She was still standing there, her face pale in the darkness.

He heard the low drone of an aircraft.

He was shouting her name when the world exploded.

———

'Her name was Stella Allen. I loved her. I wanted to marry her, but I never asked her. Not until it was too late. I didn't want to hear her say no. If I didn't ask her, there was always a chance. Something to hope for. A chance she might say yes. She was so different to me. Full of life. So certain of everything. I'd never met anyone like her before. I didn't think she wanted me. Not really. Dull and boring. Law and order. But I didn't even have the courage to ask. And then I got blown up. Half deaf. Leg shot to pieces. And I thought, Well, that's an end to it. Who'd want me now? An old man. Hard of hearing, can't walk, can't dance. Only fit for the scrap heap. But I never stopped thinking about her. Ever. After the accident, all the time I was in hospital, convalescing in Hastings, living in Dorchester. Months and months of wanting her. But not having the courage to find her. And when I came here, I saw her everywhere I looked. She was the face of every woman I ever met. But it wasn't her. Because Stella wasn't there any more.'

In the stifling gloom of the charge room, Mary – lost in thought after finishing her tale of Arthur's murder – looked up, surprised. William was staring down at his hands, palms flat on the table, the fingers long and white. The notebook, abandoned, had somehow half shut itself, the pages springing back together.

'My brother said, She won't make a policeman's wife. They'd never allow it. We had a row. I said to him, I'm going to ask her, whatever you say. And that was the last time I ever saw him. Shouting at him in the street because he said I shouldn't marry Stella. Telling him he was stuck-up, prejudiced, a snob. When he died, we hadn't spoken for two years. More than two years. I didn't even answer his letters. And I can't forgive myself. Because he's gone, and there's nothing I can do.'

William paused, his breathing uneven. 'When I heard he was dead, I went to find her. I don't know why. I just had to. I had to tell her. I went to London. Back to Silvertown, with the factories all along the river. The stink of heavy industry. Got her address from an aunt. Went down to Kent on the train. And there she was, living with another man. Frank. Ugly scar on his face, pulling his eye down. But she didn't seem to mind. Nice house, new furniture, her little boy asleep upstairs. Frank was waiting for his divorce. And then they'd marry. She was angry with me for going off without telling her. For just disappearing. And then the siren started. And Frank went to the shelter in the garden with her little boy. And when he'd gone, I said, Don't marry him. Marry me.

'But she said it was too late. Two years with no word, and then I turn up on her doorstep. What did I expect? And the siren kept going. And all the time I was talking to her, all the time we were standing in the hall, she should have been in the shelter. With Frank and her son. But even when I left, she stood there, watching me walk down the path. I should have put her first. I should have thought of her safety, not my own. But I didn't. And what kind of love is that? What kind of love doesn't think about keeping someone safe? And then there was the plane overhead. A huge explosion. Crashing in my ears. I went down, face in the dirt, hands over my head. Felt the ground underneath me shaking like an earthquake. The smell of gas and burning and brick dust. And then the thud of footsteps pounding beneath my fingers, and I heard shouting, and I pushed myself up to my knees. You couldn't see anything. There was a wall of smoke, and a red haze behind it. Thick, like fog. The bell of a fire engine ringing. I got up. But I couldn't go fast enough. It felt like my legs were wading through mud. And then, for a moment, the smoke cleared and I saw it. A pile of rubble. A great fire burning. Then the smoke came back again, blowing over it all like a veil. Sparks and cinders flying about. I tried to move forward, but I felt my arms grabbed from behind, and it was a fireman saying, You can't go in there, mate. I started shouting, Stella! Stella! And he said, We'll find her. Don't you worry. We'll get her out. I was trying to pull away, and there was a woman by my side. And she said, Come on, love. Let them do their work. And they were pumping out water as fast as they could, and it was landing on the rubble, hissing and steaming, and I shouted, She'll drown in there if you keep doing that! She'll drown in there! The woman said, They've got to put out the fire, love, or she's got no chance. And then I remembered Peter. I said, Her little boy. He's in the shelter. In the garden. She said, All right, love, I'll let them know. And she left me standing there. I looked at the water, and the red flames high in the black sky, and the smoke was turning dark, and I started coughing, and couldn't get my breath. It was burning in my lungs. And someone came and pulled me away and sat me down. They put a blanket round my shoulders. A woman came up and said, Frank and Margaret Dollis, right? And I said, No, no. Frank's in the shelter with Peter. I don't know Margaret. It's Stella Allen in there somewhere. Stella Allen.

'It took a long time to get the fire under control. And then all the neighbours were in the street, helping. All of them. The shelter at the back was covered in rubble. But they got them out in the end. I saw him. Frank. Carrying Peter. A blanket wrapped round them both, like a big grey cloak. Peter was crying. They got into an ambulance. Frank didn't turn round. I don't suppose he knew I was there.

'It was dawn before we dug her out. The blast had taken off most of her clothes. So they covered her up quickly. I remember her white arm, flung back, with the fingers all together as if she was pointing at something. Red nail varnish. They put her on a stretcher with a cover right up over her head.

'I gave them her aunt's address. I said to the woman from the WVS, They'll want to know Peter's all right. They're a close family, you see. All live together in Silvertown. Look out for each other.

'And the woman said, Are you family, too, love?

'And I said, No, not me, I don't have a family.

'I got to Bromley South about six in the morning. The conductor on the platform said, You might want to have a wash before you board the train. Your face is as black as the ace of spades.

'So I went to the Gents and looked up at the little mirror above the basin, and he was right. My hair was grey, and there was blood on my cheek. And I remember washing very carefully, as if it mattered. I took out the soap in my pocket. Stella's soap. Because she didn't need it now, dead, with her white arm flung backwards on the rubble. I got the dirt out from under my fingernails. I brushed down my clothes as best I could. By the time I finished, I just looked a bit worn. A bit tired. No different from anyone else who's been up all night. I rinsed all the dirt from the sink, and took out the plug, and the grey water rushed down the plughole. And it was all over.

'I left the soap on the sink, by the taps.

'I got back to Wareham at lunchtime. I remember Constable Meech gave me a sort of knowing look and said, Good night out? I didn't answer. But I don't expect he thought that strange. I don't talk to any of them much if I can help it. They don't like me. Coming from Dorchester head office, and then sitting down all day typing reports. Nice comfortable job. Round to the Granary on the Quay for lunch, while they're out in all weathers. Can't even get a cup of tea.'

Mary, who had sat silently through the whole account, watched him as he talked.

William took a deep breath. 'So, yes, you're right. I'm guilty. As guilty as if I killed her myself.' His mouth stretched in a kind of grin. 'Guilty in so many ways, I've lost count. I often think I should be dead myself. Because I've failed so many people. My brother. Jack. Stella. And I'm not sure why I'm alive and they're not. It seems all wrong. And I can't think what to do to put it right.'

There was silence in the room for a long time. Then Mary said, 'You don't have to do anything.'

He looked up, his eyes full of despair.

'I know you don't believe me. But it's true.'

He shifted position, wincing with pain. His voice, when he spoke, sounded old and tired. 'I am living a lie.'

She made a little face. 'You and the rest of the world. John eight, verse seven. *He that is without sin among you, let him cast the first stone.*'

Saturday

'For the love of Mike,' said Sergeant Mills, pushing open the door with such force that it banged against the wall and shuddered. 'There are enough tears in Wareham this morning to fill a lake.'

William looked up.

'Wafting about, dripping with misery. Like the Lady of Shalott. For ever cursed. Weeping for eternity.'

'Because of the Americans?'

'Yes, yes. The Americans who have carried off the hearts of our womenfolk. English flowers destined to spend their entire lives in a state of deep mourning.' The sergeant flipped back the cover of the large leather ledger, which crashed open on to the desk. 'No warning either. Which is to be expected, of course. We're always the last to know. But still supposed to deal with all the broken pieces left behind.'

'So that's why they stopped them going to the dance.'

'Yes, Constable, I'd worked that out. Making sure they all had a good night's sleep before moving out at 0500 hours. No thought, of course, what that would do to the sleep of the inhabitants of Wareham, with tanks, jeeps and lorries rolling by their windows at dawn.' Sergeant Mills shook his head. 'I thought the colonel's chief of staff was being a bit cryptic on Thursday. When he said that the colonel was sorry he'd been unable to thank me personally for all the help I'd given the soldiers from the twenty-sixth billeted in Wareham. I thought, Well, there's still time. Offer me a drink. Make me a cake. Invite me over for a fine four-course meal at Binnegar Hall.'

William said, 'So they've all left?'

'Indeed they have. From the army huts next to the school, from the manse in North Street, and from Mrs Barnes's top bedroom in Moreton Lane. The canteen's gone from the Congregational Chapel, and there's no store cupboard in Bonnet's Lane. All gone. All over. All finished. I tell you, the fish and chip shop's going to feel it. I don't think it's closed since they got here. And the cinema. There'll be empty seats in the back row of the Rex from now on.' The sergeant looked resigned. 'Of course all that's happened is that we're back to the way we were before they came. Like getting used to perpetual rain after a long hot summer. But it won't feel like that. There will be gloom and despondency, you mark my words. Because they added a bit of charm, you see. A bit of life and vibrancy. A bit of sunshine. And now we're just left with the war. And to be quite honest with you, Constable, we've all had enough. We're all very, very tired.'

'Would you like a cup of tea?'

'I don't suppose we have any cake, do we? Ginger nuts? Bread pudding?'

'Not the last time I looked.'

Sergeant Mills sighed. 'There, you see. A case in point. I only had to pass the kitchen and young Lyle Brooks would rush out with a nice bit of warm apple pie. All wrapped up in a white napkin. Sugar and cinnamon on the top. I can almost smell it now.' He stared, wistful, into the middle distance. 'Well, times move on. And I tell you what, Constable. If you've had your eye on a young lady who's been otherwise engaged in the past few months, now's the time to make your move. They tell me the dance last night was dismal. Like a wet weekend. Annie was almost in tears when she came home. Said she'd got all dressed up for nothing.' He stopped. 'Has something happened to you, Constable? You look different today. Got some of your colour back.'

William stood up. 'Before I make the tea, Sergeant, can we have a quick word about Miss Holmes?'

The sergeant's eyes opened wide in mock alarm. 'Must we?'

'I think we should. We'll have a senior officer coming on Monday unless we can satisfy the coroner that we've got enough evidence to put before the jury.'

The sergeant cleared his throat and looked appropriately solemn. 'Yes, of course. What would you like to report?'

'Perhaps we should talk in private?'

The main door of the police station opened. Mary stood on the threshold, wearing her usual black coat and hat but with a blue and white striped scarf round her neck. It gave her a jaunty, naval air.

'Ah, Miss Holmes,' said Sergeant Mills, without enthusiasm.

'I hope it's all right to interrupt,' said Mary, 'but something rather important occurred to me last night, and I thought I should come straight round this morning and let the constable know.'

'Of course,' said the sergeant. 'Go on through.' He paused. 'While it's quiet, I might nip round to Worlds Stores. See if they've got any Garibaldis. I'll only be five minutes.'

The charge room was full of light. Morning sunshine had just cleared the obstacles in the passageway and shone brilliantly through the sparkling new glass of the open sash window. Soft May air spilled into the room.

'Well,' said Mary, with delight, 'what a difference!'

William, who had been living like a mole for so long that he had become blind to his surroundings, looked taken aback.

'I think you ought to ask your Sergeant Mills whether the station budget extends to a bit of spring cleaning. All this sunshine is showing up the dust. It wouldn't take much, you know. Wash the floor and the cupboards, wipe down the walls. You don't want to live with all this old grime, do you?'

'It's not something I think about very much.'

'Well, perhaps you should.' Mary sat down, her bag on her lap.

'So what's on your mind, Miss Holmes?'

'I've been wondering whether I need to pack a suitcase.'

William looked confused.

'Now that I've confessed to murder. We didn't manage to discuss it yesterday. And I must admit, once I got home, I began to feel quite nervous. So I thought I'd come in and ask.'

'It doesn't work like that, Miss Holmes.'

'Doesn't it? I was expecting handcuffs at least.'

William lowered himself on to the bench. 'First of all, I have to write up your statement and give it to the coroner.'

'You haven't done that yet?'

'No.'

'Why?'

William looked awkward.

'You weren't listening, were you?' said Mary. 'You have no idea what I said yesterday.'

He was annoyed. 'Of course I was listening.'

'The minute I finished, you started talking about Stella.'

'I'll show you my notes, if you like. I recorded everything you said.' William paused. 'And I've already apologised. I told you, before you left the station yesterday – I didn't mean to start talking about Stella. It just happened. I didn't mean to suggest that what you'd told me wasn't important.'

Mary shrugged.

He fixed her with a direct gaze. 'The reason I haven't finished the report is that I'm not convinced you're telling the truth.'

'Oh, Constable, please.' Mary looked weary. 'Surely we don't have to go through this again?'

'It's important. I need to be sure that your statement is accurate.'

'So what worries you?'

'There's quite a long list.' He took a deep breath. 'To start with, Arthur Corben was a marbler. A stonecutter. A fit young man. Used to handling heavy materials and sharp tools.'

Mary shrugged. 'So?'

'He was much stronger than you.'

'You think I couldn't have killed him.'

'I think he would have defended himself.'

'You are forgetting,' said Mary in a cold voice, 'that I had the benefit of surprise. He wasn't expecting me to swing the shovel round and smash his skull.'

'Even so—'

'You are finding it hard to think of me as a young woman. It's a failure of imagination on your part. You should make more of an effort. What you see before you is not the woman I was then. I was twenty-three years old. Young and fit myself. Probably three or four inches taller than I am now. Because people shrink with age, you know. Become smaller versions of themselves.' She glared at him. 'But more importantly, I was angry. At that moment, when I killed him, I hated him. And surely you understand that? Hatred gives you strength you can only dream of.'

William nodded.

She looked irritated. 'But that's not enough?'

'No.'

'Why?'

William said, with great care, 'Because you told it like a story.'

'All events become stories in the end. That's what we do. We turn even horrible things into tales fit for children. Think about the rebels on Bloody Bank. Hung, drawn and quartered on the West Walls, their guts pulled out while they were still alive. But there isn't a child in Wareham who can't tell you every detail.'

'It sounded rehearsed.'

'We've been through this before. I have lived with it every day. I have thought about nothing else since it happened. I have examined every tiny part of it. I know it as well as I know my own body. If it sounds rehearsed, it's because I have spent

245

sixty-two years going over it again and again in order to make sense of it.' Her voice was rising, quivering with emotion.

'I'm not trying to upset you. I am trying to be calm and dispassionate. That's my job.'

She looked at him, her mouth set.

'Surely you don't want to be tried for murder?'

'It's not something I'm looking forward to. But I'm tired of lying. I want it all out in the open.'

'You could end up in prison. Behind bars. Hanged.'

'I'll accept whatever punishment I'm given.'

They stared at each other.

William said, 'I'm going to discuss it all with Sergeant Mills today. As soon as we have a moment with no interruptions. I'll outline everything you've told me and ask him what he thinks we should do next.'

The silence was hostile.

'Miss Holmes, I'm a junior officer. I ask the questions and record what I hear. It's up to others to decide how to proceed.'

'You must do what you think best.' Mary's voice was still angry. 'But ask yourself this. Why would I lie? Why would I go to all the trouble of telling you this long and complicated story if it wasn't true?'

'I have no idea, Miss Holmes.' William looked exhausted. 'I have absolutely no idea.'

The sun bathed the charge room in soft golden light, turning the walls the colour of clear honey.

Mary pulled on her gloves. 'Well, there's no point my staying here. I might as well go home.'

William said, 'You didn't tell me what happened next.'

'Next?'

'After they were both buried.'

She looked at him with scorn. 'The whole of the rest of my life? I told you everything the day we met. You can look back over your notes. If you still have them.'

'You told me very little. About running the pub and the forge in Langton, and then the garage in Wareham. With Lawrence of Arabia as one of your customers.'

Mary did up the buttons on the wrists of her gloves. 'And there you have it. That's all you need to know.'

'Why did you go back to using your maiden name?'

'It seemed simpler. I didn't want to be known as the Mary Ball whose husband committed suicide, or as the Mary Ball whose ardent suitor Arthur Corben mysteriously disappeared.'

'You never married again?'

She shook her head. The sun glinted off the clasp on her bag. She gave her left glove a little tug and smoothed the fabric over the back of her hand. 'Which is why, I expect, I was such a successful businesswoman. The garage had my full attention. There was no man demanding clean shirts and a cooked meal every night.' She fixed William with a glacial stare. 'It appears I have a very masculine mind. Logic, analysis, money. They found it quite frightening to begin with, the men of Wareham. But I kept a guard on my tongue. And I was easy on the eye, which always helps. As the years passed, they almost forgave me. They had to. I employed the best mechanics in Dorset.'

'And no one ever asked questions? About what had happened?'

Mary shrugged. 'There was gossip, of course, when Arthur disappeared. He had left everything behind – his clothes, even his tools. No marbler abandons his tools. There were some who thought history had repeated itself – that Arthur had asked me to marry him, and left Langton when I refused. Couldn't bear to be rejected a second time. They thought he'd probably gone back to London. I let them think that. It seemed a likely solution.

'And once he'd disappeared, there was no more talk of burial services over the unmarked grave, or moving the bones to the churchyard. Because only Arthur knew where the coffin was buried, or so they thought. So all the plotting and scheming died away. Mr Lester carried on with his lobbying and letter writing. And the law changed, in the end. In July 1882. Too late for those in Langton who had wanted the landlord back at St George's. But others who died by their own hand had the dignity of a proper burial in a churchyard from then on. So Mr Lester's zeal was rewarded. I think even his cross little wife was proud of his achievement in the end. On bad days, when I felt lost and lonely, I forced myself to think that something good had come out of the mess we'd created. That John's death had changed the law. But it was cold comfort.'

There was a pause. William stayed as still as possible so that nothing would distract her.

She said, 'It was hard after I killed Arthur. When I knew that John was dead. I tried to turn back time by going for long walks along the cliffs. All through that winter, and all through the following spring. Just as I'd done years before. I thought when the sun returned, my feelings would change. I thought the ice in my heart would melt. But nothing happened.

'And one day I climbed down the rocks to Dancing Ledge, to the flat grey shelf where the sea rises up like a great white bird with wings outstretched, and I stood there, listening to the boom and return of every wave, and I thought, It's gone. It's all gone. My heart doesn't lift at the sight of the sea. I feel nothing, nothing at all. Because there's nothing left for me here any more.

'When I told Mrs Selby that I was going to sell the Ship and the forge, she wept. She said, Why, Mary? Why leave the village? Is it because of John? Because we can't bring him back to the churchyard?

'And I leaned out and took her hands, and I said, No. It's not because of that. For a long time, I couldn't accept that he was dead. But I can now. I know that he's gone.

'And Mrs Selby said, So are you leaving because Langton is too full of memories?

'I said, The memories will be with me always, wherever I go.

'Mrs Selby looked bewildered. She said, So why go? Why do you have to leave?

'Mr Lester came to say goodbye. We sat, as usual, on either side of an empty fireplace. It felt like all the talking had been done – all the great stories of suffering and redemption and rising from the dead, all the solemn words about justice and truth and mercy. I felt dull and old and tired. All words were meaningless.

'Right at the end, he stood up. He bent down from his great height, and said, What happened, Mary?

'And for a moment I was tempted. I wanted to fall at his feet and confess. I wanted to tell him about John's great plan, and the lie of the suicide. I wanted to tell him about John's body in the coffin, and how he'd been buried alive by the one man he thought he could trust. I wanted to tell him about killing Arthur, smashing his skull to a mess of blood and bone. I wanted to tell him that my heart had turned to ice, and that God had left the Isle of Purbeck.

'But I said nothing.'

The sun had left the charge room, leaving the customary grey chill.

Mary said, 'You're right. I've lied to you. I said I wanted to confess because I was tired of keeping secrets. Tired of a lifetime of silence. But that isn't the whole truth. It turns out that Mr Lester was right all along. I was blind, from the very beginning. He could see what I couldn't. The fact is, I loved John Ball. With all my heart and with all my soul. We fought and argued and bickered and battled because it mattered. Because we were each the centre of the other's life. And once he'd gone, there was nothing left. I never married again because no one could replace him. And I have never found peace, because my husband has no grave. I want to mark his passing. I want to be able to stand in a churchyard and bow my head and see it written there, in front of me, on black Purbeck marble: *Here lies John Ball, 1856–1878. Beloved husband of Mary Holmes*. And underneath a verse from the Bible that will give me comfort in my last years. Ezekiel thirty-six, verse twenty-six. *A new heart also will I give you, and a new spirit will I put within you. And I will take away your heart of stone, and I will give you a heart of flesh.*' Mary turned and faced him, her eyes full of tears. 'I'm tired of being cut off from life. I'm tired of feeling nothing. Make it happen, William. Please make it happen. Make them listen and believe me. Because in that coffin are the bodies of Arthur Corben and John Ball. And I want to bury my husband before I die.'

———

The main office of the police station in Wareham was busy that Saturday afternoon. Constable Fripp, with his shock of red hair, was talking to one of the Land Girls billeted at the YMCA. Constable Keyes was discussing driving permits with Percy Best from the Home Guard.

'I'm afraid I'm not able to give out any information about US troops,' said Sergeant Mills in a loud voice to Mrs Bascombe, who had called in on her way to evensong at Lady St Mary's. 'Official secrets, you see. All very hush-hush.'

William glanced up through the window, across the street towards the Black Bear Hotel. On the porch above the front door, tethered to the black railings with a chain attached to a collar round its neck, the six-foot model of the bear stood up on its hind legs. Local legend said that if the bear ever fell, the world would end.

Wareham seemed empty without the army vehicles.

'All right there?' said Constable Meech.

'Just thinking,' said William.

'You can do too much of that,' said Constable Meech. 'They say it sends you mad.' But he smiled when he said it.

William, after a small hesitation, smiled back.

At three o'clock, Sergeant Mills glanced over at William,

seated behind his typewriter at his usual desk, and said, 'You wanted a word, Constable?'

William nodded.

On the table in the charge room was the end of a grey-looking loaf on a bread board, half a jar of strawberry jam, and a pair of bicycle clips.

Sergeant Mills sat down. 'So how's that report coming along then? The mystery of the ancient skeletons.'

William eased himself on to the bench, tensing against the pain. 'Miss Holmes has given me enough information for a book. But most of it's irrelevant.'

'That sounds like Miss Holmes.'

'It's hard to make any sense of it at all. Stories and gossip and bits of old history all mixed together.'

Sergeant Mills smiled. 'Like looking for diamonds in compost.'

'I wondered if I could give you a summary of where we've got to?'

'Fire away.'

William opened his jacket pocket and took out his notebook. 'She says the skeletons belong to two men from Langton Matravers.'

'Names?'

'Arthur Corben and John Ball. She says they were born in the mid-1850s, and died in the late 1870s. John Ball was a blacksmith, and Arthur Corben a stonecutter.'

Sergeant Mills nodded. 'Did you look at the parish records?'

William rifled through the pages of his notebook. 'I contacted the vicar at St George's in Langton Matravers. He says there's no record of Arthur Corben. But that's not surprising. It wasn't compulsory to register births until 1874. And according to Miss Holmes, Arthur Corben wasn't born in Langton in any case. He was informally adopted by an uncle when his parents died.'

'What about John Ball?'

'He was baptised in November 1856. There's also a marriage

certificate between John Ball and Mary Holmes dated September 1876.'

'So John Ball was her husband?'

'Yes.'

'She's never called herself Mary Ball.'

'I asked her about that. She didn't give a reason.'

'Death certificates?'

'Nothing for Arthur Corben. But one dated December 1878 for John Ball. Also a coroner's report giving full details of his suicide.'

Sergeant Mills narrowed his eyes. 'Why wasn't he buried in the churchyard?'

'According to the vicar in Langton, what Mary Holmes told me is true. In those days people who committed suicide weren't allowed a Christian burial. And on the Isle of Purbeck, the custom was to bury them outside the village in an unmarked grave. People were worried about unquiet spirits. Being haunted by their ghosts.'

'So you think one of the skeletons might belong to John Ball.'

'Miss Holmes said that her husband was very tall – six foot four. It wasn't in the newspaper report. I know she might have picked it up from gossip about the discovery of the skeletons. But I think she's probably telling the truth.'

'And the other skeleton? Why does she think it belongs to Arthur Corben?'

'Because he pushed the coffin out of the village the day after John Ball killed himself. He'd volunteered to bury him. The whole village saw him leave. There might even be other witnesses if we can find them. Although it's unlikely. So they all watched Corben pick up the handles of the cart and wheel John Ball's coffin on the road to Acton and Worth. And according to Miss Holmes, that was the last they ever saw of him. He just disappeared.'

'Disappeared?'

William nodded. 'He just left, leaving his clothes, his posses-sions, even his stonemason's tools. From that day on, he was never heard of again.'

'Because he was six feet under,' said Sergeant Mills.

'Exactly.'

'Does she have any idea what happened? How Arthur Corben died?'

'No.'

'None at all?'

'None at all.'

'That doesn't sound like Miss Holmes.'

'She was getting tired at that point in the story, I think. She's in her late eighties. It's hard work trying to remember what happened.'

Sergeant Mill looked thoughtful. 'What about the earrings and the necklace? Where did they come from?'

'I don't think we'll ever know. Miss Holmes got very confused at this point. I made the mistake early on of telling her that jewellery had been discovered in the coffin. Obviously I should have waited to see if she mentioned it herself. But I didn't. I'm sorry. After I told her, she sat and brooded and I think her memories became muddled. She told me that a ship had been wrecked on the coast near Langton Matravers a few months before John Ball died. She said it sank to the bottom of the sea, and John dived down and stole the jewellery from one of the cabins. She was very convincing. But I don't think it's true. I've looked, and there's no record of a shipwreck on that part of the coast in 1878. I think she was remembering the stories she'd heard as a child. There was an East India sailing ship called the *Halsewell* that went aground a hundred years before that, in 1786. Just off the coast at Seacombe beyond Dancing Ledge. There was a terrible storm, and a lot of people lost their lives – drowned in the waves or battered to death on the rocks. The captain stayed on board with his daughters and nieces as the ship went down because he couldn't leave them alone to die. Turner painted it. Dickens wrote about it. There's a mirror from the wreck in the church at Worth Matravers. When Mary was growing up, most people round there believed there was still treasure on the sea bed. So when she heard that old jewellery had been found in the coffin, I think she remembered the romantic stories of her youth, and imagined John diving down to the bottom of the sea.'

'The jewellery might have come from a wreck. It's possible.'

'Anything's possible. But it's hard to be sure, unless there's a record somewhere of those particular pieces. It could take months of enquiry. Years, even.'

Sergeant Mills screwed up his eyes, thinking about what William had said. 'So were they killed for the jewellery? John Ball and Arthur Corben?'

William shook his head. 'John Ball wasn't murdered. He committed suicide. There's a lot of evidence to back that up – not just Mary's statement, but the death certificate, and a letter from the local vicar in the *Dorset Country Chronicle*. According to Miss Holmes, he was an unstable character. Short temper. Often violent. They were an ill-matched couple. Argued all the time. They weren't even living together in the end. She said he used to get drunk and threaten her with a gun. Then one night, he turned it on himself.'

'No wonder she doesn't use his name.'

'I think it's possible that Arthur Corben was the one who found the jewellery. He was a stonecutter, after all. He might have dug it up in one of the old quarries. Perhaps he was going to London that night to sell it. Or perhaps he was just keeping it with him until he'd decided what to do. But whoever it was who buried Corben didn't know about the jewellery, or didn't want it, because it was still in the coffin when the coroner examined the remains. So I don't think Corben was killed for the jewellery either. If he was killed at all.'

'Someone must have killed him.'

'There were no obvious injuries on either skeleton. Slight depressions to the skull on the shorter one, but that could have happened after death. For all we know, Arthur Corben died of natural causes. Lost consciousness and hit his head as he fell. Although I think what's most likely is that he was pushing the cart with the coffin past all the quarries, tripped over a buttress or a crabstone, and fell down an old mineshaft. There's plenty of disused mines round there. And I think one of the quarrymen working in Acton found Corben's body, found the coffin with John Ball's body, panicked, and buried them both. Better than starting up a whole rigmarole of investigations and being accused of murder. And after all, if both men were dead, it wouldn't have seemed such a big crime to bury them.'

Sergeant Mills's eyes were full of mischief. 'Two dead bodies and buried treasure, and you're telling me it wasn't murder?'

'I'm just saying we shouldn't jump to conclusions.'

'Perhaps Miss Holmes killed Arthur Corben.'

William looked surprised. 'Are you serious?'

Sergeant Mills laughed. 'I wouldn't put it past her.'

'She's tiny. Like a bird. I can't imagine her killing anyone.'

'It's a great idea, though, isn't it? An elderly lady who's been keeping quiet about an evil murder for sixty years.'

William smiled.

Sergeant Mills was silent for a moment, apparently turning everything over in his mind. 'I think I should talk to the coroner on Monday. Explain that conversations with Mary Holmes suggest that the taller skeleton belongs to John Ball – and we have records to show he committed suicide and was buried in an unmarked grave outside the village – and the shorter skeleton belongs to Arthur Corben who disappeared on the day that he buried John Ball, cause of death unknown. I will also say that we have no information about the gold and ruby necklace and earrings, but that we will continue to make enquiries.'

William nodded.

'Do you think Miss Holmes would be able to give evidence in person?'

William shook his head. 'It's been hard getting this far. You know what it's like. She tells stories that seem to make sense. But they may have no bearing on reality at all.'

'The good thing,' said Sergeant Mills, 'is that the coroner's keen to get this sorted out as soon as possible. As far as he's concerned, it's ancient history. At some point he'll have to decide what to do about the jewellery. But that may be better left until time and resources are more plentiful. Let me have a word with him. I'll tell him that you spent all last week getting some kind of statement from Miss Holmes, and it's unlikely that any further questioning will produce new evidence. Has she signed it yet?'

'I wanted to talk to you first.'

'I think you should get over there now.' He hesitated. 'It's only a few minutes' walk. But if you'd rather, I can send someone to ask her to come to the station . . .'

'I can manage.'

Sergeant Mills got to his feet. 'Good work, Constable. With a bit of luck, we won't need to trouble Dorchester at all.'

'One more thing.' William looked up. 'Miss Holmes is very keen to bury her husband's body in consecrated ground. It's something that's been worrying her for years. If the coroner agrees with our conclusions about John Ball's remains, could that happen? Would the coroner agree to it?'

'I can't see why not.' Sergeant Mills smiled. 'I must say, Constable, you're very kind. Looking after Miss Holmes, even though she's spent all week driving you mad.'

William lowered his eyes.

———————

For a moment, outside the police station, William was unsure. It was some time since he'd attempted a journey as long as this.

He stood by the brick wall, looking up South Street towards the Cross. The sun was bright.

'Afternoon, Constable.' Mrs Bascombe was right by his shoulder, staring up into his face. She seemed puzzled. For the first time since he'd arrived in Wareham, he found himself studying her closely, noticing the laughter lines round her mouth, the faint dusting of powder across her cheeks, her light blue eyes. 'Off for a walk?'

William knew she was watching as he began his slow progress towards the centre of town. When he glanced round, she was deep in conversation with Mrs Legg, gesturing in his direction with wild hand movements. Mrs Legg – a small, compact body in a pink floral dress – looked anxious.

Opposite the Black Bear Hotel, he stopped to catch his breath. People he didn't know nodded and smiled, and a boy on a bicycle waved. Mr Beck from Worlds Stores touched his hand to his forehead in a kind of salute. William began to feel dizzy with all the attention.

'Lovely day, isn't it?' said Mrs Walbridge. She was holding the hand of a small girl with blond hair who was staring at him with fierce scrutiny. 'I thought I'd take Margaret to see the cygnets. Although we won't get too close, of course. Or the cob will flap its wings. They're very protective, swans. Take care of their young.'

The town was empty without the Americans. No jeeps, no lorries, no motorbikes.

It was only once he'd reached the Manor House, still some forty yards from the crossroads, that he realised he'd been too ambitious. The pain had intensified from its habitual dull ache to something much bigger. It demanded his attention. He waited, concentrating on being still. A large black perambulator came to rest beside him.

'Nice to see you out and about,' said young Mrs Farwell. 'I hope that means you're feeling a bit better.'

He was breathing fast, as if he'd been running.

'Why don't we sit for a minute?' Mrs Farwell put the brake on the pram and settled herself on to the low wall. 'It seems a shame to rush about on such a sunny day.'

Reaching behind for support, William lowered himself down. As he took the weight off his leg, pain shot through his knee and ankle with such force that he nearly cried out.

She put her hand on his arm. 'My George is a bit like you. He's in the navy hospital in Gosport. Has to learn to walk all over again.' She smiled. 'I'll have the two of them, won't I, once he's home. They'll have to learn together.'

Constable Keyes – red-faced, sweating, because bicycling is hard for a big man on a hot day – came to a halt in the road. 'All right there?'

'He's just having a rest,' said Mrs Farwell.

William looked away, waiting for the light-headedness to disappear. A pair of brown boots appeared at the edge of his vision.

'Would you like a barley sugar, Constable?' said Miss Bussell.

The pain eased. He could breathe again. When he looked up, he saw he was surrounded by a circle of concerned faces – young Mrs Farwell, Constable Keyes, Miss Bussell and Mrs Legg, who was trying, with little success, to hold back Vic Smith's dog.

'Thank you,' said William. 'I didn't realise it was such a long walk.'

Constable Keyes looked puzzled. 'From the station?'

'For me,' said William.

The dog pushed its way between Miss Bussell and Mrs Legg and laid its smooth brown head on William's knee.

When she opened the door and saw him, she looked frightened. She said, in a harsh voice, 'Have you come to arrest me?'

'No.'

'So why are you here?'

She seemed so small, framed by the doorway. Without her black coat and black hat, without the sharp angles of crown, brim and lapels, she seemed insubstantial.

He had a hand out against the brick wall, taking his weight. 'May I come in?'

'Of course.' She stood back, and he struggled past her into the narrow hallway, limping even more badly than usual.

He had been expecting a house dense with furniture and fabrics, a complicated, stuffed, Victorian decor with flounces and ferns and a stuffed bird in a glass jar. But the living room was light and bare. The walls were painted white. There were two low armchairs either side of the fireplace. On the chimney breast was a large painting framed in wood showing the sea, or possibly sky, in a blur of blue and azure and teal.

She said, 'You'd better sit down.'

He flopped into one of the chairs.

'Did you walk all the way? You look terrible.'

Sweat was running down his face into his collar.

'Cup of tea? A glass of water?'

He shook his head.

She sat down opposite him, her hands loosely clasped in her lap. Her dress was light grey, like smoke, or a cloud. At the neck was a silver brooch in the shape of a crescent moon.

She waited for his breathing to return to normal. It took a long time. 'So no handcuffs.'

'I told you, Miss Holmes. It doesn't work like that.'

'But you've talked to Sergeant Mills.'

He nodded. The colour was beginning to return to his face. 'What did he say?'

'He's very pleased. He thinks there's enough evidence to present to the coroner.'

She raised her eyebrows, surprised. 'No anxiety about whether or not I might be telling the truth?'

'None at all.'

She gave him a small look of triumph. 'As I said at the beginning, I have a lot of time for Sergeant Mills.'

'I spent this morning typing up your statement. Hoping the sergeant would approve. Which indeed he did. So I wondered whether you would mind reading it through? If you're happy, and are willing to sign it, we can send this to the coroner on Monday morning.'

She looked suspicious. 'Why wouldn't I be willing to sign it?'

'Well,' said William, 'you have to be sure that it accurately reflects what you've told me.'

'And does it?'

'I've had to summarise some of what you said. To make it a little more concise.'

'What have you left out?'

'I think you should read it.' He took the folded document from his inner pocket and held it out to her.

Her face was pinched, almost angry. 'What have you done?'

'I've recorded your statement.'

'It sounds to me like you've rewritten it.'

His voice was calm. 'You said it yourself. We make stories out of everything. This is the one that keeps you out of prison.'

She narrowed her eyes. 'What if I don't like it?'

'Try harder.'

'I want to tell the truth.'

'No, you don't. You want to bury your husband.'

She sat there, stiff-backed, glaring at him. 'I have spent all week explaining to you what happened.'

'And I have spent all week listening to you.' He wouldn't back down. 'You've made your confession. That's enough.'

For a moment, it seemed as if she were going to argue.

He said, 'I don't think you should suffer any more, Mary.'

She went quite still, as if he'd said something so outrageous she was too shocked to understand. The silence was spiky with tension, barbed with attack. He waited, almost afraid. Then, as he watched, the fight went out of her. Like a fluffed-out cat watching danger recede, she folded in on herself, becoming small and neat and aloof. Keeping her face averted, not meeting his eyes, she reached out and took the statement from him. 'I can't read while you're scowling at me. Go out in the garden. There's a bench under the apple tree. You can sit in the sun.'

He stood up quickly, without any of his usual preparation, and cried out. He groped for the back of the chair. He stayed there, bent over, waiting for the waves of dizziness to recede.

Her voice came out of the silence, cool and calm. 'How long has it been like this?'

William swayed as the pain subsided. 'A year, two years. I can't remember.'

'Will it get better?'

'It was blown into seventeen pieces. There's nothing else they can do. There are some days when it's not so bad. And then it comes back, worse than before.'

'So there can be no improvement.'

'There's no muscle any more. Just bone that's dying.'

'It will only get worse.'

He nodded.

'Cut it off.'

He flinched as if she'd hit him.

Mary sounded matter-of-fact. 'We live in violent times. I saw the young men coming back from the Great War. I've seen farming accidents, mining accidents, men thrown from horses, crushed by cars, flung from motorcycles. And now this. Another war. Men coming home missing hands and arms and feet and legs. And I tell you this. I have never seen anyone cut by knives each time he moves. I have never seen a face so drawn in agony as yours. You can't go on like this. You can't spend your life hiding away, fearful of every movement. If you were thinking clearly, you would have worked this out for yourself. Pain is not heroic, William. It is not something to be borne in silence.'

He looked at her, saying nothing.

Mary said, 'Now go to the garden and leave me in peace. I want to read this story you've written.'

He turned to the door.

She said, 'One more thing. What happened to Peter?'

He looked back.

'Stella's little boy. What happened to him?'

William stared at her.

'Yesterday, you said you didn't know what to do to put it right. You felt guilty that you'd let people down and wanted to make amends. I said there was nothing you could do.' She paused. 'Well, I was wrong. You can go and find Peter.'

'He has Frank. He doesn't need me.'

'Frank isn't his father. You told me he and Stella weren't even married. So Frank may not be allowed to keep him.'

William looked startled.

'Of course, no one will be asking too many questions. Not while there's a war on. But that's not really the point, is it? How much do you know about Frank? Was he a good man? Did he want Peter? Maybe he did. Maybe he loved him. But he might have gone to pieces after Stella died. Mad with grief. Started drinking, getting home late, leaving Peter alone in a strange and empty house.'

'She had family, too. A mother. An aunt.'

'But you don't know what happened, do you? Did someone find them? Tell them that Stella was dead? Tell them where Peter was? At the very least, you should be making enquiries.' She shrugged. 'You're a policeman. It shouldn't be too hard.'

William's eyes were full of pain.

'Don't think. Just do it. Surely you've learned that much. The worst kind of regret is wishing you'd had more courage.' Her voice softened. 'We've spent a whole week being selfish. Going back over the past, trying to come to terms with what we've lost. It's time to stop now. Because the truth is, what you and I think and feel doesn't really matter. Not in the world we're living in now. Not when so many are being killed.' Her gaze was direct. 'You told me you didn't know why you'd been spared when all those you love have died. Perhaps this is why. You're alive, William. That's all that's important. You go on living. And perhaps it's your job to look after Stella's son.'

Outside, the apple tree was in full leaf. Small green fruits were just beginning to show. Screwing up his face with the effort, William lowered himself on to the wooden seat and allowed his body to sink back so that the sun shone on his face. He thought about Peter's head on Frank's shoulder, blond hair against black jacket. He could see the flush of sleep on Peter's face, his arm flopped and abandoned. He breathed in, and for a moment, for a blessed tiny moment, the pain scuttled off. There was a silence of pain. William sat there, revelling in the nothingness, glorying in the emptiness, and he thought, The pain's ice cold, that's the worst of it. Not the warmth of blood. It's like steel. And it yawns, wider and wider, like a tunnel, like a hungry mouth, and I shout out to it, all right, all right, I give in, you can have me, all of me. But it's not enough. Because it will go on and on. And it's the fear of it that's the worst. It's the fear of it, never-ending, stretching out in front of me, cold, grey and empty.

He felt the heat burn into his skin. He closed his eyes, and the yellow light turned orange, then pink, as if someone had painted a sunrise over his sight. He allowed the colour to wash through his head, flooding his mind. And then, full of the heat of the sun, he opened his eyes. He saw the bees dipping into the wild geraniums. He saw the lilac, the irises, the white clematis clinging to the fence as it climbed. He smelled the lavender and the mint. He felt the tiny flailing touch of a fly on the skin of his hand.

Then, as usual, as he did every day, he allowed himself to remember Stella.

But this time, he let the thought of her stay. He felt the heaviness of it. The weight that crushed him. The guilt, the loss.

And he wept.

Two weeks later

Sergeant Mills was walking the beat. It was pitch black. But he'd lived in Wareham all his life. He knew these roads. He knew the houses. He even knew what lay beneath – the ruined keep of the Norman castle, the Saxon nunnery, the Church of St John. Sometimes he stood in South Street and imagined the great fire of 1762 that tore through the timber-framed houses, burning the thatch, sending out black billowing smoke and tongues of red flame that reached the sky.

He had toyed with the idea of living elsewhere. Somewhere without walls. Especially after Elsie died. He had thought for a while of making a new start – Dorchester, perhaps, or Weymouth. A different town with a different history. But it seemed in the end a foolish conceit, a way of trying to move on from death. Which of course you can never do. Elsie would stay dead whether he went to Land's End or John O'Groats. And Annie liked Wareham. Or at least saw it as home, which amounted to the same thing.

Annie, he thought. A young woman now. Knows her own mind. Hard for her, falling in love with an American soldier. And I wasn't supposed to see it, even though it was there, right in front of me, as plain as the nose on your face. And how it wrung my heart not to be able to hug her close, like I did when she was a little girl, and say, There now, Annie love, it'll be all right, you'll see, it'll all look better tomorrow. I couldn't offer her a crumb of comfort, because I wasn't supposed to know. And I couldn't blame the lad. He was just one of those smiley young men who's kind and polite to the world. Natural good manners. Didn't realise she thought it was just for her. I couldn't bear seeing the light in her face fade away. Not my Annie. She had so much hope. Even when he made it clear he had a girl back home. And then they left, in the blink of an eye, and it was all over, even the tiny chance he'd change his mind. One minute they were there, the next they had gone.

Sergeant Mills turned into Cow Lane, heading towards the West Walls. I don't like her working at the factory. All the explosives. Three pounds a week, Dad, she says. I wouldn't get that anywhere else. And I say to her, There's more to life than money, Annie. There's more to life than money. They call it the Glamour Express, the train that takes them from Wareham station. Because of all the girls. Although, she says, chance would be a fine thing, what with thick navy trousers and every strand of hair bundled up in a tight cap. They're terribly strict, she says. All the rules and regulations. No metal. No jewellery. Except for wedding rings. You're allowed a gold wedding ring. But the canteen's good. Day and night. You can get a cooked dinner at three in the morning.

Sergeant Mills's stomach rumbled. Bloody war. Always hungry. Never enough to eat. His mind began to drift. He imagined the treats of his youth: iced buns, jam puffs, spiced apple cake and gingerbread with silver stars. He saw a tea table laid out in the garden with roses on the white cups. Funny how you always think of the past in sunlight. It's hard to remember a rainy day. And then he was four years old, sitting on his mother's knee, and the rain was running down the glass of the window. The Queen had died, the old Queen in her black silks, and England was in mourning. And her heir was Edward, her eldest son, the Prince of Wales.

Sergeant Mills smiled. It's taken a week to get her story. A whole week. She's lonely, of course. Wanted someone to take notice of her. And why not? It's not often that history demands attention. Old bones. Old stories. Especially not now. It's the present, nothing else. That's all you can see. Because the killing makes it precious.

He trudged ahead, his mind full of war. He saw the faces of boys he'd known in his youth, long dead, long buried. He remembered Bert Bascombe, off God knows where, and George Farwell, blown up on a destroyer. He thought about Wareham lads like Danny Smith, Jack Thorner, Jim Cornick, Eddie Walbridge, fighting side by side with the Americans. God keep them safe. Please God, keep them safe.

He felt, for a moment, sick with fear.

But they've captured Rome, he thought. That's got to be good news.

At the end of Cow Lane, he turned up the gentle slope to the top of the earth walls. There was barbed wire all along, rolls of bristling defence, but enough room for a single man to walk alone. The black night was full of stars. All around him was soft darkness. Ahead, he could just make out the leafy burst of the mountain ash, loved by chattering flocks of starlings. Murmurations of starlings. He walked on, high above the town, the grass thick beneath his feet. The midnight air was cold on his face. The great earth mound turned the corner, and now he was on the North Walls. In front of him was the flood plain of the river. Beyond that, Sandford, Morden, Holton Heath.

Out of the darkness came a low hum. It grew louder, a monotone rumble. As he stood there, waiting, it ripped through the silence, taking over the night. The roar pounded his ears.

And now, above his head, the great black bodies of planes, bombers towing gliders, line after line of them sweeping over southern England, across the Channel, heading into France: an armada, a battery, an assault.

He looked up, amazed.

And his head was full of the sound, the thundering roll of the engines above, and he thought, This is it. The second front. It's begun.

Acknowledgements

Thanks to Hilary Sheers for her kind permission to reproduce Vera Rich's poem 'Should You Ask Me', which gave the novel its title. Born in London in 1936, Vera Rich began publishing her poetry in the early 1950s and founded *Manifold*, a magazine for new poetry, in 1962. Throughout her life, Rich translated Ukrainian and Belarusian poetry, and in 2007 was awarded the Order of Princess Olha, by presidential decree, for fifty years' service to Ukrainian literature.

Thanks for generous help with research to Nicholas Rheinberg, Clive Emsley, Jeremy Crang, Ben Buxton, Stuart Hamilton, Juliet Gardiner, Mark Connor, William Philpott, R. J. Saville, Isabelle Grey, Eric Gillespie and Andrew Woods (at the Colonel Robert R. McCormick Research Center, First Division Museum at Cantigny in Illinois), Debs Barclay, Edwina Ehrman, Richard Christmas, the Virginia Military Institute Archives, The Tank Museum in Bovington, the Discover Purbeck Information Centre in Wareham, Wareham Town Museum, the Dorset Bird Club and the Dorset Police Archives.

Thanks to my agent Veronique Baxter and to my editor Ruth Tross and her team at Hodder and Stoughton for all their support.

Finally, love and thanks to friends and family who read the first draft – Yvonne Wilcox, Alexandra Fabian, Sally Eden, Tamsin Kelly, Joe Kavanagh, Ben Kavanagh, Alice Kavanagh and, as always, my husband Matt.

Do you wish this wasn't the end?

Join us at www.hodder.co.uk, or follow us on
Twitter @hodderbooks to be a part of our community
of people who love the very best in books and reading.

Whether you want to discover more about a book
or an author, watch trailers and interviews, have the
chance to win early limited editions, or simply browse
our expert readers' selection of the very best books,
we think you'll find what you're looking for.

And if you don't,
that's the place to tell us what's missing.

We love what we do, and we'd love you to be part of it.

www.hodder.co.uk

@hodderbooks

HodderBooks

HodderBooks